BLOOD DRIVE

JEANNE C. STEIN

ACE BOOKS, NEW YORK

THE BERKLEY PUBLISHING GROUP
Published by the Penguin Group
Penguin Group (USA) Inc.
375 Hudson Street, New York, New York 10014, USA
Penguin Group (Canada), 90 Eglinton Avenue East, Suite 700, Toronto, Ontario M4P 2Y3, Canada
(a division of Pearson Penguin Canada Inc.)
Penguin Books Ltd., 80 Strand, London WC2R 0RL, England
Penguin Books Ireland, 25 St. Stephen's Green, Dublin 2, Ireland (a division of Penguin Books Ltd.)
Penguin Group (Australia), 250 Camberwell Road, Camberwell, Victoria 3124, Australia (a division of
Pearson Australia Group Pty. Ltd.)
Penguin Books India Pvt. Ltd., 11 Community Centre, Panchsheel Park, New Delhi—110 017, India
Penguin Group (NZ), 67 Apollo Drive, Rosedale, North Shore 0745, Auckland, New Zealand
(a division of Pearson New Zealand Ltd.)
Penguin Books (South Africa) (Pty.) Ltd., 24 Sturdee Avenue, Rosebank, Johannesburg 2196, South
Africa

Penguin Books Ltd., Registered Offices: 80 Strand, London WC2R 0RL, England

This is a work of fiction. Names, characters, places, and incidents either are the product of the author's
imagination or are used fictitiously, and any resemblance to actual persons, living or dead, business
establishments, events, or locales is entirely coincidental. The publisher does not have any control over
and does not assume any responsibility for author or third-party websites or their content.

BLOOD DRIVE

An Ace Book / published by arrangement with ImaJinn Books c/o Trident Media Group, LLC.

PRINTING HISTORY
Imajinn Books edition / 2006
Ace mass-market edition / July 2007

ISBN: 978-0-441-01509-2

ACE®
Ace Books are published by The Berkley Publishing Group,
a division of Penguin Group (USA) Inc.,
375 Hudson Street, New York, New York 10014.
ACE and the "A" design are trademarks belonging to Penguin Group (USA) Inc.

PRINTED IN THE UNITED STATES OF AMERICA

10 9 8 7 6 5 4 3 2 1

To my mom, the sweetest soul

For taking a chance—
Linda Kichline, Scott Miller, Sarah Landis

For guiding and shaping—
Jessica Wade and the great Berkley staff

For showing me how to be a better writer—
Jim Cole, Mario Acevedo, Margie and Tom Lawson,
Sandy Meckstroth, Jeff Shelby

For love and support—
All the wonderful people of Rocky Mountain Fiction
Writers and Sisters in Crime who, along with friends
and family, are always there to make me feel special

For all of the above and just being on my side—
Phil and Jeanette

Thank you

CHAPTER 1

MONDAY

THE GUY SQUIRMS AGAINST ME LIKE A WORM ON a hook. He's in his early twenties, built like a defensive lineman—big muscles, big gut, no neck. He keeps moaning and pressing himself against my chest and I have to hold his head to keep a good grip. Culebra said he'd been here before, but the way he's wriggling around, I'm afraid I'm hurting him.

I swallow a mouthful of blood, open my eyes, and look up at Culebra. I need more but I'm unsure if I should continue.

Culebra's arms are crossed on his chest. He isn't paying attention. In fact, he looks bored, and when he feels my eyes on him, he shrugs and says, "What?"

My thoughts reach out. *Should I stop?*

His own come back. *Have you had enough?*

No. But he keeps moving.

He rolls his shoulders again. *He's been well paid. He's here because he wants to be. He is not a virgin, you know.*

He's done this many times before. He moves because he finds it pleasurable. Watch his hands.

I do. They're at his crotch, caressing a bulge in his jeans.

Oh my god. Is he . . . ?

The lines on Culebra's face deepen as he grins. *You could make it more pleasurable for him, you know. All you would have to do is—*

I gulp two or three more mouthfuls. I know what he's going to say. All I want is the blood. Just what I need to refresh and restore. I've learned to ignore the other sensation, the thrill that spirals into powerful sexual hunger if you let it. When I finish and pull away, the kid actually groans louder and reaches up to pull my head back down to his neck.

I jump to my feet, moving so fast the kid loses his balance and his head hits the floor.

Culebra laughs. I hear as well as sense it.

I reach down and help the kid into a sitting position. "Are you all right?"

His mouth curves upward in a grin, but his eyes are clouded. He makes no move to get up. "You didn't have to stop, you know." It's a combination growl and whine. One hand remains between his legs and the other is on his neck, though there's not a mark to show I've drunk.

I always make sure of that.

I raise an eyebrow at Culebra. *Next time, I want someone who does it just for the money.*

Again, the shrug and the upturned palms. *As you wish.*

I follow Culebra out of the back room of the saloon, leaving my libidinous donor to his own devices. It's September, late afternoon, and bright sun pours through the swinging doors. In the glare, dust motes dance and twirl on an invisible draft of air.

The place is almost deserted. Two humans, friends of the guy in the back, wait for him at the bar, nursing drinks. One vamp couple sit, knees touching, at a table against the back wall. Their thoughts are hot with desire. As soon as I pick up on it, I shut down. Vampire telepathy is not always a good thing. The sexual energy they're emitting makes me edgy, especially after feeding.

We cross to the bar where the bartender greets Culebra with marked deference. The bartender is human, another of those who find it exciting to be in the presence of supernaturals. He asks what we'd like to drink.

Culebra waves him off, reaching into the cooler under the bar for two beers. Culebra owns the place. In fact, he owns the entire town. Without a word, the bartender moves away.

Culebra pops the tops and hands me one of the beers.

I take a long pull. It goes down easily, washing away the salty aftertaste of the blood, refreshing in the way that an icy drink satisfies after eating peanuts or spicy foods. Consuming liquid is the only form of human sustenance left to me.

Culebra is watching me. When I meet his eyes, he nods. *What happened back there, it's not perfect, but it's the best we can do.*

I know it's true. I don't have to like it.

He leans across the bar, sharp eyes acknowledging a response he's plucked from the air. His face is ageless, yet old, the surface covered with tiny lines and wrinkles etched by the stylus of a life I know nothing about.

He shuts me out of his thoughts now, and the ease with which he can do that makes me uneasy. I am vampire and supposedly at the top of the food chain as far as immortals are concerned. I don't know *what* Culebra is. He hasn't shared that yet. He can read my thoughts and I his, when he lets me. He is the only nonhuman creature who can hide himself so completely that I can't glean the smallest fragment of his true being. And yet, with the death of Avery, the vampire doctor who took care of me when I first became vampire, this unlikely character, with the name that means "rattlesnake," has become one of my closest friends.

He's staring again, picking through my thoughts like a beggar with a bag full of clothes—hopeful, expectant but resigned to the reality that all he's likely to find are castoffs. Nothing new and nothing that fits.

So. His mouth turns down in a frown. *You haven't spoken with Williams yet, have you?*

Williams. Chief Warren Williams of the San Diego police department. A friend of Avery's, or so I thought. Culebra thinks he should finish what Avery began—my instruction into what it means to survive as a vampire. But the relationship between Williams and me got off to a shaky start—and ended even worse. I shake my head. *What can he say to me? Nothing I want to hear. And what can I say to him? That I'm sorry I almost killed him? That would be a lie.*

He sniffs impatiently. *I suppose it has never occurred to you that he might have things you need to hear. Important things. Like your heritage and what lies ahead.*

My heritage? You mean like finding out I'm a descendant of Vlad the Impaler? That provokes a snicker that bubbles up before I can stifle it. *When did Williams put you on his payroll? Every time I come down here it's the same thing. It's becoming tedious.*

The frown deepens. *Then take me up on my offer. Stay here. Work with me. I can teach you what you need to know.*

I lay the bottle down on the counter and wave a hand. *This is what I need to know. I have a life in San Diego. My home is almost rebuilt. My business is going well. How would I explain leaving all that behind to move down here? What would I tell my parents?*

Culebra radiates aggravation. *This concern for mortals.* His tone is sharp. *I understand now why Avery found you so irritating.*

My shoulders draw tight. Culebra's mention of Avery is deliberate and cruel. I placed my trust in Avery and he not only betrayed that trust, but almost destroyed me. I thought I loved him, which made all that happened between us that much more hurtful. Culebra knows this.

I place both hands on the bar to steady myself before raising my eyes to meet his. *You cannot bait me. I owe you a debt. One I am willing to repay. But I will not relinquish whatever natural time I have left with my family and friends to stay here with you. My life is my own. I thought you understood that.*

Culebra doesn't look away. Neither does he back down. *A life that involves chasing human scum wanted for petty crimes. You deal with criminals. You are above that.*

I smile. *This town, Beso de la Muerte, "Kiss of Death," isn't this a Mexican hideaway? Isn't this home to criminals both human and otherwise who have earned your protection in one way or another? You, too, deal with criminals. How is that so different from what I do?*

Culebra has no answer. A long moment passes. He looks around the bar, then back at me and the rancor is gone. *Sooner or later you will have to accept what you've become.*

What have I not accepted? I'm here, aren't I? I will not deny myself the time I have left with those I love. Neither will Williams. Neither will you.

Suddenly, the cloud lifts from Culebra's face and his thoughts clear, become neutral. The corners of his lips curl upward. *I'm impatient. An illogical emotion for one who deals with immortals, I know. But now you had better go. The lines at the border crossing will be long. I believe your parents are expecting you for dinner.*

Something I know I hadn't mentioned. I raise an eyebrow. Again, he has pulled a bit of information from my subconscious. I scowl at him.

You are annoying, you know that?

He smiles.

I leave Culebra with a wave. The next time I see him will be the next time the hunger strikes. I won't miss the lectures.

My car is parked just outside the saloon. One dusty, slouching, wooden building in a street full of them. It's an hour's drive from the border yet no one ever ventures here uninvited. I suspect Culebra has cast some kind of protective spell over the place.

Another of those things I would have thought preposterous two months ago.

Two months. Sixty days since a fight in a dark parking lot changed me forever. Even now, when I think about it, it doesn't seem real. My partner, David, and I were on a midnight run. A simple snatch job that should have taken no more time or effort than a hundred others we've performed as bounty hunters. The guy was an accountant wanted for embezzlement. No priors. No history of violence. What we didn't know, what we *couldn't* have known, was that he was a newly turned vampire.

He overpowered David and attacked me. He intended to kill me. He didn't. Not in the normal way. But during the struggle, we exchanged blood.

I became a vampire, too.

I placed my trust in the doctor, Avery, who treated me in the hospital only to have that trust betrayed in the cruelest way. Avery thought he'd impress upon me the need to turn my back on my mortal family by burning my house to the ground and kidnapping my partner and friend, David. What he did instead was invoke the wrath of a vampire coming to terms with her new strength and power. I killed him. And now I am more determined than ever that I will not give up whatever time is left with my human family.

It's all I have.

I glance at my watch.

Culebra was right. I need to get on the road. My folks live on Mt. Helix, a bedroom community east of San Diego. They're expecting me at six and I'll be cutting it close. I press my foot down on the accelerator and let the Jag have its head. We race a funnel of twirling, dancing dust out of town.

I look back in the rearview mirror and see Culebra standing alone on the sidewalk, watching. He sends a silent message of farewell.

CHAPTER 2

MY MOTHER EYES ME OVER THE RIM OF HER coffee cup. "Anna, you look so thin. And you hardly touched your dinner. Are you on one of those silly low-carb diets?"

I almost choke on a mouthful of coffee. I'm on the ultimate low-carb diet. I put on a bright smile. "Of course not, Mom. I told you. I had a late lunch."

But I can tell she doesn't believe me. She's a high school principal who observes firsthand the symptoms of anorexia and bulimia on a daily basis. I think she might be concerned that I'm on the same path as some of her students. In two months I've lost twenty pounds. I can't check my appearance in the mirror, but my body *feels* harder, leaner, more efficient. David has commented on it, too. He attributes it to stricter workouts.

I attribute it to a liquid protein diet. Not something I can share with any human.

But now my dad chimes in. "Leave her alone, Anita.

She looks fine to me. She's trimmed down, that's all. She's been working out." He sends a pointed glance my mother's way. "Something we should try. Too much pasta and not enough exercise in this family. Anna sets a good example."

I smile at him, squeezing his hand. He looks tan and relaxed and very dapper this evening in gray slacks and a pink polo shirt. His thick silver hair is brushed back and a pair of reading glasses is perched on the top of his head. He looks like the prosperous investment banker he is.

"You should talk," my mother scolds. "Eighteen holes once or twice a week in a golf cart hardly qualifies as a rigorous exercise regime."

It's a familiar theme. Both my parents tend to eschew physical exercise and yet at sixty, my mother is the most beautiful woman I know. She's five foot five, small boned and slender. Her honey-colored hair is touched with silver and falls in a smooth, straight sweep to her shoulders.

Physically, we're similar; same color hair and hazel eyes. But she has a natural grace about her that shines from within and without. I, however, inherited my father's more earthy temperament along with his thick, curly hair. Just as well, really, since I can't use a mirror anymore. Being able to go out in the sun enables me to keep color in my cheeks, so finger combing my hair after a shower and a little dab of lipstick is the extent of my primping nowadays.

Chalk that one up on the plus side of becoming a vampire.

My dad's voice brings me back. "I drove by the cottage the other day, Anna. When do you think you'll move in?"

My smile is wide and genuine. "Next week. The finishing work is all that's left. Kitchen cabinets, a few baseboards. I've ordered furniture. When the contractor gives me the word, I'll call the store and arrange delivery."

"And the police don't know who set the fire?"

I look down at my coffee cup, toying with it a moment before answering. I know who set the fire. Avery. And I exacted my own justice. But I can't tell him that.

"The police think it was some kids," I lied. Something else I've gotten very good at. "Anyway, the insurance came through and the cottage is rebuilt, so I'm not going to dwell on who did it. I get too angry when I think about it." That part, at least, is true.

The telephone rings just then and my mother rises to answer it, patting my shoulder as she moves past. I rise with her and gather dishes to take to the sink. It gives me a chance to scrape the garlic-laden pasta sauce off my plate and into the disposal without anyone noticing the gag reflex that threatens to overwhelm me. I'm getting better at hiding such things, but I have to come up with a reason that will gently convince my mother to fix something other than pasta when I come to dinner.

An allergy to tomato sauce maybe?

I'm loading the dishwasher when she comes back into the room. An inquisitive frown tugs at the corners of her mouth.

"Anna," she says. "Do you remember Carolyn Delaney? Steve's girlfriend from Cornell?"

I turn to my mother, hoping the look on my face reflects only curiosity and not the inexplicable tingle of alarm racing up my spine. "What about her?"

She's picked up a sponge and turned to the counter. Her head is bent, but I know she's shaken. My brother was eighteen when he died, two years older than I was, struck by a drunk driver on his way to classes at Cornell University. It was fourteen years ago, but the pain from that kind of wound never heals. Carolyn had been his first real girlfriend.

My dad has risen from the table, dishes in hand, and he joins us by the sink. "What about her?" he echoes.

Mom tilts her head, turning finally to face us. "She's here in town. She called to get your telephone number, Anna. I told her you were here, and since she was calling from a gas station just a few miles away, I invited her over."

The tingle becomes a full-fledged jolt. Why would a friend of my brother's, a woman we'd met only once fourteen years ago, want to get in touch with me? I turn back to the sink, busying myself with the cleanup, thoughts racing.

"Why do you think she wants to see you, Anna?" Mom asks.

I smile and shrug. I have no idea why Carolyn is coming here tonight. And I don't want to share my suspicion that the quiet, comfortable evening I envisioned spending with my folks is about to spiral into something quite different.

CHAPTER 3

T HE MENTAL PICTURE I HAVE OF CAROLYN DE-
laney from long ago is sharp. She was a petite, blue-
eyed blonde who possessed a smile that dazzled, a radiant,
bubbly personality, and she was a *cheerleader* no less.
Couple all that with the fact that Steve was obviously head
over heels in love, it's no wonder I hated her on sight.

But to make matters worse, Carolyn exuded sexuality.
Not the high school, fumbling, experimental kind of sexuality I happened to be experiencing at the time, but the
real thing. I was only sixteen, but I could tell she and
Steve were *sleeping* together. With Carolyn, I knew her
hold on my brother went way beyond anything I could
compete with.

Like a whirlwind all that spins through my head now
as I prepare myself to come face-to-face with the female
who usurped my place in my brother's heart all those
years ago. It still rankles, especially since she hadn't had
the grace to come to Steve's funeral.

I plan to get to the door first, but when the bell rings, Mom beats me to it. I'm concerned about how my parents will react. The first and only time they met Carolyn was when Steve brought her home during a school holiday.

Mom ushers Carolyn into the living room with a hand on her arm. Carolyn has placed her own hand over it, a gesture that suggests that if my mother moves away, she might bolt. Carolyn lifts her chin and looks at my dad and me. Her expression seems to acknowledge that she knows she has changed in the years since she walked in on Steve's arm.

And that those years have been less than kind. She's overweight, with the boxy, waistless figure of a woman who hasn't seen the inside of a gym since college. She's wearing baggy jeans and an oversized gray sweatshirt that reaches almost to her knees. A tote bag the size of a small suitcase dangles from one shoulder. Her platinum blond hair has faded to dishwater, and the once sparkling eyes turn down at the corners, as if a lifetime of frowning has left them in a perpetual slump. The dazzling smile has vanished, gone without a trace.

She eases the tote bag to the floor and turns toward my father. "You're Steve's dad. James, isn't it?"

He replies with a brief nod and takes her other arm, leading her toward the couch. "Why don't you sit down? Would you like something to drink? Coffee? Something stronger?"

She shakes her head. "No. Thank you." She sinks into the couch, letting her head rest a moment against the cushions.

"Do you remember Anna?" he asks, motioning for me to join them.

But she doesn't look at me. Her gaze is on Steve's picture against the far wall.

"Are you all right?" Mom's voice is gentle.

"No." She passes a hand over her face, shielding herself from our scrutiny, as if sorry now that she made the decision to come.

The three of us find ourselves standing over her in confused wariness.

The drama is beginning to grate. Carolyn's shoulders slump with despair, but she exudes the smell of fear. Or duplicity. They smell very much alike. My senses snap to full alert. For all the waves of vulnerability rolling off Carolyn like ripples in a brook, I don't trust her. I wish I could probe the human mind as easily as I can another vampire's. But I can't. Like my parents, all I can do is wait, shifting impatiently from one foot to the other.

Finally my mother, ever the facilitator, sits down beside Carolyn. Her lips curve in an amiable smile of concern. She takes Carolyn's hands and holds them in her own, rubbing gently as if to warm them. "Carolyn Delaney. You know, it's an amazing coincidence, but we have a parent at our school with the same name. I think of you often because of it."

Carolyn drops her eyes. "It isn't a coincidence, Mrs. Strong."

Mom gives a little start. "It isn't? You're related to Trish Delaney?"

The way my mother asks the question tells me she knows the girl, and her impression is not at all favorable.

Carolyn's face flushes with color. "She's been in some trouble, I know."

My father's eyes register the shock and surprise on Mom's face. "Anita?" he asks. "You know this girl?"

Mom's eyes narrow. I know of Trish. She's missed quite a bit of school this year. We suspect a drug problem. Both the school nurse and her counselor tell me they've tried to contact you, Carolyn, many times. You never return the calls."

Carolyn's shoulders sag. "I was afraid to. Afraid if

I came to school, if you recognized me—" She bites off the words, shakes her head, and continues. "But I did try to get Trish help on my own. I made appointments for her with a counselor at the hospital where I work. But I couldn't force her to attend the sessions." Her eyes shift to me. "That's why I'm here. She's run away." She turns and looks directly at me. "I want you to find her."

My parents and I exchange looks. We don't have to speak the words aloud to know what each is thinking. Why would she come to us, virtual strangers, with a problem that is better addressed by the authorities?

I cross my arms over my chest. "You should call me at the office tomorrow. Or better yet, go to the police. They are the ones—"

"I can't go to the police. *You* have to help her."

"What do you expect me to do?" I ask, my voice sounding brittle in my ears. "I'm not a drug counselor."

A glimmer of hope sparks in Carolyn's eyes. "I know what you are. You're a bounty hunter. You can find Trish before the police and we can work out a deal for her."

I frown at her, afraid my suspicion is about to be confirmed. "What did Trish do that she'd need a deal from the police?"

But my mother interrupts before she can answer. She's looking at Carolyn, wariness darkening her eyes. "How do you know what Anna does?"

Carolyn pauses just a heartbeat before saying, "Anna's been in the papers. You know. There aren't that many bounty hunters in San Diego."

The answer placates my mother, but not me. "That still doesn't explain why you'd come here tonight, to us, instead of the authorities. I'm sorry, Carolyn. I understand how upset you must be that your daughter is in trouble. But you need a private detective, not a bounty hunter. I have my hands full chasing people who present a real danger to society, not an out of control teenager."

"That's what you think she is? An out of control teenager?"

"Well, isn't she?" Resentment is beginning to prickle the back of my neck. "What did she do? Get caught dealing? And why in the world would you come to my parents' home to ask for help?"

"I didn't know who else to turn to," she says with a quick intake of breath.

"How about the police? How about her father? How about—"

"I think Trish may have killed someone."

She says it so sadly, so quietly, that at first I think I imagined it. Mom and Dad stare at her. I feel my pulse start to race.

"You suspect Trish has killed someone?"

"It's not her fault," Carolyn says. "Not really. It's that teacher."

"Teacher?" Mom's sharp voice cuts in like a razor.

"His name is Daniel Frey," she says. "He teaches English. He mentors students, uses his 'sensitive nature' to help them get in touch with their inner selves while he's getting in touch with everything else." Carolyn's voice loses its tenuous waiver, becomes heated. "He's a drug dealer, among other things, and a pedophile—"

Mom presses both hands over her eyes as if they burn with weariness. "You have proof of this?"

The question startles me into shifting my gaze from Carolyn to my mother. "You don't sound surprised."

She lets her hands drop and turns away from me to face Carolyn. "I've heard rumors," she says. "They have never been substantiated. Daniel Frey is a tenured teacher with a good record. His students love him. Without proof of wrongdoing, there has never been anything I could do."

Carolyn's eyes bore into my mother's. "Hear me out," she says. "Help me find Trish. I'll give you all the proof you need."

"Wait a minute." I'm still reeling over the turn this conversation has taken. "Mom, Carolyn should be telling this to the police. She has no right to involve you. If she thinks it's because she and Steve were friends—"

"We were more than friends. You know that."

She says it quietly.

"Okay. You were more than friends. That doesn't give you the right—"

My mother draws a quick breath and raises a hand to stop me. "Anna. Wait. Trish is thirteen."

I don't understand the implication of Mom's words and I'm not ready to relinquish the resentment I feel toward Carolyn. Her presence here brings back a rush of bad memories and I see how it's affecting my parents. I want her gone. "So what?"

Carolyn turns away from me to face my mother. "You know, don't you?"

I blow out an impatient puff of air. "Know what?"

Mom's voice has the hollow ring of shock. "Trish is Steve's daughter."

My eyes lock on Carolyn's. "What are you talking about? Trish can't be Steve's."

Carolyn's expression shifts from uncertainty to relief. It happens instantly, like the flash of reflected light on a mirror. "Yes, she can," she says. "And she is. Trish is your niece."

CHAPTER 4

"WHAT DID YOU SAY?" I BARELY RECOGNIZE MY own voice, it's so hoarse with rage.

"It's true," Carolyn says. "Trish is your niece, your parent's grandchild."

I take a step toward her. That she could come into my parent's home and lie to them in such an outrageous way threatens what little self-control I have left. "Get out." The words come out in a growl, sounding more animal than human.

But my mother places a hand on my arm. She's staring at Carolyn, face blank with shock. Then she recovers. I see it in the set of her shoulders. Her mouth forms a thin, hard line and she steps between Carolyn and me. "Why should we believe that this child is Steve's?"

Carolyn holds up both hands in a conciliatory gesture. "I didn't expect that you would. I brought Trish's hairbrush from home. We can use the hair for a DNA test. If you don't have anything of Steve's, we can use a sample of your blood. It won't be as accurate of course, but—"

For the first time my father speaks. His expression betrays nothing, but his voice trembles. He's feeling the same fury burning through me. "Why are you telling us this now? Because she's in trouble? What do you think we can do?"

Carolyn takes one of his hands, holding on even though he stiffens and pulls back. "I'm sorry that I've upset you. I never intended to tell you about Trish. Not ever. I just planned to talk to Anna. To hire her to find Trish. But when your wife told me on the phone that you were all here together, I thought it was a sign. I had to come. I don't have anyone else to turn to. And I thought after you'd heard the story, you would want to help. She is your grandchild. I wouldn't make that up."

Mom's voice is steady. "Why wouldn't Steve have told us that you were pregnant?"

"He never knew. I didn't find out until after the accident. When Steve died, I got sick. I ended up in the hospital. That's when I found out I was pregnant."

"Why didn't you come to us then?"

Carolyn releases my father's hand. "I thought I could handle it. I loved Steve. But I made the mistake of telling my parents. They didn't share my enthusiasm. They tried to convince me to have an abortion. They were relentless. I figured you would feel the same way, that the baby was a mistake." Carolyn's expression hardens. "After all, you didn't bother to call to see why I hadn't come to the funeral."

When no one responds, she waves the air with a hand. "It doesn't matter now anyway. I ran away. I came here because I got a scholarship to nursing school. After I had Trish, I got a job at a local hospital. I raised Trish in the best way I could. We got along very well until Trish started high school. Suddenly, everything changed."

"Tell us," Mom says, when neither my father nor I seem inclined to urge her on. "You've kept Steve's child, our grandchild, from us for all these years. What you tell us now had better be the truth."

Carolyn nods and perches on the edge of the couch. "Trish and I moved here from downtown last year," she says. "I didn't like the group of kids Trish was involved with in her old school." She looks up at my mother. "I didn't know it was your school. Not until later."

Mom says nothing, but her eyes betray her skepticism. I see it and a building anger reflected on her face.

Carolyn shrugs and continues. "There was an older group of kids in the neighborhood who took a special interest in Trish from the moment we moved in. Naturally, she loved the attention. I suspected they were smoking pot and drinking. I should have stopped it then. But if Trish was doing it, too, she was very clever at hiding it. She never missed a curfew. Never neglected her chores or lied about where she was going or with whom. A couple of months ago, things changed."

She moves restlessly, pressing and releasing her palms, crossing and uncrossing her legs. "Trish has always been a good student but suddenly her grades fell. She began to stay out late, was evasive about what she was doing. Sometimes she would come home stoned or drunk. Once she didn't make it into the house before passing out on the front porch steps. I tried everything I could think of to intervene. That's when I contacted Daniel Frey, the one teacher Trish seemed to respect. I hoped that he could offer insight into Trish's behavior."

She pauses and wearily shakes her head. "He promised to watch out for Trish and asked my permission for her to join a select group of students he mentored after school. But he said his techniques were a bit unconventional and he often took students to his home for overnight or weekend sessions. If I objected to that, I could say no and he wouldn't pursue it."

At this point my mother can no longer hold her tongue. "You didn't think 'overnight and weekend sessions' an odd thing for a teacher to suggest? It didn't occur to you that perhaps you should contact someone else at the school and report what this teacher said to you?"

Carolyn lowers her eyes. "He gave me the name of a parent of one of the other students in his 'program.' I called her. She told me in glowing terms how Mr. Frey had helped her daughter. You have to understand, Mrs. Strong. I was desperate. Trish refused the help I offered through the hospital. She was slipping away and I felt I had no one else to turn to. When Trish said she'd accept Mr. Frey's help, I was relieved."

Mom shakes her head. "You've leveled some very serious charges against this teacher. Once we've found Trish, I expect you to come with me before the school board. But right now, we need to help your daughter. Do you have any idea where she is?"

Carolyn shrugs. "No. She's been gone two days. She left right after the disappearance of Barbara Franco. When I heard this morning that Barbara's body had been discovered—that she'd been murdered—I was afraid Trish might be involved."

Mom draws a sharp breath. "Barbara's body was discovered?"

The tone suggests she knew this girl, too. She catches my eye and gives a brief nod. "Another of our students. She was reported missing on Friday. God, I can't believe this is happening."

I look at Carolyn. "Why do you suspect Trish is involved?"

Carolyn bites her lip. "Barbara is the one friend Trish made here that was her same age. They really seemed to hit it off. But she was as worried about Trish as I was. Barbara came to me last week with suspicions about Mr. Frey and what he was doing with Trish. I told her that she must be mistaken. I had talked to him, that he was helping Trish. But she kept insisting that Frey was supplying drugs to kids in exchange for sex."

"And you didn't believe it?"

"Would you? Trish was getting better. There were no more late night parties. She seemed happier. But I couldn't convince Barbara. She said if I didn't do something to stop what was going on, she would. She said she would go to you, Mrs. Strong, and tell you what was happening."

I look over at my mother. "Did she?"

Mom shakes her head. "No. I wish she had."

Carolyn's expression crumbles and she begins to cry. "She didn't because I talked her out of it." Sobs shake her shoulders. "I told her she should go to Mr. Frey first. I told her he was a good teacher and it wouldn't be fair to slander his reputation with gossip. I sent her to Frey. I think he killed her and I'm afraid Trish may have helped."

We let her cry, though part of me wants to ask her why she hasn't told this story to the police. But the other part acknowledges that if what she says is true, Trish is Steve's child. She's blood. And she's in trouble.

After a minute, I go into the kitchen for a box of tissues. Carolyn accepts the box, pulls one free and mops at her face. She reaches down and pulls something out of the tote at her feet.

It's a photo album.

She holds it out to us like an offering. "Pictures of Trish. I thought you might like to see them."

Neither Mom nor Dad moves to accept it, but I can't resist. I lower myself onto the couch beside her and open to the first page.

I can't tell how tall the girl is from the school picture, or what body type she is, but there *is* a resemblance to my brother. She has Steve's dark, onyx eyes, huge, almond shaped. She's looking straight at the camera, her facial bones delicate, her mouth full. Her hair is the same color as mine, as my mother's, pulled back with a clip at the top of her head, tendrils resting on her shoulders, wisping around her face. She's smiling but not quite. An almost spectral radiance surrounds her. I can't stop myself. I suck in a breath, blow it out and hold the picture up for my parent's to see.

This could be my brother's child.

My mother's breath catches. The anger and skepticism are gone. "Oh my god."

Carolyn gathers up her things. "I know you're shocked by all this. I'm sorry. I'm only doing what I think is best for Trish."

My mother starts to rise, to show Carolyn to the door, but I hand her the album. "I'll see Carolyn out. I have some questions for her."

The reality is there are a few things I want to say to Carolyn that I don't want them to hear. The look my mother throws at me makes it clear she knows exactly what this sudden gesture of courtesy on my part is all about.

Still, she doesn't argue.

But Carolyn isn't fooled either. "Do you believe me about Trish?" she asks quietly when we're out of earshot.

I shake my head. "I don't know. It seems strange that you've been here for months, knowing all along that my mother and father are Trish's grandparents, and choose now to spring it on them."

"I explained that—"

"I know what you explained," I snap, cutting her off. "I want to explain something to you. If Trish is Steve's child, she's blood, and I'll do everything I can to help her.

But if you're trying to run a con, if you hurt my folks, I swear, I'll make your life more than miserable."

A little spark of defiance flashes in Carolyn's eyes, but she's smart enough not to give voice to it. She simply nods and starts down the porch steps. She doesn't look back.

CHAPTER 5

IT IS ELEVEN WHEN I SHOW CAROLYN OUT. MY parents and I spend the next few hours poring over the album she left. It's a small album, composed mostly of Trish's school pictures. No cuddly pictures of mother and daughter, no formal family portraits, no group photos with extended family. At one point, Mom brings out one of Steve's baby pictures to compare with Trish's. The two babies could have been twins.

But don't all babies look alike?

I see the shift taking place in my parents' attitude toward this girl. They *want* her to be Steve's.

Before long, we are all hugging each other and crying.

They ask me to spend the night with them. But one of the sad truths about being a vampire is a keen awareness of the everyday things that make us different from humans. I have to avoid mirrors, for instance. And quite naturally, my parent's home is full of them. Nighttime is particularly bad because I cast no reflection in brightly lit windows either. So far, neither Mom nor Dad have noticed how I carefully pull all the drapes just before sunset. One of these days, however, they may question why I'm so diligent. They live at the top of Mt. Helix and the view from their home sweeps from Del Mar to Mexico. I used to love it, especially at night.

So, I make my excuses and at 2:00 a.m., trek wearily home. Before I go, we decide that we should meet again tomorrow night. Mom will call Carolyn from school the next day and set it up. I hug her, knowing what she faces at school is weighing heavily on her. A student murdered, another missing, a teacher under suspicion. It seems the most logical place for me to start looking for Trish is this Daniel Frey. Mom will arrange for me to come on campus in the guise of extra security.

I hate to leave them.

I've rented a condo downtown while my cottage in Mission Beach is being rebuilt. I console myself on the drive with the thought that it makes sense for me to go there tonight because I have to be in the office early. I want to fill my partner, David, in on what we'll be doing for the next couple of days.

Tracking a *niece*—a niece I didn't know I had.

A niece who may be involved in a murder.

I reach into my handbag beside me on the seat and withdraw the picture I removed from Carolyn's album. I hold it in front of me, just below my line of sight as I drive, so I can glance at it.

There is something about the girl that fascinates me. Not just that she might be my niece, but that I feel a connection to her unlike anything I've ever experienced. Since becoming a vampire, I find my sentiments toward humans often seem to rage out of control. Culebra tells me it's natural. That as long as I have ties to human family and friends, I will be sensitive to mortal concerns.

But this is more than mortal concern. I saw the way my mom and dad reacted to her pictures.

I can't describe what I feel when I look at her. But it's powerful and strong.

And it feels a lot like hope.

CHAPTER 6

TUESDAY

By THE TIME I GET HOME, I'M EXHAUSTED—emotionally and physically. The myth about vampires being creatures of the night is just that. Some things don't change when you become a vampire. If you were a morning person before the change, you will remain a morning person. I need my eight hours, so when the alarm goes off at six, I literally have to drag myself out of bed and into the shower.

The need for that first cup of coffee is another of those constants. I don't bother to get dressed before I plug in the pot. By the time I've slipped on jeans and a sweater, the coffee is ready and so am I.

I take a cup of coffee and go to stand on the balcony that spans the front of my apartment. I have a view that extends over Seaport Village and west toward Coronado. In early morning, the bay is quiet, the motionless water shimmering like liquid gold in the sun.

I sip coffee and let the caffeine awaken sleeping brain

cells. I'm not worried about spending the day at Mom's school or my presence attracting unusual attention. Because of the murder of Barbara Franco, there will be grief counselors and police on campus. Another unfamiliar face won't be cause for alarm. The few teachers who might recognize me know what I do for a living. It's not too far a stretch to imagine a bail enforcement agent moonlighting as a security guard—especially when she is related to the principal.

And the irony is not lost on me that for the first time, my choice of occupation is not a matter of dissension between my parents and me. Not once last night did they mention how much they wished I'd give up this quasi law enforcement gig and go back to teaching.

Carolyn didn't know the particulars about Barbara's death, but I'm assuming there will be something in the newspaper. I finish my coffee, grab my purse and start down for the parking garage. There's a newspaper kiosk just outside the elevator door. I drop in the requisite coins, pull out the paper and fold it under my arm. I'm busy searching my purse for car keys when I run head first into the last person I expect to see—my sometimes boyfriend, Max.

So much for a vampire's catlike reflexes. I literally bounce off his chest. He laughs and gently holds me at arm's length.

"Hey, sunshine. Where are you off to in such a rush?"

Max is one of those big, handsome men that makes a female's heart—human or vamp—beat faster. He's six foot three and weighs in at a well-muscled 225. He's Latino, with eyes the color of the ocean. The combination of suntanned skin, dark hair, and those glorious eyes takes my breath away.

This morning he's wearing shorts and a muscle shirt that emphasize most of his best features.

Most. Not all.

He's holding my arms and smiling down at me. I gather my wits together enough to cleverly ask, "Where did you come from?"

"Originally?" he says. "Or just now?"

I shake my head. "You know what I mean. When did you get back from DC?"

He makes a move to turn me back toward the elevator. "I'll be happy to fill you in. But let's go upstairs. It's been way too long since we've seen each other and I've missed you. A lot. Want to see?"

I've missed him, too. It's been a long time since we've been together—really together. Since I became vampire, in fact. First it was because feeding and sex are so intertwined, I was afraid to let myself go there with Max.

He doesn't know what I am, of course. No human does.

And then I got involved in a thing with Avery. That didn't work out so very well. But during that time, Max was on a DEA assignment, working undercover as the driver for a Mexican drug lord. That case came to a close and he was sent to Washington to clean up the details. He's been gone the last two months.

Now, here he is.

I stare into his wonderful face, heat rippling my skin with such a strong flush of sexual desire I almost succumb to the temptation to take him back upstairs. I think I've learned to separate feeding from sex in the time we've been apart, but unfortunately, I don't have time to test the theory. I'm due at Mom's school at eight, and I need to get David working on a trace.

Reluctantly, I extricate myself from his hands. "I can't. Not now. I have to go to the office. Come with me. There's something I want to tell David and you should hear it, too. In fact, you may be able to help."

The corners of his mouth turn down. "Great. Spending the morning with you and David. Just what I fantasized about all the way from Washington."

Still, he takes my hand and follows me to my car. I use the remote to open the doors. When we're both inside and heading out of the parking garage, he asks, "Help you with what?"

"Wait until we get to the office," I reply. "I'll tell you and David both at the same time. Fill me in on your case. What's going on?"

He shrugs. "It's a wrap. Martinez's money laundering operation in Mexico is history. The dozen or so businesses he used on this side of the border will be next."

Martinez is the head of the Mexican mob—the guy Max worked for as a driver. I sneak a sideways look at his face. "But Martinez hasn't been arrested yet, right?"

Max catches the real question I'm asking. He reaches over and caresses my shoulder. "I'm not in any danger. At least not yet. Martinez wouldn't be crazy enough to come after me here, even if he figures out who I am. He may be a greedy, ruthless bastard but he's not suicidal. He'll lay low for a while. In fact, we have intel that he and his family are in Colombia. At the hacienda of one of his suppliers."

"When do you expect to go after him?"

"As soon as we have extradition ironed out. So far, the *Federales* have agreed to cooperate. For the time being, it's best to let Martinez think he's in the clear. That it was just minions like me who got picked up. When the time is right, we want to catch him by surprise."

He sounds very matter-of-fact and unconcerned, but I know as long as Martinez is loose, Max is not completely safe. Sooner or later it's bound to get back to Martinez that the driver he thinks is in jail is actually a federal agent putting together the case against him.

But right now I'm pulling into the parking lot in front of my office so the conversation is put on hold. The office is on Pacific Coast Highway, in a low slung, concrete building that used to belong to the StarKist people when tuna fishing was a thriving industry in San Diego. The building stood vacant for over fifteen years, prime water-front real estate. A consortium of businessmen, my father among them, worked out a deal to convert the property to office space. He cut David and me a deal, and we got first pick of the renovated spaces—a corner office with a deck over the water. To top it off, we have designated parking spots, a luxury unheard of this close to Seaport Village and the marina.

Nepotism is not always a bad thing.

David's vehicle, a yellow Hummer with all the chrome bells and whistles, squats in its space. I ease the Jag in next to it. Max gets the hungry look of a little boy on his face as he traces a finger along the Hummer's door as he goes past.

He catches my eye and grins. "I've been thinking of getting one of these."

Right. Just what you need in Southern California—a gas guzzling monster truck. I didn't understand it when David bought his and I don't understand it now. Men and big vehicles. Go figure.

Dad's largesse did not extend to springing for new furniture, so the office is outfitted with stuff we brought from our old digs. There's a big oak partner's desk in the middle of the room and two oversized captains chairs perched one on either side. They have to be big. My part-ner is six foot six and weighs 250 pounds. He was a tight end for the Broncos and stays in shape.

We have a filing cabinet along one wall. Next to it is an old scarred credenza with a coffee maker and mugs on top, supplies underneath. We each have computers and telephones on our respective sides of the desk. A printer and fax sit on a small worktable near the slider that leads to the deck. The only other piece of furniture is a small refrigerator, just big enough for a couple of six packs. It's not much, but it's all we need.

The smell of brewing coffee greets us as we come in.

David is busy at the credenza, his back to us. He's dressed in jeans and a Hawaiian shirt that stretches across the muscles of his back as he moves. He has the kind of smooth, olive skin that retains a tan all year long. He has short-cropped brown hair and blue eyes that can either sparkle with pleasure or cut you dead with cold precision.

When he turns around, he's got two mugs and he thrusts one out to me.

"Glad you're here. Just got a call. We've got—"

He stops short when he spies Max coming in right behind me. The animation drains from his face just as the oxygen seems to drain from the room. The blue eyes become crystalline. David's spine stiffens, his brows crease, his mouth thins with displeasure.

It happens every time. There's a dynamic at work here that I'll never understand. The two men have a lot in common. Both are big guys, both went to college on sports scholarships. David played football at Notre Dame. Max, baseball at USC. After college, David went into pro football. Max played baseball for a while until he blew out his shoulder. They're both adrenaline junkies, which explains their job choices when the sports gigs wound down. Yet, with all that, they can't stand to be in the same room.

I refuse to play their silly game. I pass the mug that David holds out to me back to Max and proceed to fill another one. "You were saying?" I prompt, ignoring the way David is ignoring Max.

David swallows a mouthful of coffee, eyes shifting back and forth from me to Max. Finally, he says, "It's not important." His eyes settle on Max. "So. Max, you're back from Washington, huh? For good?"

It's obvious from his tone what he wants the answer to be. I'm sure Max picks up on it, too, but he doesn't show it as he shakes his head. "No. There's more to be done." He puts a hand around my waist. "I just wanted to spend some time with Anna."

David looks at me. "So what are you doing here?"

That's my cue. "I asked him to come. I have something to tell you both."

I motion for them to sit down. David takes his seat, Max, mine. I perch myself on the corner of the desk. In as short and concise a way as possible, I tell them what happened last night. There's a long moment of stunned silence when I finish.

David speaks first. "I never met your brother. But I know what you've told me about him. To find out that he might have a child must have been quite a shock to your folks. How are they holding up?"

"As well as can be expected."

"Do they believe the kid is Steve's?" Max asks. "Are you sure this Carolyn isn't running some kind of scam?"

David shoots me a look that says it figures Max would ask something like that. But it's a fair question. One I've asked myself.

"I don't know," I reply. "Carolyn offered to run DNA tests. And we saw pictures. In fact," I rummage in my handbag and pull out Trish's picture along with one of my brother's at the same age. "What do you think?"

I lay the pictures side by side on the desk. David and Max lean forward.

"There is a resemblance," Max says after a moment. "It doesn't prove she's Steve's daughter."

"No," I admit. "It doesn't. But even if it turns out Carolyn is lying to us, there's a murdered teenage girl, another who's missing, and a teacher at my mom's school who may be a pedophile, or worse. I think it's worth looking into."

Max is shaking his head. "This is a job for the authorities. If the girl has been kidnapped, the FBI should be called. They are far better equipped to handle this sort of thing than you and David."

David frowns indignantly, but I speak before he has

a chance. "You're right. If we knew Trish had been kidnapped, I'd be the first to make the call. But maybe she's hiding because she knows something about what happened to her friend. Her mother is afraid if the police find her first, they'll assume she's involved. If we find her first, we can make a deal with the authorities if we need to."

David quickly nods in agreement. "What do you want me to do?"

I pick up a notepad and begin to jot down the names as I explain. "The murdered girl's name is Barbara Franco. I don't know anything about what happened to her except that her body was discovered yesterday. Could you call your contacts at SDPD and find out what you can? I brought the newspaper. There may be something there to get you started. I'll be spending the day at Mom's school. I want to see this Daniel Frey in action. Mom will give me access to his personnel records, but you could run a check on him, too. I plan to follow him after school. See what he does. Where he goes. We can meet back here, say at six?"

David takes the pad from my hand. "I'll get started right away."

"What can I do?" Max has gotten to his feet.

I'd actually forgotten for a moment that he's in the room. "Thanks, Max," I reply, smiling up at him. "I appreciate your wanting to help." There's a pause while I try to come up with something for him to do, but it's an awkward moment.

Max puts the coffee mug down on the desk and stands up.

"Well, I should probably check in with the boys downtown. Maybe we can have dinner tonight."

His eyes are guarded, but I catch the flash of disappointment. I walk him to the door. "I'm sorry I can't spend the day with you," I say, reaching up to hug him. "I mean it."

His body relaxes against mine a minute before he straightens up and reaches for the doorknob. "I'll be at my old office in the Federal Building if you need me," he says. "Let me know about tonight."

He nods over my head to David, and then he's gone.

MY MOTHER'S SCHOOL IS IN LA MESA, ABOUT FIFteen miles east of San Diego. This is the first time a student at Valley Vista High School has been murdered. I have a feeling the media will be out in force.

And they are. I count four news vans in the visitor's parking lot. Mom advised me to park in the faculty lot, so I make my way around a swarm of reporters and concerned parents to the back of the school. Most of the parking spaces are filled, leaving me to assume teachers, administrators and staff are already assembled at the meeting Mom had called for eight o'clock.

As I make my way on campus, I'm approached by a uniformed security guard. He asks for identification, which I produce. He ticks my name off a list on a clipboard and asks if I know my way to the administration building.

I assure him that I do. He doesn't acknowledge that my last name is the same as the principal's, which leads me to believe he's been hired for temporary duty.

Valley Vista High is a typical Southern California school. Open, sprawling; the buildings are buff colored, one-story stucco rectangles with red-tile roofs. Like most schools in the district, it's a closed campus, meaning students are not allowed to leave at lunch. Because of this, there are lots of "green belts" outfitted with benches and tables. Made of concrete, not wood. Prevents hormonally charged teenagers from carving their lascivious desires into the benches and tables. It is not impervious to tagging, however, and no matter how tight the security, a determined kid can sneak spray paint on to campus and mark his territory like a mongrel pup.

A maintenance man is busy scrubbing last night's artistic endeavors off one of the benches as I pass. He looks up and gives me a nod, then returns to his labors. Here in the back of the school, at least, it's business as usual.

Not so in the front office. I spy Mom through the door of her office. She's talking with a couple of uniformed policemen. They are standing behind someone who is seated with his back to me. When she spies me, she crooks a finger, inviting me in.

I'm barely through the door when the person in the chair turns to face me. My heart gives a little jolt. It's the Chief of Police, Warren Williams, and the last time I saw him, I nearly killed him.

CHAPTER 7

WARREN WILLIAMS IS A VAMPIRE. A REALLY OLD vampire who has integrated himself so well into human society, he can hold an office like chief of police and no one, except other supernaturals, knows the truth. The confrontation he and I had two months ago resulted in his retreating into a comalike trance called "stasis." I don't quite understand everything about that conflict. And I don't want to. At the time, Williams told me that I was "the one" and made references to a mysterious calling that neither he nor Avery ever explained. After Avery died, Williams regained full health. He has tried often to contact me, presumably to mend fences, but I wasn't ready to see him.

I'm still not.

Williams rises from the chair and holds out his hand. He seems to bear no scars from the fight we had. In fact, his grey green eyes meet mine and I detect no malice simmering in the depths. All the same, I take his hand warily.

He smiles and says, "Miss Strong. Nice to meet you. Your mother tells me you've volunteered to help on campus today."

His thoughts project a different message. *Anna. We need to talk. Avery's affairs must be settled. People are beginning to question his disappearance. The hospital wants to start an inquiry.*

I drop his hand, smile, and ignore the undercurrent. "Nice to meet you, too." I glance at my mother, then back to him. "I don't know the particulars of Barbara Franco's death. I assume you're here to fill us in."

His eyes narrow, darken. *You can't ignore this. I want you to meet me tonight. At Avery's.*

No. If that is the reason you are here today, you have made a mistake. You should have sent someone else. I will contact the hospital. I will send them Avery's final message—his letter of resignation. That should buy us more time.

I move away from him and around the desk to stand beside my mother. "What happened to the girl?"

Williams watches me for an instant. Then the storm passes and his eyes settle once again into pools of calm. *Perhaps that will work. For now. But we must talk. About you.*

He catches the imperceptible nod with which I acknowledge his remark. I know he's right. I need to end the nagging once and for all.

He catches that, too.

He gives me a cold smile and motions for Mom and I to sit. There is another visitor's chair in the corner and I pull it over so that my mother and I are facing Williams, the desk between us.

"Barbara Franco's body was discovered early yesterday morning by a jogger in Cuyamaca State Park," he begins. "She had been beaten, sexually assaulted and strangled. At this point, we have no suspects and no motive. She had no male or female lovers. There are no known sexual predators in her family or in their close circle of friends. At least none that we know of. We are, of course, looking into that."

He pauses a moment and looks at me.

Instantly, I understand. *You think she may have been killed by a supernatural?*

There are some indications. I have my people working on it. We'll know after the post mortem.

You will let me know?

I will be in contact.

All this passes between us in the length of a heartbeat. I feel my mother move restlessly beside me. I know she's battling with the decision we made last night to keep the information about Trish and Frey and the possible link to Barbara's murder from the police. If Barbara's death was caused by a supernatural, though, neither Trish nor Frey may have had anything to do with it.

And Trish may be in greater danger than we imagined.

But I'm not willing to bring Williams into my confidence about Trish. I speak before Mom can. "Will you have people on campus all day?"

Williams nods, his expression wary. He suspects I'm holding something back, but I've shielded my thoughts and he can't penetrate the mental barrier. He says, "Detectives will be questioning students and faculty. Your mother has offered us the use of a counselor's office."

I put a hand on Mom's arm. "Let's let Chief Williams get his men set up. You need to address the faculty, don't you?"

She draws a deep breath and passes a hand over her face. "Yes. Chief Williams, my secretary will take your detectives to the counseling office. Would you like to say something to the faculty? Or to the students when we meet later this morning?"

We've all risen from our chairs. Williams considers

the question for a moment. "I'd like to speak to the students if it's all right. Maybe one of her friends can shed some light on Barbara's last day."

Mom glances at her watch. "The student assembly is at nine. We've called a minimum day, so students will only be on campus until noon. That way if they wish to speak to a detective or counselor, they can do so this afternoon."

She shows the policemen out of her office and closes the door before turning back to me. "I should have told him about Trish and Frey."

I know the reason for her anxiety. I also know why she didn't say anything. A decision I agree with. "You didn't say anything because you don't want to involve Trish until we know for sure what happened. You're protecting her. It's all right, Mom."

"But what if she's in danger? God, Anna. If anything happens to her and I could have prevented it—"

I put an arm around her shoulders. "Carolyn is her mother, and she asked us not to say anything. The police are on the case now. They're trained to investigate this type of crime. If Frey is involved, they'll find that out, too. In the meantime, let me see what I can do. I've got David running a background check on Frey, and I plan to follow him when he leaves campus today. Remember, Trish is a troubled teenager. Her running away may have nothing to do with Barbara."

There's a discreet knock on the door. Mom's secretary is back, and she points at her watch. Mom acknowledges the gesture and tugs at the hem of her suit coat.

"Are you coming to the meeting?" she asks.

I nod. "I'll stand in back. Before we go, though, can you get me that file on Frey?"

Mom shuffles some papers on her desk and retrieves a thick manila folder. "I pulled the file this morning." Then, like an afterthought, she reaches into a bookcase behind her desk and pulls out the most recent of a string of year-books that fills the bottom shelf. She opens to the faculty section and points. "Here's a picture of Daniel Frey." She glances up to meet the gaze of her secretary, standing expectantly by the door. "I'd better go."

Her tension is palpable. I try to make my smile en-couraging. She squeezes my arm in an acknowledgement of the effort and leaves me alone to study the photograph on the desk.

It's a studio photograph, a head shot of a man in his early forties with short, salt-and-pepper hair and a smile made perfect by generous lips and straight, white teeth. There is inherent strength in the face and a certain stud-ied sensuality. Daniel Frey projects humor, sensitivity, intelligence and sexuality. A combination that would be irresistible to teenage girls.

Hell, a combination irresistible to females of any age or species. The vibe I'm getting is strong enough to make me run my fingers over the page.

I snap the book shut and replace it on the shelf. I'll look at the file later. It's time to see if this guy is as good in person.

The faculty meeting is being held in the theater on campus. Mom is up on the stage, her smooth, pale hair shimmering under the lights. She's composed, profes-sional and concerned as she fills the staff in on what has happened.

Once again, I'm taken with how beautiful she is and how proud I am to be her daughter. Two months ago I resented my parents and their inability to accept what I chose to do with my life. Now because I know our time is limited, my feelings have changed.

I shake away the melancholy and let my gaze sweep the room. Daniel Frey is easy to spot. He's in the middle of the auditorium, surrounded by female faculty mem-bers. His expression is serious, engaged, as he listens to my mother. Suddenly, he turns in his seat and his eyes go straight to mine.

Hello, Anna. I've looked forward to meeting you.

Daniel Frey is in my head.

I never felt it coming. One moment I'm thinking about my mother and the next, Daniel Frey is in my head. The shock knocks me off guard and raises the hair on the back of my neck. I'm exposed and vulnerable. Any kind of weakness, whether it's surprise or fear, is a dangerous thing. Something you learn very quickly as a vampire.

I shut down my thoughts, but I'm sure not quickly enough to prevent Frey from knowing what I'm feeling. He has turned away from me, looking back toward the front, his own thoughts as impenetrable as a cave on a moonless night.

A second jolt hits me as I realize that only once before have I been locked that completely out of another's thoughts. We vampires can conceal our thoughts from one another if we choose. But this is different. Daniel Frey is not human. Nor is he a vampire.

He's like Culebra.

And I don't know what that is.

CHAPTER 8

WHEN THE FACULTY MEETING IS OVER, AND the auditorium empties, I remain in the back. Frey stands to allow his fellow teachers to file past him and out the door. He remains standing. He's dressed in an outfit that looks both designer and expensive—summer-weight wool pinstripe slacks, raspberry-colored sweater with a striped shirt underneath, black leather coat that hits at midthigh. He didn't buy that outfit on a teacher's salary.

My mother, the last to leave the stage, joins me. Frey follows her. He has not projected a single thought nor has he made an attempt to read mine.

Mom looks at Frey. "Good morning, Daniel." Then she turns to me. "I'm going back to the office. Are you coming, Anna?"

Frey holds my attention, not with his thoughts, but with his smile. It's inquisitive, guarded.

I shake my head at Mom. "No, you go on. I have a few questions for Mr. Frey."

Frey's expression changes, his smile now resonating concern. When he speaks, his voice is velvet edged and smooth as a rose petal. "I'm glad you're here to help your mother. I'll tell you everything I know about Barbara, though I'm afraid it isn't much. She isn't one of my students. Do you want to walk with me to my classroom?"

I nod and Mom leaves us with a surreptitious glance. When Frey's back is turned, she mouths, "Be careful."

I mouth back, "I will."

That's not necessary, you know.

Frey's voice. This time it doesn't come as such a shock, though it reminds me again that I need to be careful in projecting my thoughts.

If that's possible with a creature like Frey.

I follow him down a sidewalk that leads from the theater to his classroom. He has a corner room, by the student parking lot. He opens the door and allows me to precede him inside.

The English classrooms I remember from my high school teaching days were painted institutional gray and decorated with portraits of literary figures scattered among bulletin boards bursting with colorful trivia. Frey's classroom is painted pale yellow and there are no bulletin boards, no portraits. Nothing on the walls at all except a small framed sign. A human would have to get close to read it. Since I don't have to pretend to be human, I read it from the doorway.

"Life may not be the party we hoped for . . . but while we're here we may as well dance."

I shoot Frey a look with raised eyebrows. *Interesting philosophy. Who came up with it?*

He shrugs. *Don't know. Somebody sent it to me in an e-mail. I liked the way it sounded.*

We move to the front, wending our way through student desks lined up eight to a row and stretching from

Frey's podium in front of the blackboard to the back.
I count forty-eight.

Unusually large class size, isn't it?

He shrugs. *Kids seem to want to take my class. And
there's a perpetual teacher shortage. Good teachers leave
to pursue other things.*

He says the last with a pointed look back at me. Has he
picked up the fact that I used to be a teacher from my
mother or out of my head?

Frey opens a door beside the blackboard and motions
me into a tiny office. It's not much bigger than a broom
closet and it's outfitted with a desk, chair and a bookcase.
He offers me the chair and slips out of his jacket, tossing
it onto the bookcase before perching on a corner of the
desk. He can't close the door because his feet are in the
way.

For some reason, it's a comfort that he can't close
that door.

"You don't have to be afraid of me," he says.

"Maybe if you told me what you are, I wouldn't be."

He tilts his head and looks at me, surprise widening
his eyes. *You really don't know? How long have you been
a vampire?*

Not the first time I've been asked that question in that
same tone. I didn't like it much the first time, either. I
blow out a puff of air. *Obviously not long enough. Are you
going to answer my question? What the hell are you?*

He stands up and when he extends a hand toward me,
I jump up, too. Sudden fear elicits a reflexive growl of
warning that comes from deep inside me and curls my
hands into fists at my side. It stops him. He holds the
hand palm up in a gesture of conciliation. Slowly, he
points to the desk and I realize he was reaching for something on it, not aiming a blow at me.

I'm both relieved and embarrassed. *Go ahead.*

He picks up a small round stone, red as blood, and

holds it in his palm. He closes his eyes, mumbling something in a language I don't understand. At first, I'm so busy watching his face that I almost miss it. Then I see. His hand. Nails lengthen into claws, the palm becomes a leathery pad, and fur the color of midnight surrounds the . . . paw.

I press myself against the wall, unable to take my eyes off what looks for all the world like a panther's paw. *What are you?*

Daniel Frey moves, drawing my attention back to his face. He opens his eyes, places the stone back on the desk and waits. In a moment the transformation is complete. He flexes the fingers on his very human hand before answering.

I'm a shape-shifter.

Shape-shifter? How much of your shape can you shift? Just the hands?

He laughs. *Of course not. I didn't think it prudent to give you a full demonstration when I have students due in a few minutes. A panther on campus would be hard to explain. I'm surprised you didn't know right away.*

So many questions form in my head that I don't know what to ask first. *Can you change into anything else? Once you've changed, how do you hold that stone to change back? Don't you need the moon to change?*

He picks up the last question first. *The moon? You're thinking of a were. An entirely different species altogether. And no, I can't change into anything else. I don't really need the stone, either. It merely speeds up the process.*

I know I shouldn't be surprised at this. Shape-shifters. Werewolves. Vampires. What other creatures are there that I've yet to discover?

Frey answers, though the question is rhetorical.

Let's see. I can name several right off the top of my head. Ghosts, for instance. Angels. Demons. Dragons.

Dragons?

— Not many left. But there are a few. In remote jungles, mostly. And lost islands.

I sink back down in the chair. Why do I feel as if we should be having this conversation on a moving staircase at Hogwarts, not here in a California classroom?

Frey is smiling at me. *Now* that's *fiction. The school, that is, not the existence of witches and warlocks. They exist—*

I hold up a hand to stop the flow. I'm quickly reaching information overload. And yet, he's telling me things Culebra has not. I want to keep him talking. *How many shape-shifters do you know? Around here, I mean. Do you travel in prides?*

He resumes his perch on the corner of the desk. *No. We're pretty much solitary creatures. It's hard enough for one big cat to prowl the city undetected. It would be impossible for a pride. Besides, we're not all cats.*

Oh?

There are all kinds of shape-shifters. Some change into dogs. Birds. Snakes.

That's when it clicks, like tumblers in a rusty old lock that yield when you're given the right combination.

Culebra. Rattlesnake.

It's so clear.

Culebra? Frey snatches the name out of the air. *Who's that?*

I shake my head. I'll think about Culebra later. I need to get back to the reason I'm here. I don't waste time forming the words, just let Frey pick the story out of my head. All of it—including Trish's disappearance. I want to see and "feel" his reaction.

His face betrays nothing as he "hears" about Barbara and Trish and why Carolyn suspects he is involved with her daughter's disappearance. I'm not specific about Carolyn's accusations. I frame it in terms of rumor and innuendo. His mind is not closed to me and what he projects is hurt and puzzlement and a growing anger.

Exchanging drugs for sex? Why would she think that? Why would anyone think that?

My mother tells me those rumors have been around for a while, just never substantiated. In my experience, a story like that usually has some basis in fact.

Frey draws himself up, fury hardening the lines around his eyes and mouth. *I help students. I don't give them drugs and I certainly don't sleep with them. I can't believe your mother thinks that I might. Finding women to have sex with has never been a problem for me. And I do prefer women to girls.*

I didn't say my mother believes it. I'm just saying she's heard it. I raise my eyebrows. *And I've seen some of to-day's high school "girls." They're pretty mature for their age.*

Nonetheless, I wouldn't do that. There have never been "sleepovers" or "weekend seminars." I've spoken to Trish a couple of times. She was a troubled kid. I could see that. But she wasn't ready to open up. And I never spoke to her mother. Not once. God. Why would she make up things like that?

I shrug. *Who knows?* I pause briefly before asking, *And what about Barbara Franco? Did she come to see you?*

No. And if she had, I would have told her what I just told you.

He answers directly and without any prevarication that I can detect. However, my experience with shape-shifters has been limited. Even Culebra has kept his true nature from me. I don't really know what they are capable of.

Culebra again? Frey shrugs. *Shape-shifters can be as deceptive as any other being—human or otherwise. We can lie. So can vampires. But I think you already know that.*

Irritation tightens my jaw. *I hate this. I want you to stop getting into my head uninvited. I can prevent it with vampires. Is there a way to stop you?*

Why should I answer that?

A show of good faith. You expect me to believe you, and this would go a long way toward establishing credibility.

He leans toward me, his own irritation evident. *That would require a great leap of faith on my part. I don't know you. I don't trust you any more than you trust me. I think you should go. I have students coming.*

Do you know where Trish is?

The question seems to catch him off guard. Something flickers in the depths of his eyes, ripples the calm, dark waters of his thoughts. But he recovers quickly and the hesitation is like the flutter of a hummingbird's wings—so fast you think it might be an illusion.

Would you believe me if I said I don't? I hope she is safe. Now, I want you to go. Students are arriving. They will need my full attention.

I glance past him to the open classroom door. I don't see anyone.

He taps the side of his nose. *I don't have to "see" to know they are coming.*

And as if on cue, a car door slams in the parking lot. Then another and another. It's thirty minutes until class time. I guess Daniel Frey can smell a human's approach as easily as a panther in the jungle can smell a tethered goat.

CHAPTER 9

I TAKE A SEAT AT ONE OF THE LUNCH TABLES IN front of the theater and watch as silent, somber-faced teens file into Frey's classroom. I don't know what I expect to glean from this eavesdropping, but I don't know what else to do. Daniel Frey blindsided me with his seemingly honest demeanor, to say nothing of the shape-shifting trick. I told him much more than I should have, given the circumstances. And he told me nothing.

Good work, Anna.

Frey meets the students at the door to his classroom, ignoring my presence, though I know he feels it. His thoughts flicker out once or twice as if testing my reaction to the scene.

I don't have one. Yet. All I have are more questions.

As many boys as girls form a crowd that soon spills out of the classroom and into the grassy quad right below my bench. For some reason, I figured his appeal would be strictly to girls. But the students gathering are a mix of jocks and nerds, model-pretty cheerleaders and mousy bookworms. They're all drawn to Frey, and through him, to each other. He's like a modern Pied Piper. I'm not sure if that's a good thing or bad.

Watching the scene takes me back to my own high school experiences. The first two years, I was happy, basking in the reflected glow of a big brother who was immensely popular. Then, in my junior year, he was gone. First off to college, then—gone. Really gone.

I understand the sense of loss, the emptiness. Some of these kids may have been friends of Barbara's. But even if they aren't, no teen expects to have a classmate die at fourteen—let alone be murdered. It's unnatural and unnerving. Frey seems to have a knack for letting them know the sadness and fear they are feeling is a normal part of the grieving process.

Either that, or he's setting them up for one of his "special programs."

As nine o'clock approaches, he shepherds the kids toward the auditorium where my mother and Chief Williams will address them. I follow as far as the office. I don't see the point in hearing another recitation of what I already know. I'll come back to question Frey again after I see Carolyn.

I duck into Mom's office to call David. He answers on the first ring.

"Any luck with the names I gave you this morning?" I ask.

I hear a rustle of paper. "Who should I start with first?"

"How about Daniel Frey?"

"An interesting character, that one," David replies. "He's forty-two years old, born in Boston, educated at Harvard. Came west about ten years ago after teaching at an inner-city school in Boston. Unblemished record. The decision to come to San Diego seems to have coincided with the death of an uncle in an automobile accident. He inherited a little money, bought a condo in Mission Valley, and has lived here ever since."

I give an impatient huff. "What's so interesting about that?"

"I contacted the records office at Harvard. There's a Daniel Augustus Frey listed as having attended all right. But they show him graduating in one of the school's early classes. That would be in the late, what? 1800's? Which makes him closer to two hundred than forty-two. What kind of shape is the old geezer in?"

I detect the humor in David's voice, but somehow I can't bring myself to laugh. Neither can I explain to David that Frey may in fact be two hundred years old. I have no idea of the life expectancy of a shape-shifter. "So," I say instead, "must be a mistake."

"Don't school districts check that kind of thing?"

"They should. My hunch, though, is that he got his job here based on an exemplary record in Boston. Who knows how thoroughly the Boston school district checked his credentials when he applied there? Anything else? Any mysterious disappearances around the time he left?"

David's voice echoes with disappointment. "Nothing. And Frey doesn't have as much as a parking ticket on his record. Fact is, he has never applied for a driver's license. How the hell does he get around in Southern California without a driver's license?"

Good question. On all fours maybe? "I'll be able to answer that when I see you this evening," I reply. "I plan to follow him when he leaves school. What about Barbara Franco?"

What he tells me is pretty much a repetition of what Chief Williams told us this morning. "One interesting coincidence, though," he adds. "The Franco's moved from Boston about the same time as Daniel Frey. They lived in different parts of the city, though, and of course Barbara would have been too young to be one of his high school students."

"What about a sibling? Any brothers or sisters?"

"Nope. Barbara was an only child."

I start to thank David and sign off when he interrupts by asking quietly, "Don't you want to know what I found out about Carolyn Delaney?"

A muscle at the corner of my jaw twitches. I don't remember asking David to run a check on Carolyn, and his tone is less than positive. "Sure. What?"

"She's not going to win any Mother of the Year Awards." His voice is guarded. "In fact, she's been in trouble with the law several times. Five years ago she was caught shoplifting, and Social Services was called because she had Trish with her when she was stopped. She's been picked up for misdemeanor drug possession and a couple of DUIs. But so far, none of the charges have stuck."

He pauses as if waiting for a reaction. I don't have one, not yet, so I prompt, "Go on."

"This isn't the first time Trish has been reported missing. She's run away before. Twice in the last year. The authorities found her both times, and since she refused to say why she ran away and her mother took her back, there was only routine follow-up."

I let this information sink in. I'm getting that same feeling of uneasiness I had when Mom first told me Carolyn Delaney was trying to get in touch with me. "Any way you can follow up on that with Social Services?" I ask after a moment. "And on the Carolyn stuff, too?"

"Will do."

"And David, when Max and I walked in this morning, you said you'd had a call. Do we have a job?"

"Not to worry." His breezy tone makes me imagine he's sitting back in his desk chair, waving my concern away with a handful of paper. "Nothing I can't handle on my own."

"Which means what?"

"Which means just what I said. I can handle this one on my own."

I don't like the sound of that. "Who's the skip?"

"Nobody who'll give me trouble."

"David, who's the skip?"

There's an exaggerated sigh from the other end of the line. "Jake Verdugo."

"Jake the Snake?" As I say it, I get a chill. Maybe the name is literal.

"He's just a small-time hood. He's been spotted in Lakeside. I figured I'd run down there this afternoon and grab him."

"By yourself."

"Why not? You don't think I can handle the little shit? He's barely five feet tall."

"Take Max."

I can't believe I said that, but once it's out, it makes sense.

Obviously, though, not to David. There's a silence at the other end of the line so dense it's almost palpable.

"David? Are you there?"

No answer. He must really be pissed. I'd better talk fast.

"Listen. You know Jake's reputation. He may be small, but the .45 he carries isn't. You'll take him down. Just use Max for backup. Please. Or I'll come downtown right now and we'll go together. I can always follow Frey tomorrow. He isn't going anywhere."

"And what about your niece?" he snaps. "You going to risk losing a chance to find her just so you can babysit me on a job?"

He is pissed. I'll have to bring out the big guns. "Babysit you? After what happened a few months ago, I thought we decided we wouldn't take unnecessary chances. Call me crazy, but going alone after a guy who knows this is the third strike against him and has sworn not to be taken alive sounds like an unnecessary chance to me. If you don't agree to let Max go with you, I'm coming."

It's an unfair argument. David is awash in guilt about the night we were attacked by the man who turned me into a vampire. Of course, he doesn't know that I was turned. All he knows is that a white-collar criminal who shouldn't have given us any trouble knocked him out and assaulted me.

There's a protracted sigh. "How do you know Max will agree?"

"He'll agree. Give me five minutes to call him."

"Be sure he understands I'm only doing this for you, and that he'll be there strictly as backup. That's all. I can handle the rest."

I assure David that I will make Max understand his role in the operation and hang up. When I talk to Max, he immediately agrees to help. He doesn't question why he should or whine that David doesn't treat him well. He simply says he'll call David as soon as we hang up and that he'll see me tonight.

It's one of the reasons I like him so much.

Once that's done, I sit back in Mom's desk chair and digest the information about Frey, the Francos, and most disturbing of all, Trish and Carolyn. Carolyn left some salient points out of her story last night, like the drug bust and DUIs. She also neglected to say anything about Trish having run away twice before. She led us to believe Trish's drug problems came about because of the bad influence of some new friends. Maybe those new friends weren't the only ones responsible.

I grab a piece of paper from a pad on Mom's desk and scribble a hasty note. I don't tell her where I'm going, just that I'll be back before noon.

I think it's time Carolyn and I have a private chat.

CHAPTER 10

CAROLYN AND TRISH LIVE IN ONE OF THE FEW less-than-prosperous areas of prosperous La Mesa, about three miles from the school. The neighborhood is low income, and the address is an apartment building hidden behind a screen of scruffy junipers. The asphalt in the parking lot is cracked and buckled. Only two vehicles occupy spaces, a battered Volkswagen and a rusted Chevy sitting on blocks. Neither one looks capable of going anywhere. I pick my way around bottles and cans littering the walkway to a "security" gate that hangs open on broken hinges. Beyond it is a pool littered with decayed leaves that smell as if they've been there since last fall. The place has the forlorn feeling of neglect.

I know nurses are underpaid, but I can't believe this is the best Carolyn can afford.

I enter through a courtyard strewn with plastic pool chairs yellow with age. I maneuver around them and make my way to a row of mailboxes attached to the wall under a portico of crumbling stucco. Carolyn hadn't given us the apartment number. In fact, she hadn't mentioned that she lived in an apartment at all. But I find a mail slot with "2A" and the name "Delaney" printed in a thick-tipped black marker. There are stairs with rusty banisters on either side of the courtyard, but no indication which apartments are to the right or left. I choose left and start up.

I'm rounding the top of the staircase when a door opens and a man with a broad back and stocky shoulders backs out of a doorway and right into me. He slams the door and then turns with a glare.

I'm not sure which of us gets the bigger shock.

It's No-neck from Beso de la Muerte.

The glare disappears. Like a puppy given an unexpected treat, he wriggles with delight. "Wow, what are you doing here? Did you come to see me?"

But I'm looking past him to the door. "2A." I narrow my eyes and frown. "Not in your wildest dreams. Do you live here?"

He grins. "Me? Nah. I'm just here collecting rent for the guy who owns this building. Broad inside was late paying up."

"Then why would you think I'd be here looking for you, Einstein?"

"Don't have to be a smartass," he whines. But the grin changes to a leer and he gives his crotch a tug. "Sure you don't want a taste? I have plenty left—and you kind of cheated me before."

I don't know what makes me angrier. The implication that part of the "rent" he collected from Carolyn was sex or that I owed him something of the same. I grab him by the scruff of the neck and throw him against the wall. "Does Carolyn know what you do in Mexico?"

He tries to pull away, the same stupid smirk on his face. "Come on. What difference does that make? Sex is sex. I just like the added thrill of doing it with vamps. You're the first one who wouldn't spread her legs—"

Before he gets another word out, I have him upended over the balcony. I know it's not the smartest thing I could do. What if someone catches me dangling a two-hundred pound gorilla by one ankle over a balcony? But sometimes you have to give in to base impulses.

And I now have his full attention.

The smirk is gone. The kid is white with fear, so scared he can't speak. I yank him back up and again slam him against the wall. Hard. "Does she know about Mexico?" I ask again.

He swallows, Adam's apple dancing as he tries to find his voice. "Yes. She thinks it's cool."

"Does she know about me?"

"How could she? I didn't know who you were. I still don't."

I let my fingers find his windpipe and squeeze ever so gently. "And we'll keep it that way, won't we?" He gives a shaky little nod but I'm not convinced. I exert a little more pressure. "You won't mention seeing me here. In fact, you won't come back here. Ever. If you do, I'll find you. I can do it. Trust me, it won't be hard. Do you understand?"

It's amazing how being strangled clarifies thinking, even in the densest individual. He blinks his eyes in rapid-fire succession. At the moment it's all he can do, I've cut off his air supply.

I release my hold and he falls to his knees, clutching his throat and coughing.

"I take that as a 'yes.' Now get out of here."

He slinks down the stairs. I watch him go, but not with any feeling of satisfaction. I know his type. He'll go home, change his shorts and plot revenge. But he may go to Beso de la Muerte to get it. I'll let Culebra know what happened. I don't want this idiot kid to take out his anger on an unsuspecting vamp. Culebra will know how to handle him.

From the balcony I watch the kid squeal out of the parking lot in the Volkswagen. I wouldn't have thought it capable of such speed. I let another minute or so go by just to make sure he doesn't come back. Then I knock on Carolyn's door. I hear a rustle from inside, a murmur that sounds something like, "Fucking kid. What's he want now," and the door swings open.

If I thought Carolyn Delaney looked bad the first time I saw her, the way she looks now is a hundred times worse. She's wearing a worn terry robe so stained and tattered I can't be sure if the color is dirty brown or faded gray. The robe gaps open at the waist, breasts spilling out of a lacy bra that looks like she might have had it since her college days. Only now there's way too much breast and not enough bra and the effect is not pretty. Her hair is unwashed and uncombed, her face splotchy. She smells of sex, musk and tobacco.

The expression of horror when she recognizes me is no doubt mirrored on my own face at seeing her like this.

She pulls the robe closed, runs a hand through her hair, and stands blocking the door. "I didn't expect to see you here," she says. "How did you find me?"

"You gave us your address. Last night. Remember?"

"I gave you my telephone number, too," she grumbles. "I expected you would call if you had any news."

Her attitude is beginning to annoy me. "Carolyn, are you going to let me in or not?"

But as I say it, I move toward her and she has no choice but to step back, waving a hand in a reluctant invitation to come inside.

Cautiously, I do. The idea of being in a closed room with this woman is about as appealing as having sex with No-neck. But there is a reason I'm here—Trish—and I force myself to swallow back the revulsion.

As if it finally dawns on Carolyn that maybe I'm here for some important reason, like the whereabouts of her daughter, and she should show a little maternal concern, she says, "Do you have any news about Trish?"

I'm looking around the apartment and wondering how a nurse could live in such squalor. There are dirty dishes on every conceivable surface, including the couch and tattered chairs scattered around the room. Empty beer and soda cans litter the floor. An ashtray, whose first life was a jam jar, is so full of butts and ashes the contents spill over onto the grease-stained pizza box it's perched upon. Makes me wonder what her work area at the hospital is like, or how often she washes her hands.

When my gaze sweeps back to Carolyn, I make no attempt to hide my disgust. "This is where you and Trish live?" I almost add, "No wonder she ran away," but I don't, though I dearly want to.

She responds with self-righteous anger. "We don't all live in big houses on Mt. Helix," she says. "Or in beach houses. Some of us have to struggle to get by."

I'm stuck on the "beach houses" part of her tirade. "How do you know where I live?"

"You told me. Last night. Remember?" She throws my words back at me, hands on hips and head cocked to one side.

Echoing my own words doesn't distract me, though. It only ratchets my dislike of this woman up another notch. "No, I didn't tell you that last night. And I do remember. So, I'll ask you again. How do you know where I live?"

"What does it matter?" she snaps right back. "Aren't you here because of Trish?"

She's right, but she seems to know more about me than I like. I want to pursue it, but I'm standing in this dump for a far more pressing reason. "Yes, I'm here about Trish. But no, I don't have any news. What I have are questions. Like why you didn't tell us last night about your trouble with the law? And that Trish has run away—twice? Those are pretty important details to have left out."

Her face reddens. "Maybe I didn't tell you because I knew you'd have the same contemptuous look on your face that you do right now."

When I don't respond, she continues with a huffy sigh. "Yes. Trish has run away before. I was involved with someone she didn't get along with."

I flash on No-neck. "The guy I just saw leaving?"

"No, not him. I live here alone now. I mean, alone with Trish. That's why I'm so worried about her. Something really bad must have happened to make her leave like this. I may not be the best mother, but I always provided a home for Trish. Made sure she had food and clothes and a roof over her head."

"And supplied her with drugs?"

Carolyn looks genuinely taken aback. "Why on Earth would you ask that?"

"Come on, Carolyn," I snap. "Did you think I wouldn't find out that you've been busted for possession?"

"I wasn't charged," she says. "And the drugs weren't mine. They belonged to that guy I told you about. The one Trish didn't like. I kicked him out right after that. For Christ's sake, I didn't know I was carrying drugs. He'd slipped them into my purse."

It's not lost on me that she's changing her story. She kicked the guy out because he got her in trouble, not because of Trish. There's enough conviction in her reply, however, that I grudgingly concede her that point, especially since David confirmed the case was dropped. "What about the DUIs?"

I can see the wheels turning as she decides whether to confirm or deny. I make the decision for her.

"Tell me the truth. A case may not get to court, but

there's always a paper trail. I'll find out one way or the other."

She shrugs. "I used to have a drinking problem."

"Used to?"

"I got help. Through the hospital. I completed a rehab program and my record was expunged." She shoots me a resentful look. "Or at least it was supposed to be."

"How have you managed to keep your nursing job through all this?"

Her eyes skitter away and then slide back. "I'm a good worker," she says.

Another glance around the room and my skin starts to crawl at the thought that this woman renders care to the sick. I shake the disgust away and pull my thoughts back. "I'd like to see Trish's room."

A defensive look creeps into her eyes. "Why?"

"Because I might be able to find something that would give us a clue as to where she's gone. Or why."

"There's nothing to find," she says sharply. "I've looked."

"Yeah, well I want to look, too." I don't give her a chance to argue, but turn toward the short hall that leads from the living room, assuming it's the way to the bedrooms.

She's right on my heels. I put a hand on the first door and she stops me. "That's my room," she snaps.

I don't tell her how happy I am that I don't have to see the horror that must be her bedroom. I step instead to the next door. The knob has been removed from the door, leaving only a large, round hole. "What happened here?"

She rolls her shoulders. "Trish leaves her room locked. When she disappeared, I had to get inside. That was the only way I could think of to do it."

I open the door. There are also two deadbolts that lock from the inside. Trish felt she needed to deadbolt her bedroom? I know teenagers value their privacy, but most don't resort to deadbolts. I wonder who she was trying to keep out.

I push the door back and move inside. Carolyn doesn't follow me, a flush creeping into her cheeks. When I look around, I understand why. She should be embarrassed. This room belongs in another house. The bed is made, the furniture clutter and dirt free. Schoolbooks are stacked with neat precision. There is a bulletin board with a few pictures, but only of Trish and others whom I assume are school friends, no family photos. The things in her dresser drawers are folded. The closet yields shoes lined up in a row, clothes clean and pressed and hung up by category: shirts, skirts, pants, coats.

Hardly the room of a teenaged doper. Her wardrobe is meager, and somehow that makes me sadder than anything else I've seen so far.

But I don't find anything that gives me a clue as to where she might have gone. No diary. No notebooks with scrawled notes on the covers.

I close the door respectfully behind me and turn again to Carolyn. "When Trish ran away before, where did she go?"

Carolyn's shoulders hunch a little. "What does that matter?"

"You're kidding right?"

She frowns and purses her lips. "Where she went before doesn't matter. She's not there now. I checked."

"Not where, Carolyn? I want an answer."

She strikes a defensive pose. "She went to my parents, okay? But she's not there now."

I feel my jaw muscles clench. "I thought you said last night your parents didn't want anything to do with you or Trish?" But the truth strikes me as I say it. "It's not Trish they don't want anything to do with, is it? It's you."

Carolyn glares at me with reproachful eyes. "What do you want me to say? That my mom and stepdad are disappointed in me? That my life didn't turn out the way any of us had hoped? Okay. I've said it. Now what are you doing to find Trish?"

"You're sure she's not with them?"

Reproach veers to anger. "Yes. I called them. Now they have something else to blame me for. My mother is on her way here right now to make sure I don't screw anything else up."

"On her way from where?"

Rancor colors her face and words. "Where she lives with her rich husband," she replies. "Boston."

"Boston? How did Trish manage to get to Boston?"

She gives an impatient huff. "Where she lives *now* with her rich husband. She used to live in L.A. They moved to Boston two months ago."

"Why Boston?"

"What does it matter?" she snaps. "You asked if Trish is with them. She isn't."

"Did you know Boston is where Daniel Frey is from? And the Francos as well?"

She flicks at a wisp of hair. "So what? There are lots of people from Boston. I was born there. So were my folks. Big deal."

Her attitude is seriously pissing me off. I toy with the idea of telling her about my chat with Frey this morning, how he denied having any conversation with her at all, but at this point, I don't know who to trust. Better to keep it to myself. In spite of the revulsion Carolyn raises in me, I need to keep the lines of communication open.

Carolyn reaches for a pack of cigarettes. I take it as my signal to leave. The atmosphere in this place is fetid enough without adding smoke to the mix. I don't see any point in our getting together again this evening, either. I'll tell my mother not to call her when I get back to school.

I wonder just how much I'll tell her about the mother of her only grandchild.

Probably not much.

CHAPTER 11

ON THE WAY BACK TO SCHOOL I MULL OVER THE recurring theme—the Francos, Daniel Frey, and now Carolyn's parents—all with a connection to Boston. Carolyn acted as if it's a coincidence. She may be right. California is one of those places that draw easterners with the promise of balmy winters and sun-soaked beaches. Just the same, I think I'll ask David to dig around a little more.

It's a little after twelve when I pull in at the school. Mom is holding a press conference on the steps in front of her office. Chief Williams is beside her. A crowd of students gather to the side, some weeping and some talking in low voices. The TV news cameras swarm in to catch it all.

I drive around back and park in the same lot as this morning. Most of the teachers must have left for the day because there are far fewer cars. When I get to Daniel Frey's classroom, however, he is there with a half-dozen students. He detects my presence immediately. He wraps up his conversation and the students drift out. No one pays the least bit of attention to me though they make their way around me like the wake around the bow of a ship.

He joins me at the doorway. "I need a ride home. Why don't you take me." He doesn't ask it like a question.

I raise an eyebrow. "And why would I want to take you home?"

An impatient frown tugs at the corners of his mouth. "Look, we both know you plan to follow me. I let my driver go. Will you take me or not?"

"Fine. I'll take you home. But I want to stop by the office first."

Frey has his coat over his arm, and with his free hand, he pulls the door to his classroom closed and locks it. "I need to check messages. Let's go."

I pick through his thoughts, looking for some hint of deception but finding none. I feel him doing the same to me, so I send him this message: *You are either being honest with me about your innocence or you are the most accomplished liar I've ever met.*

He smiles, not warmly, and slips his keys into the pocket of his coat. *I could say the same about you—being an accomplished liar, I mean.*

I haven't lied to you. In fact, I've told you a lot more than I should have considering the circumstances.

Or maybe you felt you didn't have a choice. He twirls a finger at his head. *Because of this.*

We approach the office just as the press conference is coming to a close. Frey goes to the receptionist to check for messages and I wait for Mom in her office. Williams is at her side when she comes in.

He closes the door behind him. "I got a call from the medical examiner's office," he says. "Barbara did die from strangulation. A belt was used, with a metal buckle that left a clear imprint. And a distinctive one. We found marks on her body where she had been hit with it. There was skin under her fingernails. She fought back. And semen on her clothes. Multiple donors. We have DNA samples that we will run through our databases. If we don't get a hit, we have more than enough to make a match when we catch them."

Williams' tone is detached, professional. I'm used to it, but I can see how it's affecting my mother. She's thinking of Trish and her shoulders are rigid with tension. Williams can read the signs and will if I don't distract him. His sharp eyes are watching her.

I reach out to him telepathically. *Barbara went down fighting.*

His eyes shift to me. *Yes, she did. But there are other things we need to talk about, too. We need to meet privately.*

He's not letting any of those "other things" into his thoughts. *I know what you're doing. It won't work. Barbara was killed by humans, not by supernaturals. You want to meet about Avery, not Barbara. I can't do it now.*

In the instant it takes for this to pass between us, my mother presses her fingertips gently against her eyelids and draws a deep breath. "What can we do, Chief Williams?" she asks.

Without hesitation, he switches mental gears. "I'll have detectives on campus this afternoon and tomorrow. But if you hear anything, or if a student goes to a counselor or teacher because he feels more comfortable talking to someone familiar, let us know immediately. In cases like this, what we learn in the first forty-eight hours often determines whether or not we catch the killer."

Mom nods and extends her hand. "Thank you for your help today," she says.

He shakes her hand, offers his to me, and leaves with no parting shots.

Several teachers and parents have gathered outside Mom's office door. I take just a minute to let her know I don't think we should meet with Carolyn tonight but that I will call her later, after I've checked in at the office. She doesn't ask why, which is an indication of how distracted she is. I don't add that I'll be taking Daniel Frey home for the same reason I decide not tell her what I saw at Carolyn's this morning. Mom has enough on her plate right now without adding to her anxiety.

Frey is waiting for me at the back door to the office. We are at the edge of the parking lot when I realize David told me only that Frey lives in Mission Valley. Big valley and a lot of condos. *Where are we going?*

He gives me a sideways glance. *So, you've already checked up on me. I guess I shouldn't find that surprising.*

He directs me to the freeway and then to take the off-ramp at Friar's Road. During the twenty or so minutes it takes to get there, we don't exchange a word, or a thought. I can't tell if Frey is in my head, so I keep my own thoughts carefully neutral. When we pull into his condo complex, he hands me a magnetic card that I slip into a reader, allowing us to enter the gated community.

It's a very upscale community, perched above Qualcomm Stadium, with a view that extends over the shopping complexes that make up Mission and Fashion Valley Malls and to the city. He directs me with a terse, turn right, then turn left, pull in here. "Here" is a numbered space that I presume is his. Empty, of course, since he doesn't have a driver's license.

So, you know that, too, huh? You have been busy. The look he gives me is a mixture of anger, contempt and disgust. The vibe he's sending off, though, is tinged with something odd. Disappointment. Like I've let him down in some subtle way.

I shake my head and smile at that. *You've been hanging around teenagers way too long. The "I'm disappointed in*

*you" shtick doesn't work on me. I plan to find out every-
thing I can about you. Now if you have nothing to hide, as
you keep insisting, why not invite me in? You can answer
some questions and make my job that much easier.*

His fingers are wrapped around the door handle but he
pauses and half turns to face me. *You have questions? Is
that all?* His smile is brittle. *Sure. Why not? That way you
can search the place, too, and you'll know I'm not holding Trish captive in a broom closet.*

Sarcasm comes through, even in telepathic communication. He realizes instantly that Trish's disappearance
doesn't merit ridicule. He backs off with an apologetic
shrug. *I'm sorry. I will do everything I can to help you
find Trish. She's a good kid and I don't want anything
to happen to her.*

I cut the engine and grab my purse to follow him. I believe him when he says he wants her to be safe. But that
doesn't mean I'm convinced he didn't play a part in her
disappearance.

Or that I trust him.

CHAPTER 12

FREY'S HOME IS LIKE HIS CLASSROOM—STARK AND monochromatic. We enter through a foyer devoid of furniture, though it's big enough for several pieces, and pass into the living room. The walls, the furniture, and the carpet all echo the same color—gray, a shade as elusive as smoke. No art on the walls. No books with colorful jackets. Nothing in the room to break the monotony except rainbows of light that skitter into the room from a dozen small globes hung from a balustrade on the deck outside. The deck faces due west, and I imagine the colorful light show must perform its dance from morning to night.

It's nice, isn't it? Frey's tone is a purr. *The moment I walked into this place, I knew it was exactly what I wanted. The sun all day long.*

His face is turned to the window, uplifted, his eyes closed.

In that moment, I see the cat in his nature as clearly as if he'd completed the shape-shift he'd begun in his classroom.

I wonder if he curls up in front of that window and— I clear my head of that disturbing thought before the image becomes too clear and Frey picks up on it.

What else do I know about cats? Isn't there something about the way they see color—or more precisely, the way they *don't* see color? Explains the monochromatic themes of his home and classroom, and something else.

Is that why you don't drive? You can't distinguish colors?

He's followed my line of reasoning and replies with a deliberate roll of his shoulders, his face remains tilted to the sun. *Part of the reason. It's not that I can't distinguish colors exactly, though the subtleties are lost on me. But I have no desire to drive. The highways here are always congested and the people who use them drive like maniacs. I hire someone who takes me to and from school, and since I live right across from a shopping mall, I rarely need other transportation.*

He rouses himself to face me. *Would you like to see the rest of the place?*

I nod and he beckons me to follow him. He leads me down a hall with two closed doors, one on either side, and stops in front of the door on the left. He opens it and gestures me through.

It's a library, simply furnished with floor to ceiling bookcases on three walls, two comfortable easy chairs with goosenecked reading lamps perched behind them, and a small table in between. This room reflects the teacher in Frey. The shelves are lined with literary classics whose covers are worn and in some cases, cracked and peeling. There is a subtle odor—the kind you smell in antiquarian bookstores—dust, old paper, the perfume of aged leather.

I run a finger along the spines of the closest shelf. Expensive collection for a high school teacher. *Are these all first editions?*

He smiles but says nothing.

He seems to be waiting for me to make some kind of move. I shrug at his nonresponse and reach for one of the books. A copy of *Rebecca*. I open it to the first pages and read, "Last night I dreamt I went to Manderley again." But something isn't right. I hold the book closer to my eyes. Is it a trick of the light or my imagination? The words seem to float above the paper rather than being imprinted upon it. I look up at Frey.

Again he smiles and nods toward the book in my hands.

When I look back at the page, the letters are fading like a blackout in a movie and in their place, some kind of strange markings have emerged.

Frey, what is this?

He takes the book from my hand, laughing at my startled reaction. *It's my security system.*

What do you mean?

He fans the pages gently. *If you were human, you would see nothing except the Du Maurier text. Because you are not, you see what really is.*

Which is?

Frey closes the book. His fingers trace the top of the binding while his eyes sweep the shelves. *These are my textbooks.*

Textbooks? The writing looks like ancient hieroglyphics. Are these textbooks on Egyptian history? Logical, I guess, considering how they felt about cats.

He laughs, but I suspect it's not at the humor in what I've said, but the absurdity.

No. Not Egyptian history. This book—he hefts it—*is a text on locator spells.*

Locator spells? I glance around the room. *All these books are about magic?*

And very dangerous stuff in the wrong hands.

I let my gaze wander over the shelves. There must be

two hundred volumes, all bearing the names of modern classics. *How did you come to be in possession of such a collection?*

He sighs. *It was a legacy. Like how you came by Avery's property.*

He says it with quiet nonchalance, as if everyone knows about Avery and me.

But I know that isn't true. A cold knot twists the pit of my stomach.

How do you know about Avery and me?

Again, the shrug that ripples his shoulders and seems to shake off my questions. But after a moment, he does reply. *The supernatural community is close-knit. We hear things. If you took the time to learn more about us, you'd know that.*

I haven't been a vampire long, but I've learned one important thing. Secrecy is the key to staying alive. I thought the only ones who knew of my nature were Culebra and Williams and now, Frey. And the half dozen or so members of a shadowy group known as the Revengers who seek out vampires to kill them. But Avery set the Revengers upon me and they haven't bothered me since his death. The realization that there are others out there who know what I am scares me more than a little.

Frey picks up on all this. *No one who knows of your true nature would try to hurt you. Avery was an anomaly. An aberration.*

That observation provokes a bitter laugh. *Frey, the truth is, anomalies and aberrations are what we are, too, you and I. The only way I can face each new day is to keep reminding myself that I have a family who loves me and of the good I can do with these powers. I suspect it's the same with you, since you are a teacher.*

His eyes warm, and his mouth curves in a wry smile. *That's the first personal thing you've said to me. I think you're beginning to trust me, Anna Strong.*

I'm not and it's not at all what I intended. I hold up my hands.

Don't kid yourself. I'm not that easily won. And we seem to be getting sidetracked from the reason I'm here. I gesture to the book in his hand. *You said that book was a book on locator spells. Could we use it to find Trish?*

We can try. I need something of hers to hold while I work the spell. Do you have anything with you?

Only a photograph. Her mother gave it to me last night. Will that do?

Frey shakes his head. *Only if she was the last one who touched it.*

I'd already reached into my purse to withdraw the picture. With a shrug, I slip it back inside. *Okay. Maybe the picture won't work. But I'll get something else. What type of thing works best?*

Anything personal. Frey turns to return the book to the shelf. *Nail clippings. A lock of hair.*

Trish's hairbrush. Carolyn brought it over to my parent's house last night. Did she leave it? I don't remember. But I'll certainly find out. The fact that she brought the hairbrush over and suggested the test is important, I think. It means that she truly believes Trish is Steve's.

I'll get you something. Can I come back later?

Of course. I want to find Trish, too. Come back as soon as you can. I'll be home all evening.

He follows me as I retrace my steps to the front door. I'm searching the bottom of my purse for the car keys when my cell phone rings. I snatch the keys up with one hand, and the phone with the other.

"Hello?"

"Anna?"

I recognize David's voice. "Hey. Sorry I've been gone so long. What's up?"

There's just the briefest of hesitations before he says. "Can you get out to the beach house?"

My heart jumps. The last time he asked me that, the place was burning to the ground. "Jesus. What's wrong?"

He hesitates again and another spasm of alarm races up my spine. "David? What's going on?"

He exhales loudly into the phone. "It may be nothing. I just got a call from that dentist who lives next door to you at the beach. He left a message at the office this morning, but when he hadn't heard from you, he called my cell. He says he saw a light in the cottage last night. He went to investigate, but the door was locked. The place seemed secure so he didn't call the police. He thought you should know because of what happened before. If you want, Max and I can meet you there. We'd go ourselves but at the moment we've got our hands full with Jake."

When he mentions Jake's name, I hear a scuffling in the background and something that sounds like "fuck you." There's a moment of dead air and then David is back. "Anyway, we're on our way to SDPD to turn him in."

I hitch my purse up around my shoulder. I don't have to ask why my neighbor called David and not me. He's the type that refers to women as "little ladies." "Finish up with Jake," I tell David. "I'll go on out to the cottage."

"Do you want to wait for us?"

"No." I know from experience how long the paperwork can take. "I'm sure it's nothing. I'll see you and Max back at the office."

I hang up and turn to Frey. "I have to go. I'll try to get back tonight, but it may be late."

He nods and opens the front door to allow me to pass through. "I hope there's nothing wrong at your home."

He has picked the story out of my head. I should be used to it by now, but it irks me. It's dumb and childish, but I turn the tables. I look him square in the eyes, smile, and conjure up the image I remember from a long ago trip to the zoo. It involved a randy old lion and his less than enthusiastic cage mate.

I don't get the reaction I want. In fact, Frey's reaction is far from embarrassment. Sexual energy blazes out and I feel my own face flush hot.

He's laughing as he shuts the door.

CHAPTER 13

IT'S LATE AFTERNOON AND I LUCK OUT BY HITTING the freeways in that all too brief period between the lunch crowd exiting Mission Valley and the downtown commuters heading home. Under these conditions, Mission Beach is only a twenty minute drive from Frey's condo. I make it in fifteen.

I've lived in Mission Beach most of my life. The community is an eclectic mix of old, new, and no money. The differences are reflected in the architecture, and nowhere is that more obvious than where I live. Isthmus Court is bordered on one side by the boardwalk that runs along the beach and on the other by Mission Beach's main thoroughfare, Mission Boulevard. My cottage, a gift from my grandparents, was the only original bungalow on the block—until it burned to the ground two months ago. My neighbor lives in the type of monstrosity that new money seems to love—a big stucco box that rises three stories on its tiny lot. When I decided to rebuild, I used his architect.

I was in a hurry to get going, I wanted my home back, and though I wasn't sure how it would work out, the guy surprised me. It turns out that he hates the cookie-cutter look of the new stuff as much as I do. He was delighted to do something different.

So here I am, approaching the newly fenced yard surrounding my place. To my neighbor's great disappointment, the only concession I made in the rebuild was to add a second story master bedroom with a wrap around deck. Otherwise, the red clapboard cottage retains all the simple charm of the original. And the house is small enough that I have a front yard and a patio in back. A rarity in this neighborhood.

I glance at my watch. It's almost four and there are no workmen in sight. They've no doubt left for the day. I use my key and step inside.

The place smells of new paint and freshly sawed wood. A glance around the living room confirms that the floorboards are finished. The polished oak floors gleam in the late afternoon sun. I retained the craftsman touches of the old place, too, built-in bookcases, wood-framed windows.

In the kitchen, the cupboards are hung. The pungent odor of stained wood fills the air. I get a thrill when I see the contractor's note on the counter. "All done, Ms. Strong," it reads. "Welcome home."

I find myself smiling until the reason I'm here reasserts itself in my head. If someone is trespassing, I'll damn well find out. I'm not going to lose my home again.

It's time to check upstairs. I leave my handbag on a kitchen counter and go on up. It's carpeted here and I detect different odors—glue, paint, wool. Something else. It stops me dead at the doorway, tenses my muscles and raises the hair on the back of my neck.

It's nothing I can see. The room is empty. But there are faint footprints on the carpet. Not the prints of work boots. Bare feet.

And the smell is the must of unwashed hair and skin.

The footprints track across the carpet and out the sliding glass doors to the deck. There are no curtains up yet so I have a clear view outside. There's no one out there. But the door is unlocked and when I lean over the railing, I realize how easy it would be for someone to climb down onto the garage roof and jump to the grass below— especially if they're in a hurry to get out. The back leads to an alley. An easy, convenient escape route.

I'm wondering how I can remedy that when I catch a small movement out of the corner of my eye. It's a reflection in the side window of the garage, fleeting, like a cloud passing over the sun. But it's enough. Perhaps my barefoot intruder hasn't left after all.

I lock the door to the deck and move quickly outside. There are no windows facing the rear of the house from the garage so it's not hard to sneak around to the front. I haven't installed the security code on the garage door yet, since I haven't been using it. When I hit the open mode and the door slides up, someone small and blond dashes around me, racing for the alley.

But quick as she is, I'm quicker. I reach an arm around her waist and whirl her around.

Eyes, big with alarm and panic, flash up at me.

Eyes I recognize. They belong to Trish.

It's so unexpected, I almost let her go.

Almost.

At first, Trish struggles. I've caught her off guard. I hold her against my chest, saying nothing, waiting for her to calm down.

At last she does. The energy drains from her like water down a pipe. She sags against me, resigned. After a long moment, she draws herself up and pulls back.

I let her go, dropping my hands from her shoulders, but staying close enough to thwart another panic attack. She's small boned and fragile, wearing jeans that sag around her hips and an oversized sweatshirt. Her hair is loose around her face, dirty and uncombed. Her nails are unpolished, bitten to the quick.

She blows out a breath and swipes at her eyes with the back of her hand. But she doesn't look up at me. "You know who I am?"

"Yes."

Again, the quick intake of breath, the forceful exhalation. This time, though, she squares her shoulders and those luminous eyes meet mine. "Are you going to take me back?"

I know what I should say. I know what I should do. But something in this girl's quiet desperation sounds an alarm that pushes all those rational responses out of my head. I rack my brain for something that would put a teenager at ease. I can only come up with a lame, "Are you hungry? We could go down the street to the Mission for something to eat."

She starts to nod, but the gesture turns into a shrug. "Ryan is getting food. He'll be back in a minute."

"Ryan?" Suddenly, I'm hit with the suspicion that maybe Trish isn't as innocent as I've assumed.

My tone must reflect this because Trish frowns. "It's not like *that*. He's been helping me. He got me away from—"

She stops short. "God. What's the use? If you're going to take me to jail, let's just get it over with."

Her eyes dart over my shoulder, flashing an unintentional warning. I whirl around as a blur of teeth and fur launches itself at me. A dog. A large dog that seems bent on tearing my throat out.

Instinctively, the animal in me responds. It's no match. The dog is a German Shepard mix, eighty pounds or so, but in the time it takes me to reach out an arm, I've locked my hand around the dog's throat. I use its momentum to throw it to the ground, my own teeth gnashing in conditioned reflex before reason takes over. I lean over the dog, exerting just enough pressure to render it helpless. When the adrenaline stops pumping, I glance back at Trish and the boy who seems to have materialized from God knows where to stand beside her. Their faces are stamped with the same emotions—shock, fear, no understanding of what they just witnessed, and no clue how to react to it.

"I assume you're Ryan," I say, breaking the stalemate. "Want to call off your dog?"

CHAPTER 14

ONE OF THE GOOD THINGS ABOUT BECOMING vampire is that your physical abilities are remarkably enhanced. Things like speed and strength. Everything with the dog happens so quickly, the two astounded teenagers who witness it literally don't believe their eyes. Ryan's mouth hangs open and Trish has a dazed, confused look that would be comical if the circumstances weren't beginning to tick me off.

"Yo, Ryan," I snap again. The dog is starting to recover, squirming and growling as he tries to shake off my hands. "I mean it. Call off your dog or he's going to get hurt."

The kid finally responds. His mouth opens and closes a couple of times before he gets the words out. "Cujo. Down."

Cujo?

I feel the dog relax and ease my hands away. In a flash, the same dog who was hell bent on ripping my throat out is lapping at my face like it's a burger-flavored icepop.

With a shudder, I jump to my feet, scrubbing at my face with the back of my hand. There's nothing I hate more than dog slobber.

Cujo scrambles up, too, and wriggles his way to Ryan's side, his whole body vibrating to the beat of a wildly wagging tail.

Ryan reaches down and cradles the dog's head. "Good boy."

By now, I've recovered enough to be angry again. Trish has moved to Ryan's side and the two take turns patting the dog and telling it what a good boy it's been. Ryan is the same height as Trish with similar coloring. But his clothes are clean and pressed and he's obviously bathed in the last few days. Whatever their relationship, he hasn't been camping out here with her.

I suck in a breath. "Okay, you two. Enough. What's going on? Trish, what are you doing here? How do you know me?"

Trish throws me one of those looks that makes me remember all over again why I left teaching. The disdain only a teenager can exude. "My mother," she says.

"I just met your mother. Last night. What could she possibly have told you about me?"

The words are out before anxiety twists my gut. Could Carolyn have told Trish that we are related?

But the expression on Trish's face is not the expression of one meeting a long lost relative. There is no friendly curiosity reflected there, only defiance.

"She told me what you are. A bounty hunter, right?"

I nod.

"You hunt people down. Bring them to jail."

"Mostly. Yes."

"And she sent you to find me. She told you that I ran away. That I was doing drugs and drinking and a lot of other terrible things."

When I don't say anything, she sighs. "It's what she

always tells people. It's what makes them bring me back to her. But the last time, she told me if I ran away again she'd send Anna Strong, this big, bad bounty hunter after me. She said she knew something about you, something that meant you'd never stop looking until you found me. And you'd take me to jail."

Carolyn told her that? I want to ask her how long ago this was, but her tone has morphed from defiance to desperation. "I came here to tell you my side of the story. I saw that you were remodeling and the place was empty. I decided to stay here until you came back. I haven't hurt anything. You can see for yourself. I'm sorry I ran. I was just afraid you'd be mad that I stayed here and you wouldn't let me explain."

Trish's words suddenly catch in her throat and she stops.

Ryan holds out the bag he's been clutching in his hand. "Can we talk while Trish eats?" he asks. "I can only bring food once a day and she hasn't eaten since yesterday."

Trish's drawn face softens when she looks at Ryan. I can hear her stomach rumble, so I nod. "Of course. Go ahead."

The two kids sit cross-legged on the floor of the garage and rip into the bag. He's brought bologna sandwiches and chips and the biggest bottle of some dark soda I've ever seen. Typical teen fare. Not a piece of fruit or carton of milk in the mix.

I sit down beside them and watch them eat. Cujo sneaks his way to my side and lies down with his head on my lap.

And I hate dogs. Go figure.

For a minute, Ryan and Trish are just two teenagers devouring their junk food with the gusto of youth. I let her finish one sandwich and start on the second before I interrupt.

"Trish?"

She looks up at me and I see the shadow in her eyes.

"What's going on?"

She stops chewing, the sandwich suspended in a hand that begins to shake.

Ryan's eyes flash. "She's not going back to her mom," he says. "If you make her, we'll just run away again. This time we'll leave the state. We'll go to Mexico. You'll never find us."

His tone is fervent and desperate, a kid trying to explain the demon threatening his best friend to an adult he suspects doesn't believe in them.

But I'm not most adults.

"Did someone hurt you?" I ask softly.

Ryan reaches out a gentle hand and touches her shoulder. "Tell her," he says. "Or I will."

Trish's hand descends slowly, the sandwich falling from her limp fingers while tears spill onto her cheeks.

"It's what we decided, remember?"

"We don't *know* her," she mumbles.

He nods toward me. "Yeah, but look at Cujo. He likes her, so she can't be all bad."

I put a hand on Cujo's head, trying to emphasize the dog's obvious good judgment, but he looks up at me and rolls his tongue like he's ready to plant another big doggy kiss on my face. I gently but firmly push his head back down before he can.

Ryan's eyes lock into mine. "And if she was going to take you back, she'd have called your mom by now, right?"

The question is directed at me. I nod. "But I can't really help you until I know what happened."

Trish's eyes go flat, passionless. "My mother," she says simply. "My mother happened to me."

She stops, recomposing herself. I don't try to rush her or ask another question. My own insides are churning. I suspect I'm not going to want to hear what she has to say.

And I'm just as terribly convinced that my first instincts about Carolyn Delaney will prove to have been accurate. I didn't like or trust the woman from the moment she walked into my parent's home.

Trish picks up a paper napkin from the small pile on the floor and wipes her eyes. "My mother wasn't always—" Her voice falters, breaks. She scrubs at her eyes again and lifts her chin. "She used to be a pretty good mom. We'd do things together. Go to movies. Shopping. We didn't have much money, but that didn't matter."

There's nothing more disturbing or more pathetic than a child defending her parent. It should be the other way around. Always. Ryan places an arm around Trish's shoulders. The simple act seems to give her strength. She sits up a little straighter.

"Anyway, I guess the trouble really started when my dad left a couple of years ago. He just walked out on us. Mom says she doesn't know why he left. She woke up one morning and he was gone. No note. Nothing. He just left us."

My shoulders jump. "Your dad?"

Misery, as intense as the pain in her voice, slumps her shoulders. "I used to think it was something I'd done. That it must have been." She looks at Ryan and his smile of reassurance lifts the weight a little. "Ryan says it wasn't of course. That sometimes adults do stupid things that have nothing to do with their families. He almost makes me believe it."

She looks so sad, I want to put my arms around her and tell her that there's another family she could belong to. A good one that would never abandon her. But that would involve telling her that her mother has been lying to her for thirteen years.

If she has been.

One thing is for certain, though, Carolyn has been lying to someone.

"I'm sorry about your dad," I say, stumbling over the word "dad." "But you haven't told me why you ran away. Was it because of what happened to your friend?"

Trish's brows draw together. "My friend?"

In the same instant, Ryan draws a sharp breath and shakes his head at me. "I haven't had a chance to tell her about that." His tone makes it clear that he doesn't think I should, either.

But it's too late. Trish looks from his face to mine. "What are you talking about?"

Ryan stiffens, the look he throws me is dark with anger. "Trish has enough to worry about. She doesn't need to hear about that other thing."

Trish is staring at Ryan now with burning, reproachful eyes. "What other thing, Ryan?"

He looks away, refusing to meet her gaze or answer.

So I do. "I'm sorry, Trish. I thought you knew. It's Barbara."

"Barbara?" She repeats the name with the same puzzled inflection. "What about Barbara?"

I don't know how to make this easy. One thing I'm sure of, Trish either doesn't know that her friend is dead or she's an Oscar-worthy actress. I take hold of one of her hands. "Barbara is dead, Trish. The police found her body this morning. I'm sorry."

"Oh my God," Trish's anguished cry echoes in the empty garage. She snatches her hand out of mine and rounds on Ryan. "You knew about Barbara. And you didn't say anything?"

Ryan doesn't meet her eyes. He busies himself with his dog, calling him over, breaking off a bit of the sandwich in his hand and holding it out to him. He watches Cujo with fierce intensity until he can bring himself to look at Trish again. "I'm sorry," he whispers. "I couldn't tell you."

Trish's face crumbles. Fat tears wet her cheeks and her

shoulders shake with sobs, but she doesn't make a sound. It's only when she draws a deep, shuddering breath that the wail erupts. She buries her face in her hands. "Oh my god, oh my god. I'm next. I'm next. I'm next."

She keeps repeating the litany, ignoring me when I gather her to my chest, stroke her hair, and croon soft promises that I'll keep her safe. She doesn't struggle against me or try to break away. She holds herself rigid, arms wrapped tightly around her own waist.

I look over her head at Ryan. He's trembling as he stares at us. Neither kid has asked how Barbara was killed. It's as if they were expecting it. "You'd better tell me what's going on, Ryan."

He looks close to tears, too, but he doesn't break down. "It's the guys from the Web site," he says, voice flat.

"Web site?"

He nods, staring at his friend. "They want the computer back."

"Computer?" I sound like a parrot.

Ryan climbs to his feet and heads for the back of the garage, Cujo at his heels. For the first time, I notice clothes and a blanket in the corner. He shuffles through the stuff, and when he turns back around, he has a laptop in his hand. Wordlessly, he brings it back to us, kneels down and powers it up. His fingers fly over the keyboard until the expression on his face tells me he's found what he's looking for. It's a mixture of revulsion and fury that sends the color flooding into his cheeks. I know because he's turned the computer around to face me and I'm experiencing the very same things.

It's Carolyn, standing behind her daughter, a leather leash in her hand. The leash is attached to the collar around Trish's neck. Trish is spread-eagle on the bed, her face partially obscured by a scarf, but recognizable nevertheless. She's naked. And there's a man's hand between her legs.

The rage that rises up in me is unlike anything I've ever experienced. Swift. Uncontrollable. I lash out, sweeping the computer from Ryan's hand and sending it crashing against the wall. I can't stop shaking; my whole body vibrates with hot fury. I see the fear in Ryan's eyes as he watches me, feel Trish flinch away and move next to him. They both cower, shivering, out of reach. Cujo, too, whimpers and backs away. My wrath is scaring them but I don't know if I can rein it in.

But I also know I must. I'll tuck it away, secure it in a dark part of my mind, so I can recall it later.

When I face Carolyn.

CHAPTER 15

IT TAKES A MINUTE BUT WHEN I CAN SPEAK WITH-
out screaming, I hold out a hand to Trish. "I'm sorry,
but I have to ask. Your mother made you—" I gesture toward the ruined computer. "Do that?"

She nods, her face flushing to deep crimson. "I didn't
want to."

She speaks softly, yet her humiliation and resentment
ring through. "She said I wouldn't be hurt. Not really.
And we could make a lot of money. Since my dad left,
we've had a lot of bills and not much money to pay them.
She said I'd only have to do it once."

In the sadness of her tone, I recognize the depth of her
anguish caused by the betrayal. It's no surprise when she
whispers, "It wasn't only once, though."

Ryan has recovered enough to step between Trish and
me, and he's glaring again. "You see why she can't go
back there? Those men, the ones who make Trish do
things, they know all their records are on that computer.

They want it back. They went after Barbara because she knew—"

I hold up a hand. "Wait a minute. How was Barbara involved? Did she—"

"No." Trish's voice cuts in like a whip. "She didn't do *anything*. She came to my house one day after school. After the men left. She saw me crying. I know I shouldn't have told her, but I had to tell someone. I wanted to kill myself. She told me to go to Mr. Frey. To tell him what was happening. That he could help."

Again, the realization that everything Carolyn told us was a lie flashes like a white-hot bolt through me. "Did you go to Mr. Frey?"

She blanches and shakes her head. "No. I couldn't. So Barbara said she'd tell him." Her voice breaks. "I guess she never got the chance."

Through the rage boiling inside me, I fight to keep calm. "Do you know who might have told the men what Barbara was planning to do?"

Again, the shake of the head. But she doesn't look at me and her fragile body seems to shrink in on itself. It's more of an affirmation than mere words. I know what she suspects. Somehow Carolyn found out. It was her mother.

I don't know what to say. I know I must stay calm, think rationally. For the kids. The reality, though, is that I want to find Carolyn and rip her lying head off her shoulders.

Trish is weeping again, making no sound. The sight pulls me back. I have to get her to safety.

"Ryan, does anyone know that you've been coming here to see Trish?"

"No." He's got his arms around Trish's shoulders. "I've been careful. My folks think I'm just taking Cujo for a walk. We don't live too far from here. It's been easy to sneak away."

"But what about the men after the computer? Do either of you know who they are?"

He and Trish both shake their heads. Trish speaks first. "There were always two of them. One took the pictures, the other—" Her voice drops off. "Anyway, they never spoke to each other when I was in the room. The one with the camera would tell me what to do. When it was over, they'd take the video, load it into the computer and leave."

"How did you manage to get the computer?"

Trish shrugs. "They'd leave it with the camera."

Ryan jumps in. "Trish was smart. She snuck the computer out when she ran away. Her mom was at the hospital. She wouldn't have noticed it was gone. They kept the thing hidden in a box in the back of a closet. She didn't realize Trish knew where it was." He says the last with a kind of adolescent pride in the bravery and ingenuity of his friend.

The plan in my head forms in slow motion. My options are limited. I can't leave Trish here and I certainly can't take her to my house or my folks'. My mother would be obligated to inform the authorities. And the authorities would take her back to Carolyn. I want to get to Carolyn first. That leaves only one option.

I place a gentle hand on Trish's shoulders. "Do you trust Mr. Frey?"

She looks up at me, eyes red rimmed and world weary. "I don't know him. Not really. But he was always nice to me. I think he suspected something was wrong. He tried to get me to talk to him about it. But I couldn't. I couldn't."

"I'm going to suggest something to you. If you don't want to do it, I won't make you. But I think, at least for now, it would be for the best. You can't stay here. Your mother knows about this place. It won't be long before she thinks to come check it out. I'd like to take you to Mr. Frey's. I think he can help us."

Trish's eyes widen. "Won't he get in trouble?"

Probably, I think. But frankly, better him than my mother. And when I recall the claws on that paw, I know he can protect Trish better than any human. All this runs through my head in the instant it takes me to say, "He can handle it. Don't worry about Mr. Frey."

I turn to Ryan. "Ryan, I want you to go home. You've been a good friend to Trish, but I don't want to put you in any more danger. Give me your telephone number and I'll call you as soon as Trish is safe."

"No." He says it with firm resolve. "I won't leave Trish."

I don't have time to argue. "I can't take you with us, Ryan, so here's what we'll do. I'll tell Mr. Frey that you're going to call him. You whisper a code word to Trish now. When you call, if she's safe, she'll give you the code word. If she doesn't, you know something is wrong and you can call the police. Here." I tear two scraps from the paper bag and look around for something to write with.

Ryan produces a pencil from the pocket of his jacket and hands it over. I start to write.

"This is Mr. Frey's address and my cell phone number. Call it in about twenty minutes and I'll have Frey's number for you." I hand it to him with the other piece. "You write your number for me."

"I'll want to talk to Trish when you call," he says flatly. He finishes writing and holds the second piece out to me. "Deal?"

"Deal." I pocket the scrap. "Now I'm going to get my purse from inside and lock up. You give Trish the code while I'm gone."

The kids don't make a move until I'm out of the garage. I glance back and see them standing close together, Ryan's mouth at Trish's ear. I only hope they're not plotting a getaway.

I make a beeline for the house, on the alert for anyone or anything that might be watching. I neither see nor feel another presence. I almost wish I did. A good, physical confrontation would go a long way toward alleviating the blistering fury building with the intensity of a firestorm deep in my gut.

My purse is on the kitchen counter, just where I left it. As I reach down, my cell phone bleeps in monotonous rhythm. The message light flashes. On the move again, I check the text message. It's from David. *Max and I r back at office. Shld we come 2 the house?*

I glance at my watch. The message came in about fifteen minutes ago. I'd better call and let them know I'm all right and to stay put. I lock the front door with one hand, and hit speed dial with the other. David picks up on the first ring.

"Hey, Anna. Are you at the cottage? Is everything all right?"

No. It certainly isn't. But what to tell David? There's laughter in the background. Max's voice and someone else's. I recognize the voice immediately. "Gloria's there?"

"She just got here. Listen, we were thinking of heading to Sammy's for dinner. I take it nothing's wrong at the beach house or you would have called, so how soon can you get here?"

To have dinner with Gloria, David's bitchy, model girlfriend? How about never? I suck in a breath, blow it out. "You guys go ahead. I may be awhile."

David's voice turns serious. "What's the holdup? Everything is all right, isn't it?"

"No, David. Everything isn't all right. Did you forget about Trish?"

There's a moment of awkward silence. "Sorry, Anna. Did you find out anything from that teacher?"

"Yes. And I'm on my way back there now. So go on to dinner. Tell Max I'm sorry. I'll try to connect with him tomorrow."

He starts to say something else, but I've already snapped the cell phone closed. Aggravation like acid mixes with the seething rage twisting my gut. Gloria's here. Just what I need.

The kids are standing in front of the garage door, now closed, when I get back. Trish is holding her clothes in both hands and Ryan has the blanket wrapped around what could only be the computer in his.

I hold out my own hand to him. "You need to let me take that, Ryan."

He shakes his head and steps back. "No. It's the only evidence we have. You might have thought you ruined it, but I'll be able to retrieve stuff from it."

I let my hand fall to my side. I don't have time to argue about this. The longer we stay here, the greater the risk that someone might see Trish. I want these kids to trust me, but I don't want to put Ryan in any more danger.

When I can't come up with any clever reason why he should give me the computer, I tell him the truth. "I'm afraid for you, Ryan. If you keep that computer, the men may come after you or your family. Do you want to take that chance?"

He gives me a slow, sweet smile and gestures to Cujo, sitting with a stupid dog grin at his side. "I have two other dogs at home," he says. "Cujo is the smallest. I think we'll be safe."

I get a flash of Cujo flying at me, teeth snapping, and admit he's a pretty good deterrent. "Keep Cujo with you—even in your bedroom tonight, understand?"

"I always do."

"Do you want me to take you home before we go to Mr. Frey's?"

He shakes his head. "No. If you do, my folks might wonder who you are. I'll be fine."

He and Trish exchange a look I can't begin to under-stand. Some kind of teenage telepathy. I feel a flush of warmth for this scrawny kid who is willing to risk so much to protect his friend. But it's time for us to go. Without another word, Ryan and Cujo walk down the alley and disappear around the corner toward the boardwalk. Trish and I head in the opposite direction, toward Mission Boulevard and my car.

CHAPTER 16

THE TENSION IN THE CAR IS A POTENT COMBI-
nation of Trish's distress and confusion and my
nearly uncontrollable rage. It makes for an uncomfortable, silent ride. I have more questions for Trish, but one
look at her anxious, drawn face and I don't have the heart
to ask them. So instead, I concentrate on the drive, and
when we pull into Frey's condo, I stop just outside the
gate and turn to face her.

"Are you all right with this?"

She looks at me and her eyes reflect a sorrow born of
betrayal. "I have to be," she says. "I can't stay at your
place anymore. And Barbara trusted Mr. Frey. I guess I
will, too."

Her hands are clasped around the bundle of clothes
in her lap, pressed so tightly together, her knuckles are
white. I touch them briefly with my fingertips. Her skin is
nearly as cold as mine.

Frey answers when I punch his unit number on the

keypad. When he hears my voice, the gate goes up immediately. He's waiting for us at the door.

It doesn't take more than an instant for him to pluck the story out of my head. His eyes reflect concern when he turns to Trish. He takes the clothes from her hands and says gently, "I'm sorry about Barbara. And I'm sorry for what you've been through."

She gasps, her expression turning from guarded wariness to vigilant distrust. "How do you know—" Then her face crumbles. "Barbara. She did tell you, didn't she? Then you know it's all my fault. She's dead, and it's all my fault."

Trish's sobs wrack her body, and once unleashed, she's swept away by the sorrow. She buries her face in her hands and gives way to the anguish.

I don't know what to do. I touch her shoulder, but this time, she doesn't come into my arms. She pulls back and I let my hand drop. Frey and I know Barbara never got the chance to come to him. If she had, she'd be alive. But how to tell Trish that without explaining how Frey knows so much?

Frey's eyes shift from Trish to me. *I'm sorry. I should have thought before I spoke.* His eyes narrow. *You want her to stay here.*

Yes. You can protect her.

So can you.

He's read my intentions and his disapproval comes through. *You are going after her mother.*

Yes.

Do you really think that's wise?

Just as wise as trusting Trish to you. I can trust her to you, can't I?

But before he can respond, Trish gulps in a shaky breath of air. She wipes at her face with her shirtsleeve. "I'm sorry. I didn't mean to do that."

Frey's smile is gentle and reassuring. "Would you like to wash your face?"

She nods. "Yes, please."

Frey gestures with his right hand. "The bathroom is right down the hall. Do you want me to show you?"

She shakes her head. "No. I can find it." But before she does, she turns to me. "We'd better call Ryan. He'll be worried."

Ryan? Frey asks.

Curiously, he hadn't picked the entire story out of my head. Maybe he reads only what triggers the most violent emotional reactions.

Something to remember.

A friend of hers, I explain, digging my cell phone out of my purse. Out loud, I add, "Give Trish your telephone number here, so her friend will know she's safe."

Frey recites the number. Trish takes the phone and turns away from us, retreating to the privacy of the bathroom to make her call. In a second, we hear water running. Trish is taking no chance that we might overhear her conversation with Ryan.

Frey turns reproachful eyes on me. "You should report this to the police."

"Believe me, I will. But I have to have a little talk with Carolyn first. I need to know if Trish really is my brother's daughter."

"Because Trish mentioned a dad?"

I nod and gesture toward the bathroom. "Can she stay here? It won't be for long."

He nods. "Of course."

"Frey, keep her safe. I'm depending on you."

The corners of his mouth turn up in a small, tight smile. *And if I don't, you'll make me sorry.*

This time, I'm glad my intention rings through appropriately.

Trish is back then, handing me the cell phone. She's washed her face and tucked her hair behind her ears. "I'd like to take a shower if it's all right," she says to Frey.

He nods, and she gathers up her small bundle of clothes.

I put an arm over her shoulders. "I have to go now. I'll be back in the morning. Mr. Frey has my telephone number." I glance up at him and he nods that he got it. I knew he would.

Trish looks up at me. "Thank you for believing me," she says.

Her eyes are still clouded with sadness but a little of the desperation is gone. I touch the clothes in her arms. "When this is over," I tell her, "you and I are going shopping."

She allows a smile to touch the corners of her mouth. "I'd like that."

I wait until she heads back to the bathroom for her shower to take my leave. I feel Frey watching as I head for the door. His thoughts reach out to me. *What do you plan to do?*

I stop, hand on the door. *I'm not sure yet.*

Frey's expression is thoughtful. *I don't need to tell you to be careful.*

No. You don't.

But in the car, when I'm alone, the shaking starts. It's swift and relentless. The enormity of what I'm feeling about Trish and what has been done to her demands release.

Laying my head against the steering wheel, I let the tears come. I don't try to temper it or hold back. I don't try to reason or understand. I just let the sobs overtake me. Emotional eruptions this strong were a rare occurrence for me when I was human. Frankly, it catches me by surprise now. And it doesn't last long. When I can't cry anymore, I sit up. I'm glad I carry a box of tissues in the car. I happen to like the sweater I'm wearing.

Then, the emotional storm spent, I lean back in the seat to contemplate my next move. It's been hours since

I talked to my mother. It's past six o'clock, so I put in a call to her at home. Voice mail picks up. I hang up without leaving a message. I don't know what to say. Then it occurs to me that she may have left a message for me on *my* home phone. When I dial in, I find that she has. Seems Carolyn contacted them. She and my father decided to meet Carolyn for dinner after all. She tells me where, but I have no intention of joining them. I couldn't be in the same room with Carolyn and not betray my feelings. And it's not as if my parents are in any danger from her. She likes to bully children, after all. I'm sure Carolyn asked them out because she is trying to win their favor.

She doesn't realize how futile it is, of course. But she will soon. The next time we speak.

I decide to go home. A hot bath and a good night's rest are what I need. Vampires, like humans, have their emotional limits and I've reached mine.

I don't realize how weary I am until I trudge out of the elevator and get right up to my door before something stops me—light shining around the edges of the door. And I hear music.

I know I didn't leave a light or the radio on when I left this morning.

The exhaustion vanishes. I sling my purse across my chest bandoleer-style and lean closer, listening for any other sounds from within. All I hear is the beating of my heart as it pumps adrenaline. I know if I use my key to unlock the door, I'll alert whoever is inside. I'd rather catch them by surprise than the other way around.

I gather strength and lunge at the door, hitting it hard. Wood splinters with a deafening crack and the doorknob knocks a chunk out of the plaster wall behind it.

I leap inside, a snarl escaping my lips.

And there, standing at the door to the bedroom, is . . . Max.

He blinks at me. He's got a drink in one hand and

a towel in the other. He shakes his head as if to clear it and blinks again.

I blink, too. He's naked. His skin glistens, and his hair is slicked back. He must have just stepped out of the shower.

We stare at each other for a minute, and then he smiles.

"Wow, Anna," he says. "That was quite an entrance."

CHAPTER 17

NATURALLY, MY FIRST REACTION IS TO RAIL AT
Max. Ask him what the hell he's doing here and
why he didn't leave me a message letting me know?

But he's naked. And a naked Max is a joy to behold.

"I thought you were going to dinner with David and
what's her name," I say, my throat suddenly dry.

He lets the towel drop and takes a step toward me.
"Are you sorry I didn't?" His voice is husky, too.

Suddenly, that craving I had awhile ago for a little
physical activity comes screaming back. I don't say anything at all. I kick the door shut behind me, prop a chair
against it to hold it closed, and I'm on him.

Max responds just the way I hope he will. He doesn't
waste time with words, either. He tears at my clothes,
pulling off my sweater, fumbling too long with the zipper
on my jeans. I lose patience, push his hands away, and
peel them off myself.

His words are breathless in my ear. "You're so cold."

"Then warm me."

He does, with his hands and mouth. Vampire physiology is a funny thing. Sexual arousal sends heat to the skin, and in a heartbeat, I'm burning. We're on the floor, legs intertwined, my breasts crushed against his chest. My senses spin, come alive, with the scent of his freshly showered skin. I can't wait. I writhe against him, mouth seeking his, hands guiding him inside. He's ready, too. He mounts me and I welcome him in, reveling in the pleasure that I feel in every cell of my head, heart and body. Since becoming vampire, I've dreaded having sex with Max. Afraid the exquisite combination of blood and sex I had with Avery would make human sexual experience pale in comparison. Avery told me that it would.

Max and I find the tempo that binds our bodies together and sends us soaring higher and higher. When Max comes, and I feel his love flow into me like warm honey, the release shatters the night around us into a million glowing stars.

And I remember.

Avery was a liar.

CHAPTER 18

M AX ROLLS OFF ME AND COLLAPSES WITH A groan onto the carpet. I lie quietly beside him, listening to his breathing, listening to the pounding of his blood, listening to the beating of his heart. Suddenly, he sits up and his face hovers over mine, an expression of concern twisting his features.

"My God, Anna. I didn't use a condom."

I actually laugh out loud. "It's okay, Max. It's safe."

"How can you know that?"

Because I'm no longer human and bearing children or contracting STDs is not something a vampire has to worry about. Of course, I can't say that to Max. All he knows is that we've always been careful to use condoms, so what I say to Max is, "It's not the right time of the month. Trust me."

"You're sure?"

There's an unmistakable tinge of disappointment in his voice. He lays a hand on my abdomen. "Making a baby with you wouldn't be such a terrible thing. Maybe it's time we thought about it."

An alarm shrieks in my head. I sit up now, too, quickly, and point to Max's glass on the floor beside him. "Fix me one of those, will you? I'm going to take a shower."

Before he can respond or ask if he can join me, I'm out of the room. The turn this conversation has taken is too bizarre and fraught with consequences Max can't begin to comprehend. When did he get so *serious*?

When I get out of the shower, I slip into the best buzz kill I can think of—a pair of man-tailored flannel pajamas and a bathrobe, belted tight. No exposed skin.

Max eyes me when I rejoin him, holding out the drink and raising an eyebrow. "Nice outfit. Very sexy in an L.L. Bean kind of way."

I take a sip of the drink, scotch, straight up, and perch myself on the couch, tucking my robe around my legs. Max has slipped on jeans, but he's shirtless and I avert my eyes because those pecs and biceps have a predictable effect on me. Already, my skin is heating up.

He sits beside me and casually slips a hand between the folds of my robe. His hand feels warm through the fabric. "I didn't mean to scare you," he says.

"Scare me?" I act like I haven't a clue what he's talking about.

"The baby thing." He pauses. "Ever thought about it?"

I pretend the drink is in the way and move just out of reach. Max snuggles closer on the couch and the hand is back. This time his fingers play with the waistband on my pj's, wiggle their way inside and inch downward.

I squirm away. "Max, you can't be serious. You have a job that keeps you gone for weeks. I have a missing teenager to look for. No, I haven't thought about it."

My tone has the desired affect. He pulls away and reaches for his drink. I can tell he's embarrassed. I clear my throat.

"So, Max. Let's talk. How did you and David make out today?"

He eyes me. I've gone for the let's get past this silliness and on to something else tone. It seems to work because he takes a drink and says, "Piece of cake. It was fun. David's not such a bad guy after all." He takes another sip of the scotch and adds, "We discovered we have something in common."

I snicker. "You and David? Let's see, it can't be that you're both jocks and adrenaline junkies. That would be too obvious. So it must be that you're both in love with Gloria."

He raises an eyebrow. "Close," he responds. "We both love you."

I almost choke on a mouthful of scotch.

Max laughs. "I don't mean we both love you *that* way. I mean David thinks of you as a sister. He wants to protect you. He's having a hard time getting over what happened a few months ago. He says he'll never forgive himself for that."

Another topic I'm not about to get into. Neither David nor Max knows the true story of what happened that night and they never will. Just as David will never know that I saved him from certain death at Avery's hands—or teeth.

But what does Max mean about loving me *that* way. What's going on with him?

I give myself a mental shake. Later. Right now, there are more important subjects we need to discuss.

I temper the panic out of my voice. "I need to talk to you about something important, Max."

He leans back on the couch cushion and waves a hand in a "go ahead" motion.

"What do you know about kiddie porn?"

An eyebrow shoots up. "Kiddie porn?" Then there's a reflective pause. "Does this have anything to do with that girl who was killed?"

"I'm not sure. Not yet. I just need to know what can be done about catching somebody involved in selling their own kid to men for money."

I couldn't control the revulsion in my voice if I wanted to. I keep seeing Trish's shattered face.

Max sits up a little straighter. "Do you think that's what happened to Barbara Franco?"

I hold up a hand. "No. I don't believe Barbara was involved in kiddie porn directly, but she may have been killed because she knew someone who was."

Max gets that stern cop look in his eye. "And you're afraid Trish might be next? You need to go to the authorities with this," he says. "I'm not kidding, Anna. This is serious business. And it involves the worst kind of scumbag—"

He's gearing up for a lecture. One I'm not the least bit interested in hearing. "Listen, Max. I promise you. I will go to the authorities the minute I have something concrete. What I want you to tell me is what kind of evidence you'd need to put these people away."

He's frowning and glaring in that male authoritarian way that makes me want to smack the look right off his face. But that wouldn't get me the answer now, would it? I smile and purse my lips and nod encouragingly at him.

His expression softens. "Computers," he says. "These guys do big business on the Web. They can try to delete their files, but there's an evidence trail that can be recovered from the hard drive. That's usually what puts them away."

The good news and the bad news. I have a mental picture of that laptop flying from Ryan's hand and bouncing off the wall of the garage to land in a crashing heap on the concrete floor. My bad. On the other hand, Ryan didn't seem that disturbed by what I'd done. In fact, he said he'd be able to retrieve data from it. Is that possible?

"What happens if the computer is . . . say. . . . dropped?" I ask.

Once again, Max is staring at me with cop eyes. "What computer are we talking about, Anna?"

"I'm just talking theoretically here. If a computer is broken, can you retrieve data from it?"

He nods slowly but with reservation, as if he's afraid answering my question could be construed as encouraging behavior he doesn't condone. "It's possible. Depends on how badly it's damaged and how good the guy working on it is." He crosses his arms over his chest. "Want to tell me why we're having this conversation?"

But he's given me what I need. Now it's time to change the subject. "We don't have to be making a baby, Max, to have fun with the process, do we?" I place my drink on the coffee table and slip the robe off my shoulders.

Evidently not. Max uncrosses his arms and watches. By the time I've lost the pajamas, the only hard drive he seems interested in is the one between his legs.

This time we go slowly. Long, lingering kisses. Fingers that coax and tease. When the tension gets too much, when we're both more than ready, Max slides his hands under my bottom and I arch up to meet him.

I let Max do the work, move to his rhythm. I listen to his heart, see the pulse drumming at the base of his jaw. I lick at it, taste the salt of his sweat as it pools there. My mouth forms around the spot, sucking gently. Max groans and moves closer.

Suddenly, Avery is there again. This time, his words send a shiver through me. *Think of how good you can make it, Anna. It will be the most wonderful sex Max has ever had.*

I touch the pulse point with burning fingers. Max's blood rushes right there, beneath that fragile sheath of skin—a sheath I can easily pierce. My hands pull his head closer. He doesn't resist. He's hurtling past the point of return.

But I can't do it. I can't bring myself to drink from

Max. If I do, I risk whatever tremulous hold I have left on what's human inside me. And in the instant I realize that, I've lost him. I'm like a surfer who waits a second too long to make the cut. Max is swept away from me on the wave of his passion, and I'm left behind, alone, to watch.

CHAPTER 19

MAX IS AWARE THAT OUR LAST COUPLING WAS not as satisfying for me as the first. The expression in his eyes makes it obvious that he's afraid it's his fault, that the talk of having a baby has broken something in our relationship.

I can't tell him the truth. I can't tell him that what happened was not his fault at all. The temptation to drink from him almost overwhelmed me. I can't believe how close I came to doing it.

I don't want to think about that now, and I don't want to tempt fate again. Instead, I smile and tell him I'm tired. Which is true. And that things will be different after a good night's sleep. Which I can only hope is true.

He gets up and goes into the bathroom to brush his teeth. I collapse on the bed and wait for him to finish. Can't share the bathroom anymore—especially one with large mirrors. Not when you're a vampire. When the phone rings, it's a little after ten.

It's my mother. "Did I wake you?" she asks anxiously.

"No. I'm just lying here—resting. How was your dinner with Carolyn?"

"She never showed up." Mom's voice is a mixture of aggravation and concern. "We tried calling her, but there was no answer. Why would she stand us up? The dinner was her idea."

After what I learned about Carolyn today, nothing she does surprises me. To my mother I respond, "Maybe she got called back to the hospital and didn't have time to get in touch with you. I'm going to see her tomorrow. I'll ask her what happened."

"I got your note this afternoon," Mom continues. "So I didn't expect to hear from her at all, which is why the invitation came as such a surprise." There's a pause. "Any word on Trish?"

This is one of the things I hate most—lying to humans I love. It doesn't get easier, and I see no way it will ever change. But I can't share what I've learned with anyone yet, especially not my parents. "I expect to have some word soon, Mom. Please try not to worry. How's Dad taking all this?"

There's a sharp intake of breath. "Not well. He acts like he doesn't believe Trish is really Steve's. But I can tell he's scared to death for her."

A thought strikes me. "Mom, did Carolyn leave Trish's hairbrush with you?"

Again, a pause. In my mind's eye, I see Mom walking into the living room, looking around. "Yes," she says at last. "It's here."

"I'll pick it up tomorrow. I think we should run that DNA test. You have one of Steve's baby teeth, right? I remember seeing it in a scrapbook or something."

The laugh is small and sad. "I have one of yours, too. The first you lost."

I let a heartbeat go by before responding. "Will you

leave Steve's tooth with the hairbrush? I think they can get a DNA sample from it."

It seems to take Mom a long time to answer. But finally she does, in a soft, firm voice. "I'll leave everything on the dining room table in case we're not here when you come. We're returning to full schedule tomorrow at school and I expect it will be a long day."

I promise to call her and check in and then we ring off. Max slips into bed beside me and we snuggle together under the covers. He falls asleep first and I disentangle myself from his arms and lie staring at the ceiling, waiting for sleep to dull the terrible anxiety I feel for a young girl I've known less than a day.

CHAPTER 20

WEDNESDAY

I AWAKEN ONCE, EARLY, WHEN MAX GETS UP IN response to the chirping of his cell phone. I drift back to half sleep, aware that Max has gone into the bathroom and that he's showering and dressing. Then he's leaning over to kiss my forehead.

"I have to go," he says. "I got a call. There's been some trouble with Martinez's extradition. They want me back in Washington."

I struggle into a sitting position. "Is everything all right?"

But his eyes seem to be focusing on everything in the room but me.

"Max, is everything all right?"

His lips draw up and I imagine he thinks he's smiling. But the smile doesn't reach his eyes nor does it smooth the wrinkles from his brow. "Of course everything is all right," he says a little too cheerfully. "Why wouldn't it be?"

"I hope you lie better than this when you're on the job."

He smiles—a real smile this time—and his shoulders lose some of their stiffness. He perches himself on the edge of the bed and tucks a lock of my hair behind my ear. "It's Martinez. They've lost him."

"Lost him? How do they lose one of the biggest drug dealers in Mexico? I thought he was vacationing with his family in Colombia? Wasn't somebody watching him?"

His shrug morphs into a hand dipping into a jacket pocket. His cell phone again. He listens for a minute, snaps the phone shut without saying a word and leans over the bed once more.

"Sorry, babe," he says. "I really do have to go. I'll call you when I get to Washington, okay?" His brows draw together in an expression of concern. "About last night? I didn't mean—"

I reach up a hand to touch his cheek. "It's all right, Max. You be careful, you hear? I'm not through with you yet."

He smiles, relief softening the lines from his face. "Glad to hear it."

I walk him to the door, noting as I pull the chair away from it that I'll have to call building maintenance to get it fixed. They'll want to know what happened, I'm sure, so I'll have to come up with something.

I kiss Max and watch until he disappears behind elevator doors. I have a bad feeling. Not about what happened between us last night, though it's a concern. But if Martinez figured out Max's role in the bust that dismantled his money laundering operation, he will come after him.

Not something I can do anything about. Max is a big boy who is certainly capable of taking care of himself. I push the door shut. My priority has to be Trish.

I debate whether to call Frey or go to the condo. My plan this morning is to track down Carolyn, but the urge to see for myself that Trish is all right is just too strong. A quick shower, a tug of my hairbrush through wet hair, clean jeans and a cotton sweater, and I'm out the door. Trying to close it reminds me that I have one more stop to make first.

Burdick, the building maintenance supervisor, has a ground floor apartment. He's a fussy little man with eyes too close together in a fat, round face. I've never liked him. He always looks at me as if he'd like to see me served up on toast. I won't miss him when I leave.

But I needn't have fretted about concocting a story for him. He neither asks nor seems to care *how* the door got broken. He just assures me there will be a hefty bill to pay, leering like he's waiting for me to offer to work the damages off in trade.

His attitude snaps my temper like a rubber band, but I manage to rein it in before doing something stupid that would most likely land me in jail. For once, my brain engages before I put my impulse in gear. This sneering little man will never know how close he came to having something else to fix. Like the window I almost throw him through.

With the bad taste of my encounter with the building manager in my mouth, I head for Frey's. This time, I hit rush hour traffic. I drive a Jag, low slung, low profile. I find myself behind a huge, diesel-burning pickup whose tail pipe is eye level to my windshield. I don't breathe air anymore, but I can *smell*. The fumes are so noxious I look for an escape route. Behind me is a kid in a Toyota who is close enough that I can see the pimples on his face. There's a bus on one side and a garbage truck on the other.

I'm trapped.

The knot in my stomach tightens.

Relax, Anna. I haven't seen you this uptight in a long time.

The intrusion into my head is unexpected, but the voice is familiar.

Why, Casper. I haven't heard from you for weeks. Where have you been?

Here. There.

That narrows it down.

There's a chuckle. I'm scanning cars all around, trying to get a bead on the illusive voice that drops in and out of my head at will. The one thing I'm sure of is that Casper, the nickname I gave him because he's like the friendly ghost in the cartoons, only shows up when I'm in trouble. I have no idea who or what he is or how he's doing what he does.

I give up trying to locate him. *It's that bad, is it?* I ask.

It could be.

Want to be a tad more specific?

I can't be. Just keep your head.

If you mean that literally, I intend to. A spasm of alarm. *You* don't *mean that literally, do you?*

Control your emotions. Don't let them lead you off the path.

Control my emotions? I thought I'd been doing that. The building super is in one piece and Carolyn has her head. But before I can snap back, Casper is talking again.

You'll be faced with some tough decisions in the days ahead. The choices you make will affect the lives of those you love most. Remember who you are.

Who I am? An image flashes in my head. Last night with Max and what almost happened. Is that what Casper means?

The spasm of concern becomes a full-blown paroxysm. Casper has never been so explicit or so agonizingly ambiguous. *Who are we talking about? My parents? David? Max?*

There's no reply.

Damn it. I'm banging my hand against the steering wheel in frustration. *Casper? What did you mean?*

But there's only a vacuum of silence left in the place Casper occupied in my head. He's gone, having dropped the kind of subtle hint he knows will get to me. A hint designed to set my nerves and teeth on edge.

A hint that I might be a threat to someone I love.

Great.

The kid in the Toyota behind me is leaning on his horn. Traffic is moving, finally. I put the Jag in gear and inch forward.

I expect Frey to answer right away when I reach his gate. He doesn't. I try again and again. I keep punching his unit number on the keypad until a knock on the passenger window spins me, startled, toward the sound.

A uniformed guard has come out of nowhere to peer inquisitively into the car. He motions for me to roll down the window. Which I do.

"Is there a problem, miss?" he asks.

I shake my head, too surprised to turn a coherent thought into coherent words.

He has a half smile on his weathered, sixty-something face. "Who are you here to see?"

"Daniel Frey. Unit 7B."

Now it's his turn to shake his head. "Mr. Frey is gone. His driver picked him up about an hour ago. Same as every school day."

Gone? Would he have taken Trish with him?

"Could you tell, was he alone in the car?"

This time a nod. "Just like always, Mr. Frey and the driver."

It never occurred to me that Frey would leave Trish alone. What was he thinking? I assumed he would get a substitute for the day. Panic sparks, but it's fleeting, to be replaced by a darker, more heated emotion. Anger. How could he leave Trish alone? She must be frantic, listening to that buzzer ring again and again and having no way of knowing who it is.

The guard leans toward me, waiting for some indication that I've heard him and will do the logical thing—leave.

So, I do. I thank him and back away to make a U-turn in the driveway. But I pull out only as far as the road. Dipping into my purse, I pull out my cell and dial the condo. After four rings, a machine picks up. I sit impatiently through the brief instructions to leave a message after the beep blah-blah.

At last. The beep.

"Trish? Are you there? It's Anna. It's all right to pick up, honey. I know Mr. Frey left for school. I just want to know you're all right. Trish? Are you there?"

But the seconds tick by and the machine eventually clicks off. There's no answer from Trish. What the hell is going on?

As soon as I disconnect from that call, another comes in. Without glancing at the incoming number, I open the connection with a terse, "Frey? This better be you."

"No," David says. "Sorry. It's me. Your partner, remember? Though it would be easy to see how you might forget the number. You haven't used it much lately."

Guilt momentarily replaces impatience. "Sorry. Didn't check the number. Things have been kind of crazy."

There's a pause, like he's waiting for me to expand on the subject. When I don't, he says, "So. Did you see Max last night?"

A lightbulb blinks on. "You let Max into my apartment, didn't you?"

This time the pause is a beat too long. "Are you mad about that?"

I blow out a puff of air. "No. Not mad. But you owe me a new door."

"What?"

I wave an impatient hand at the phone. "Never mind. Is there a reason you called?"

"You mean other than wondering if my partner is going to put in an appearance today?"

This time the impatience is David's. And rightfully so. "I'm sorry. I should have checked in first thing. Is there anything important on the docket today?"

"Does that mean you're not planning to come in?"

When I don't answer, he heaves a protracted sigh into the receiver. "It's all right. I know you have a lot going on right now. Just do me a favor. Call me tonight, okay? Let me know what's happening. I'm worried about you."

"Why would you worry about me?" It comes out much sharper than I intend.

"Why?" His tone mimics mine. "Maybe because we're partners and that's what partners do. You've shut me out of this. I don't like it."

There's a pause before he adds, "Anna, don't get me wrong. Finding out you have a niece who disappeared under suspicious circumstances is a lot to deal with. But we do have a business to run. I need to know if I can count on you, or if I should get someone else to help out until you're ready to come back to work."

He says it in a rush, like it's an unpleasant speech he's been practicing. And the implication that I've *chosen* to be absent from work makes my mouth fall open in disbelief. Then the lightbulb goes on again. "Did Gloria tell you to say that?"

Silence.

"Gloria is there, isn't she?"

Gloria. Of the long legs and big tits. I can see it in my head, Gloria, sitting on David's lap, making sure the head he's using isn't the one on his shoulders.

She hates me.

Okay, I hate her right back. But she doesn't usually

have this kind of effect on David. There must be something else going on.

Then I know. She met Max yesterday. And if Max acted the way most men do around her, she's convinced that Max would be a much more appropriate partner for David than me. In her convoluted way of thinking it would make perfect sense. Why settle for one man lusting after you when you could have two?

"Tell Gloria it was a good try," I say in a voice you could pour on pancakes. "But it won't work. She's not getting rid of me that easily. And, just so you both know, Max left for Washington this morning. I have to go now. Oh, and David? Tell your girlfriend I said she's depriving some village of an idiot."

I hear a quick intake of breath. "Anna, I'm—"

I hang up before he, or Gloria, can say anything else. I'm angry. At Gloria. At David. At myself. I realize I wanted David to do some more checking on the Franco/Frey/Delaney connection, but I'm not about to call him back.

The cell phone rings again. The office number flashes. Still pissed, I ignore it and bury the phone in my purse.

There is one good thing that comes from the conversation, though. Any guilt I had about shirking my responsibilities at the office vanishes with the image of Gloria whispering encouragement in David's ear. We'll need to have a conversation about that later, David and I, but now I'm free to pursue Carolyn with a clear conscience.

But damn that Frey. I have to see Trish first. Make sure she's all right, that I didn't scare her to death by buzzing the condo like that.

I look around. I'd pulled over right in front of the complex. A high, brick wall surrounds it, parking lot and all. Now, getting over the wall won't be a problem. I could probably jump it without breaking a sweat. But it's daylight and this is a busy street. The only shrubbery consists of low growing bushes and a vine of some kind that snakes over the brick. Nothing that would afford me cover.

At least nothing that I can see from here.

I start the car and ease into traffic, following the brick wall for several blocks until it makes a right turn and extends away from the main road. I turn right, too, and almost immediately find what I'm looking for.

This block is lined with trees, big, leafy trees with lots of low hanging branches. I won't have to climb.

I just have to jump.

I must admit, I've come to enjoy some of my newly acquired vampire traits. The superhuman strength. The improved visual and sensual acuity. The ability to leap onto tall tree branches in a single bound. It takes me less than a minute to get over that wall and drop onto the grass on the other side.

And I luck out. There's no one peering out of a window to see me take the jump or to sprint across the grass to the sidewalk. I then saunter purposefully toward Frey's unit. I'm just about at the building when I see them.

Two men. Tall. Husky. Wearing dark suits and walking just as purposefully as I am toward Frey's front door. And they're coming from the direction of the parking lot. How did they get by the security guard? They're closer to Frey's than I am and don't seem to have spotted me, so I hang back behind a tall, fragrant bougainvillea bush to watch.

Suit One rings Frey's bell, then steps back. He puts his hands behind his back and rocks a little on his heels, smiling toward the peephole in the door. His expression is friendly, expectant. He waits a moment. Then rings again.

Suit Two, meanwhile, is a step behind him. He's looking around. I make sure I'm in the shadows when his eyes sweep in my direction. They scan right over me, keep going. I detect no unusual or supernatural vibes, and when I surreptitiously try to probe his mind, I get nothing. He's human. He turns back to his partner and nods.

It's eight o'clock on a Wednesday morning. It's obvious that most residents are at work, but it takes balls to break into someone's apartment in broad daylight. But that's just what these guys try to do. Suit One takes a small leather case out of his pocket and extracts a thin, metal wire. While Suit Two stands watch, he goes to work on the door.

That's when I lose it. Trish is inside. All I can think of is protecting her. In two strides, I'm at the door. Before surprise can register on their faces, I've grabbed both of them by the scruffs of their necks and flung them to the ground. I crouch over them, teeth bared, beyond all reason, snarling like an angry mother bear.

CHAPTER 21

T HEN TWO THINGS HAPPEN AT ONCE. THE NEIGH-
bor to Frey's right opens his door. "Hey," he shouts.
"What's going on?"

In the same instant, Suit One puts a knee to my chest
and heaves.

The sudden appearance of the guy in the doorway dis-
tracts me. Suit One's knee catches me off guard. Before I
can recover, I'm flying off of him to land in an ungraceful
heap at the neighbor's feet.

He reaches a hand down, but rather than help me, it
gets in the way of my leaping up and the two of us do a
kind of weird dance trying to get disentangled. By the
time I get my feet back under me, the suits are up and
away.

The neighbor is a kindly looking old guy, with a Mr.
Rogers smile and a shock of wiry white hair peeking
around the edges of a faded baseball cap. He frowns at
me. "Are you all right, miss?" He pushes the cap back

and scratches his head. "What just happened? Should I call the police?"

I'm looking after the Blues Brothers, who are racing back toward the parking lot.

The neighbor puts a hand on my arm. "Were those men coming out of Daniel's apartment?" he asks. "He's not home, you know. He's at school."

I'm trying to regain my balance and pull at my sweater, which has ridden up embarrassingly high. My eyes are following the suits, and just as I decide to go after them, the old guy says, "Wonder if they were talking to that sweet young niece of Daniel's?"

That snaps my attention back. "Niece?"

The old guy's little prune face is wreathed in a wide smile. "Met her last night. Daniel was taking her to dinner." He taps a forefinger near the corner of his right eye. "These old eyes don't miss much. I was right there at my window when they came out. Just like this morning. Naturally, I did the neighborly thing and came out and introduced myself. Daniel said the girl was visiting from Boston. That's where he's from, you know."

I don't share with him what I know—or what I want to do to Daniel when I get my hands on him. I can't believe he'd expose Trish to danger by taking her out in public.

The guy now has my complete attention. "What did the girl look like?" I ask, trying not to sound as concerned as I feel.

"Oh, she's a cute little thing. About thirteen, I'd say, a little thin. Blond hair down to here." He touches his own shoulders. "Beautiful eyes."

"Did you get her name?"

"Trish," he replies promptly. "Course, it was strange that Daniel came back alone. I meant to ask him about that this morning, but he left before I could."

Came back alone? That's all I need to hear. I thank Mr. Rogers for his help. He starts to say something else, but I don't wait nor do I try to keep the speed down as I race back to the car. This time I leap the fence with barely a backward glance. Let any pain in the ass who saw *that* try to explain it.

By the time I get to Mom's school, I'm sick with anger and trepidation. I park in the faculty lot and go directly to Frey's classroom. His radar picks me up before I reach the door.

Anna. She's safe.

He's standing at the podium in front of a class of about forty students. It's the only thing that keeps me from marching in and tearing his throat out. *I can get all the information I need from drinking his blood.* I fire the thought at him like a bullet.

I know that, he tells me. *So calm down and listen. Trish is safe. I took her to a place where she can be protected twenty-four hours a day. I'll take you to her after school.*

You'll take me to her now.

I can't. I have students here. And you have more important things to deal with. Go see Trish's mother. Find out who hurt Trish. Until we put those men away, she will never be safe.

While we're "talking," he's actually lecturing the class in his real voice. Something about parts of a sentence. I watch, biting on my lower lip, uncertain what to do next. Then he's in my head again.

Close your eyes.

What?

Close your eyes. I'll show you that Trish is all right.

I have no idea what kind of parlor trick he's about to perform, but I follow his instructions. I close my eyes. A picture starts to form like an image appearing out of the fog. Trish. Sitting at a desk. She has a book open in front of her and a woman sits beside her. The woman points to something in the book and they both laugh. A real laugh. Trish looks relaxed and—happy.

Is this a trick? Where is she? Who is she with?

I'll show you this afternoon. Anna, you have to trust me.

No. I don't.

The picture dissolves as we speak. I shake my head to clear it and rub at my eyes. There's a curious tingling in the back of my neck, like a subtle muscle ache after a heavy work out.

Sorry about that, Frey says. *It's an unfortunate side effect of the visions.*

He pauses, picking something else out of my head. *There were men at my condo this morning. They were looking for Trish, weren't they?*

It's my guess. Believe it or not, your neighbor scared them away. He also told me about meeting your "niece." You should have told me what you were planning.

You wanted Trish safe. She is. Carolyn Delaney may be able to tell you who those men were. You need to speak with her. Now.

Our eyes lock together over the heads of his students. Amazingly, the kids seem completely oblivious to my presence. Perhaps a being who can project images can also cast spells that anesthetize those around him to everything except that which he chooses.

Daniel Frey has a lot of interesting powers.

I shake my head again. The cobwebby remains of the vision fade like an overexposed photo. The vision seemed very real. And Trish looked happy. But I won't know for sure if it was more than a trick until I see Trish for myself.

My eyes find Frey's again. *Okay. I'm going to trust that Trish is all right. For now. I'll be back at three to pick you up. If anything happens to her, I'll kill you. Slowly.*

He allows a tiny smile to touch the corners of his mouth, the only acknowledgment of my statement.

But he believes me. My telepathic powers may be limited compared to a shape-shifter's, but not my physical ones.

And so I'm back on the road again. I feel like I've spent most of the last few days in my car. My nerve endings tingle with anxiety for Trish, tension over the prospect of facing Carolyn, and anger toward the sick fucks who take pleasure in stealing the joy of life from children. I only hope I can restrain myself when I find them. These last two months had me convinced I could lead a "normal" life. Working with David, visiting with my parents, going to Culebra when I needed to feed. It almost felt natural. But in just two days, I've been knocked off kilter.

First with Max and now with a rush of murderous rage toward Carolyn that scares me. Not because I'm afraid I can't control it, but because I'm not sure I want to.

Coming face-to-face with Carolyn will be a supreme test of self-control. But I need to keep foremost in my head that she has the key to protecting Trish. She knows who, besides herself, exploited her daughter. I will choke on my anger if I need to. I will be calm and reasonable in my approach. I will point out rationally why it is in her best interest to tell me what I need to know.

My fingers are gripping the steering wheel so tightly, the knuckles are white. My teeth ache from a clenched jaw.

So much for calm and reasonable.

Carolyn will talk to me.

One way or the other.

The apartment complex is just ahead. As I make the turn into the parking lot, a police car blocks my way. A young patrolman slouches against the door. He straightens up at my approach, and indicates with a wave of his hand that I should pull over to the side of the road.

I do, my eyes on the scene behind him. There are more police cars, strobe lights flashing. And a lot of uniforms and plainclothes cops milling around. But there's no urgency in their manner. And when the coroner's wagon pulls around me and the patrol cop waves him in, I know why.

CHAPTER 22

CAROLYN IS DEAD. I DON'T KNOW HOW I KNOW it, but I know it as well as I know my own name. She's dead, and the realization that I've lost an important link, maybe the only link, to securing Trish's safety has me banging the steering wheel with the palms of my hands in frustration.

The same young cop who waved me away from the parking lot is now watching me with open curiosity. He calls one of the plainclothes cops over and points to me.

I shut off the car's engine and wait for the detective to approach.

I know a lot of cops at SDPD, but mostly the uniforms who work at the jail, not the detectives who put the fugitives there in the first place. The guy who approaches is fiftyish, heavy set, with owlish eyes and a bulbous nose dominating a round face. His expression is neutral, giving nothing away, but the lines around his eyes tighten slightly when he looks at me as if taking a mental snapshot.

"Can I help you, ma'am?" he asks.

There are a lot of ways to answer that question. Possibilities flash like a slide show in my head. But there's only one answer that might gain me access to information. The realization that it will also shine a spotlight on my family's relationship with Carolyn is not lost on me. But Trish is the most important consideration and I know my mother would agree.

"I'm here to visit a friend. Carolyn Delaney."

I say it like I don't suspect what's going on.

The detective, however, knows better. The cop watching us from the parking lot has no doubt relayed my stupid display of frustration. He opens my car door and motions for me to get out. "Would you step over here with me a minute?"

It's not really a request and I respond accordingly. He touches a hand to my elbow and steers me to the coroner's wagon.

"How well did you know Ms. Delaney?" he asks.

"Well enough. Detective, what's going on?"

He studies me for a minute, though it's obvious that it's not as if he's unsure how to proceed, but more like he's unsure how to handle me. It doesn't take him long to come to a decision. "I'm afraid I have some bad news for you. We found a body in Ms. Delaney's apartment. We assume it's your friend. Would you mind making the identification?"

Do I have a choice? If I say no, he'll more than likely send me on my way.

I nod, and he waits beside me in silence while we watch the coroner and his men exit Carolyn's apartment. Two EMTs carry a stretcher with the shrouded body down the steps. The detective opens the door of the wagon and stops them when they get to me.

"Are you sure you want to do this?" he asks. "She's pretty badly beat up."

Again, I nod. After all the anger I've felt toward Carolyn, I don't expect to feel anything when I see the body. The attendant peels back the blanket, just to her shoulders.

Carolyn's face has been slashed, tiny cuts crisscross her cheeks. Cigarette burns scar her lips and eyelids. Her nose is smashed.

Shock sends a shudder through my body. Not of revulsion because of what's been done to her, but of anger because it's what I wanted to do. What I *wanted* to do.

I look up at the detective, my mouth so dry I'm not sure I can form the words. I swallow hard and say, "It's Carolyn."

He motions to the attendant, who cover's Carolyn's face again and loads her body into the van. The detective and I move to the side and watch in silence as it pulls away.

Only then does he turn his full attention to me. "I'm Detective Josh Harris," he says. "SDPD. And you are?"

"Anna Strong."

He has withdrawn a small spiral notebook from an inside jacket pocket. He takes his time fumbling in another pocket for a pen, shuffles pages in the notebook until he, presumably, finds a blank page, and with precise, even strokes, begins to write. "That's Anna s-t-r-o-n-g?"

I nod.

"Address?"

I give him the apartment address and follow it up with my telephone number. Easy stuff so far.

"And your relationship to the deceased?"

Now comes the tricky part. How much to tell him? How much does he already know?

He picks up on my hesitation. "Is there a reason you're reluctant to answer that question?"

Not exactly. I'm reluctant to mention Trish, who is, after all, the reason I'm here.

Detective Harris' sharp little eyes bore into mine. He's shifting from one foot to the other as if tired of waiting for me to answer. "Let me tell you what happened to your friend," he says. "It may facilitate your decision to help. She was tortured by someone who took his time and who enjoyed his work. When he tired of cutting and burning her, she was beaten, raped and strangled. The apartment was torn apart. From Ms. Delaney's condition, I can only assume her attacker didn't find what he was looking for. The neighbors say she had a daughter. She's been gone for a couple of days. I don't think I have to explain to you how important it is that we find her before this guy does."

A pause follows his words. Then he adds, "So let me ask you again. What is your relationship to the deceased?"

I see no way to avoid the question. "We didn't have a relationship, exactly. We just met. Her daughter, Trish, is a runaway. She asked me to find her."

"Are you a private detective?"

I shake my head. "No."

"Then why would she go to you and not the police?"

"Because I may be related to Trish. Carolyn told my family that Trish was my brother's child."

"And when did she tell you that?"

"Two nights ago."

"And you didn't know before two nights ago that your brother had a child?"

"No. He died before Carolyn could tell him she was pregnant. It was a long time ago."

The eyes narrow. "That doesn't explain why she would go to you and not the police."

I choose my words carefully. "She came to me because she knows what I do for a living. I'm a bail enforcement agent."

He raises an eyebrow. "Bounty hunter?" His tone lacks high regard.

"Yeah. Bounty hunter. She thought knowing I was related to Trish would be an incentive to find her."

"And did you?"

"Yes and no."

He frowns, the eyebrow ratchets higher. "What does that mean?"

"I found her. But she got away from me." Kind of.

A frown deepens the lines around his mouth. "You're a bounty hunter and you lost a thirteen-year-old girl? You must be very good at your job."

His sarcasm trips a flash of temper. I swallow it down like a dose of bitter medicine. He's just waiting for an excuse to haul my ass into headquarters and I know it.

When I don't rise to the bait, he follows the remark with, "I'd like to see some identification."

I motion to my car. "It's in my purse."

"Then let's go get it."

He marches me to the car and opens the passenger door so I can lean in and grab my purse from the seat. I withdraw my wallet and show him my driver's license and carry permit.

"You packing now?" he asks, perusing the licenses. His expression is indifferent, but there's an edge to his voice that wasn't there before.

"No. My gun is in a safe at my office. I had no reason to think I'd need it today." Actually, since becoming vampire, I pretty much have no reason to need it at all.

He glances up. "You don't mind if I check your car out then, do you? Just to be sure."

That flame of temper is sputtering back to life. "Be sure of what? That I'm telling you the truth? You have no reason to question it."

"Then you do object."

"You can search anything of mine you want, Detective. With a warrant."

He rocks back on his heels a little, studying me like a

bug on a pin. He thinks glaring at me will send me into panic mode. He forgets I'm not a civilian. Forgets what I do for a living. I've pulled this same trick myself once or twice to get what I want.

So we stand there staring at each other like two schoolyard bullies, each waiting for the other to blink first. Then Trish's face is in my head, followed by my mother's voice scolding me for acting like a child. And she's right. I need this jerk. I shake my head.

"Detective, if it will make you feel better, go ahead and search my car."

The abrupt change of attitude catches him off guard. A flash of surprise softens his face before he reasserts control and the surly mask is back. Without a word, he walks around to the driver's side, peers inside, moves the front seat forward to let his eyes sweep the back, passes a hand under the seat, front and back. Then he moves over to the passenger side to repeat the process. When he's done with that, he opens the glove compartment and the console. He walks around to the back of the car.

"Will you open the trunk?"

I do, pressing the button on the remote that triggers the trunk lock. After a moment, he slams the lid shut with the palm of his hand and rejoins me.

"Thank you for your cooperation, Ms. Strong." He glances toward the apartment. "Was Ms. Delaney married?"

"Not that I know of. Delaney is—was—her maiden name." I don't bring up Trish's mention of a "dad."

"Did she have a boyfriend?"

"I don't know. We'd just become reacquainted after fourteen years. She didn't share a lot with me."

Harris closes his notebook and slips it back into his jacket. He pulls out a small leather case, withdraws a business card and hands it over. "I will be in touch with you if we need anything else. I don't think I need to tell you to contact me if you find the girl."

The feeling behind his innocuous remark is clear. Once again, it's an order not a request. But before I can respond, a long, black limousine whispers by and comes to a halt at the driveway to the apartment complex, stopped there by the same uniformed cop who waved me off earlier. A back window slides down and a carefully coiffed gray head peers out at the policeman.

"What's going on, officer?" an imperious female voice asks.

The limousine is as out of place here as an elephant on a barstool, and that is clearly reflected in the cop's tone as he counters, "And what is your business here, ma'am?"

The door opens and a woman steps out. "I'm here to see my daughter," she replies. "Carolyn Delaney."

Detective Harris and I both react the same way to the woman's pronouncement. We take two or three steps toward the car. But then, Harris stops, and with a hand on my arm, pulls me to a halt beside him.

"Where do you think you're going?" he asks.

I gesture toward the woman. "To see Carolyn's mother."

"Do you know her?"

"No, but—"

He shakes his head. "You're not going anywhere near her. You can leave now or you can stay here. Right here. At your car. I'm going to talk to this woman. Alone."

He's glaring at me, daring me to argue.

If I piss him off, he might make me leave, and I really want to see how Carolyn's mother will react to the news of her daughter's death. I nod and hang back. What he doesn't know is that I'll be able to hear every word they say. A vampire thing.

Harris approaches the woman and flashes his badge. "I'm Detective Harris," he says. "And you are?"

She turns toward him, a look of polite indifference on her face. She's about five foot, slender but not skinny, silver hair done up in a twist at the back of her head. Her face is pale, thin; her regal cheekbones are touched with color and there is a hint of red on her lips. She's dressed in black slacks and a dark gray wool blazer. A blush of red silk peeks out from the jacket cuffs, and on her feet she wears black tasseled loafers. Understated elegance. There's a plain gold band on the ring finger of her left hand, but there are diamond studs the size of garbanzo beans at her ears.

Maybe not so understated.

She clasps her hands together and tilts her head up. "I don't know that who I am is any of your business, Officer," she says.

Anger flashes across Harris' face, but he recovers quickly. He responds, ignoring her sarcasm. "You told the officer that you are here to see your daughter, Carolyn Delaney. Is that correct?"

"And if it is?"

"Then I'm afraid I have some bad news for you, Mrs. Delaney."

"It's Mrs. Joseph Bernard," she says. "It hasn't been Mrs. Delaney for a very long time." Then she sighs and shakes her head. "What has Carolyn done now?"

Harris softens his voice. "She hasn't done anything, ma'am. There's no easy way to say this. Carolyn was killed last night."

There is no response from Carolyn's mother to Harris' words. No gasp. No physical reaction. No change in facial expression or body posture. She stands there staring up at Harris as if waiting in resigned tolerance for the punch line of a bad joke.

It's Harris who finally breaks the uncomfortable stalemate. "I'm sorry for your loss," he says.

The only acknowledgement of his words is a slight

movement of her head and shoulders, not quite a shrug, not quite a nod.

He tries again. "I need to ask you some questions."

For the first time her eyes shift away from Harris and her gaze falls on me. "Who is that young woman? Is she a friend of Carolyn's?"

Harris glances back at me. "She said she was an acquaintance of your daughter. Her name is Anna Strong."

Before Harris can object, Carolyn's mother is coming at me with long, purposeful strides. She stops in front of me. "Anna Strong?" she says quietly.

I nod. "I'm sorry about—"

But that is as far as I get. Faster than I can counter the blow, she slaps me hard across the face.

CHAPTER 23

OF COURSE, SHE CAN'T REALLY HURT ME, BUT because I am caught unawares, my head snaps back and my upper teeth puncture my lower lip. She has a gleam of satisfaction on her face as she watches me wipe a trickle of blood off my chin.

It's the last bit of satisfaction I intend to allow her at my expense.

The sound of the slap, like the crack of gunfire on the still morning air, is more startling than the physical blow itself. Everyone in hearing distance stops what he's doing and turns to look at us.

Detective Harris, right on her heels, doesn't react in typical cop fashion to an assault taking place in front of him. He comes to an abrupt halt a few feet from us and just stands there. Watching. It almost makes me as angry as being struck because I know what he's doing. He's waiting to see if either of us will say something he can use against us later.

But since Mrs. Bernard must suspect it, too, he's disappointed. We both stand staring at each other in rigid silence.

Finally, he approaches, pulls her back away from me and holds one arm in gentle restraint. His eyes are on me. "Are you all right, Ms. Strong?"

It would be touching if his expression or voice actually reflected concern. They don't.

I nod, wiping again at my chin. I almost bring my fingers to my mouth to lick the blood. It might be worth Harris' shock to see the expression on Mrs. Bernard's face if I did. But I stop myself, satisfying my rage by simply glaring at the woman.

Harris' attention turns immediately to Carolyn's mother. She stands quietly, not struggling, not doing anything, really, except staring back at me. "Would you like to explain why you just assaulted this woman, Mrs. Bernard?"

Her eyes never leave my face. "This woman's brother ruined my daughter's life. He was an irresponsible, unprincipled young man who took advantage of a sweet, innocent child. He got her pregnant and abandoned her."

"Abandoned her?" My voice shakes with fury. "He *died*. I met your daughter, Mrs. Bernard, when she and Steve were dating. She might have been a lot of things, but sweet and innocent were not among them."

A spasm of anger contorts her face, and this time, Mrs. Bernard pulls hard against Detective Harris' restraining arm. "How dare you?" she says. "You didn't know my daughter."

"And you didn't know Steve."

Harris has had enough. He tightens his grip on Mrs. Bernard's arm and locks me in a steely gaze. "Do you want to press charges?" he asks.

When I shake my head, he says, "Then I suggest you leave, Ms. Strong. If I need anything else from you, I'll be in touch."

Leaving is the last thing I want to do. I've learned nothing about Carolyn's death to help me track the men responsible. But I also realize that I have what those men were looking for—the computer. Or at least know where it is and I suspect I know what they look like—the two at Frey's apartment.

I have much more than the police.

Not once am I tempted to tell Mrs. Bernard about Trish. After all, not once has she thought to ask about her.

MY LIP HAS STOPPED BLEEDING. I FEEL THE TINGLE as it repairs itself, the swelling recedes, the torn skin knits together. In about ten minutes, when I touch the place where Carolyn's mother hit me, there's not a trace of the wound left.

All that's left is the sting of anger.

I pull into my parent's driveway. I use my key to let myself in and find Trish's hairbrush and Steve's baby tooth, wrapped in a cotton cocoon, where my mother promised to leave it—on the dining room table.

Unwrapping the tooth, and seeing the fragile, tiny reminder of my family's loss, I feel another surge of resentment toward Carolyn's mother. She condemned Steve for what happened to her daughter with no regard for my feelings. I'm glad my parents weren't there to experience her bitterness. But at least her words confirmed one thing for me. She believes Steve is Trish's father. So why would Carolyn lie to Trish all these years? It's obvious there was very little contact between Trish and her grandparents. If there had been, Trish would have learned about Steve a long time ago.

So was Carolyn lying when she said Trish once ran away to her grandparent's? I can't imagine Mrs. Joseph Bernard showing anything but contempt for her daughter's bastard child.

Too many questions and too few answers.

My fingers close around my brother's tooth. Maybe there's one question I can get answered.

I don't have the slightest idea how to go about getting a paternity test done. I could ask my family doctor, but she's been calling me to come in for my annual physical exam and that's something I won't be doing anytime soon. Maybe the phone book?

The first entry I look for—DNA testing—yields no results. But "Laboratories-Medical" has a boxed ad with "Paternity Testing" in big, bold letters. I call the 800 number and am greeted by a woman who introduces herself as "Marty." I explain my situation and the voice at the other end replies in a sympathetic tone.

"I'm sorry," she says. "But the simple truth is, we wouldn't be able to use a baby tooth. There's a lab in Canada that runs tests using bone and teeth, but it's an expensive process and takes a long time. As for the hair, it's also problematic. We need at least ten to fifteen strands with the follicles attached, and the hair should be no more than ten days old."

I pick up Trish's hairbrush. Being a typical teenager, the brush looks like it hasn't been cleaned—ever. There are a lot more than fifteen strands twisted in the bristles. And since Trish ran away just two days ago, I have to assume at least some of the hair is recent enough.

"Okay. The tooth won't work. What else could we try?"

She asks about the father's death and I explain what happened to Steve and when.

"Were you given your brother's clothes?" she replies. "The ones he was wearing at the time of the accident?"

I have to think about that. I have a vague recollection of going to New York with my parents to claim Steve's body. I was made to sit on a folding chair in a cold waiting room at a morgue somewhere near the college campus. I close my eyes, conjuring the scene, remembering how scared I was at the way my folks looked when they were taken away from me, and how I bit my lip to keep from crying when they came back, shock and unbearable sadness stamped on their faces.

But my father was holding something when he came back. He had his right arm around my mother's shoulders, but in his left hand he was holding something.

A brown paper bag.

I have to shake away the vision to be able to speak again.

"I think we may have the clothes."

The voice at the other end of the line softens. "If there is any blood, the smallest spot, we can use that. As long as the clothing has not been sealed in plastic, the specimen is viable."

I thank Marty, tell her I will get back to her when I find the clothes, and hang up. I rub at my face with the palms of my hands. I know where the clothes will be if my parents haven't disposed of them. But the prospect of going through Steve's belongings fills me with a despair that spreads like ice through my body. The only thing that propels me forward is Trish. The image of Carolyn's mother, cold, arrogant, flashes in my head. I can't help feeling that proving Trish is Steve's child and keeping her away from that woman is the only thing that can save her.

Houses in California don't have basements. As a result, garages and attics become repositories for the flotsam of life, things one step away from being relegated to the trash or donated to charity. Since my folks actually use the garage for their cars, I know where to go to find Steve's things.

The attic in this house is accessed by a pull down ladder in the ceiling of the guest room. I'm queasy as I climb the rungs. The last attic I ventured into was Avery's. What I found there foreshadowed what I fear is my future—the remains of his relationships with mortals. Literally, the remains. While I don't expect to find bodies in my parent's attic, as in most families, there's always the possibility of stumbling across a skeleton or two.

It's hot in the attic. Heat is trapped here under the eaves. And it's dark, though that poses no problem. I actually see better in the dark than I do in bright daylight. A holdover, I guess, from when vampires really were creatures of the night. I gauge each step carefully, balancing on the joists, not wanting to risk plunging through the ceiling tiles if my foot slips. There isn't much up here. A mound of old bedding and drapes. Some books piled on a wooden pallet. In the corner, a stack of cardboard boxes.

I make my way toward the boxes, knowing that if Steve's clothes are here, that's where I'll find them.

The first couple of boxes I open contain school things—yearbooks, yellow, lined note pads, binders, report cards with tape at the edges where they had been fastened to the refrigerator. I shuffle through the stack, touched by sadness. He never got anything but *A*s—ever. It was irritating to me when we were growing up. *A*s were an occasion for me, not the norm. But now it's just another reminder of what Steve might have accomplished had he lived.

What Trish might accomplish if given the opportunity.

But I'm getting ahead of myself. First things first.

The third box yields what I'm looking for. The only thing it contains is a large, brown paper bag. With shaking fingers, I curl back the top and look inside.

Steve's clothes are folded neatly. I withdraw a shirt, jeans, boxers, a pair of socks. At the bottom, Nike sneakers with frayed laces. There's no blood that I can see on the shoes. I recall that Steve was hit so hard he was literally knocked out of them.

My fingers are trembling so badly I lace my fingers together and squeeze for a minute. Then, carefully, I unfold each item and lay them one by one on top of the boxes. Jeans, shirt, boxers. No blood. It seems impossible. How can one be hit by a car and not shed a lot of blood? But the words come back to me—internal injuries.

The last things are the socks. The left one has a frayed edge where something has been cut out. I feel a tingle of excitement. The police must have kept that piece for the driver's trial. But it turned out there was no trial. The driver plea-bargained his offense. Because of his youth, he was given a sentence of two years in a juvenile facility and five years probation.

Which means right now, he's out there living a life he stole from my brother.

But if I let myself dwell on that, I'll get angry about it all over again. Right now, I have more important things to get angry about.

The right sock is folded in two. It's not necessary to unfold it to find what I'm looking for. There's a stain, brown now with age, on the cuff and another on the heel.

Blood, even old blood, evokes a visceral reaction in a vampire. It's instinctive and uncontrollable. It's my brother's blood that I "feel" on the sock. But it sets my teeth on edge, anyway, and triggers a need I have to fight. I bring the sock to my face and inhale because I can do nothing else. The smell is of salt and earth and the essence of his life. My nerve endings are on fire with the hunger.

So, I do the only thing I can. I wait for the thirst to fade. And when at last it does, I replace Steve's clothes in the box and close it up. I slip the sock back into the same bag my parents carried home with them all those years ago.

Time to stop looking back and face what lies ahead. It's what Avery tried to make me understand. And Cule-bra. As a vampire, I will remain forever same. My human family will not. At some point, when it becomes obvious that I am not aging, I will have to leave. And once more my parents will be forced to endure the loss of a child.

This time, it will be me.

Trish *has* to be Steve's.

CHAPTER 24

I CALL MARTY BACK. SHE GIVES ME DIRECTIONS TO the lab. I carry the tooth away with me because I don't want to take the time to write my mom a note explaining why I didn't. I have what we need to get the DNA test run, and the results are all that matter.

The lab is located in a medical complex up on Fourth Avenue, Pill Hill. The University of California runs the hospital here, a busy one, and it takes me awhile to find a parking space and hoof it back to the lab. I fill out the requisite forms, turn over the brush and sock, and write a check for "expedited services." I'm told I can return in forty-eight hours for the results.

Forty-eight hours. It'll be a long two days.

Back in my car, I don't realize how tense I am until I glance at my watch, see that it's only noon, and heave a sigh of frustration. Frey won't be available until three. I'm so antsy, my skin prickles. I'm not that far from the office, but after the less than satisfying conversation I had with David this morning, I'm not sure I want to go there. And if by some god-awful chance Gloria is with him, the urge to bite her—*really* bite the living crap out of her— may be too strong to resist.

I slump into the seat. For the first time I wonder how I'm going to break the news of Carolyn's death to Trish. As despicable as she was, Carolyn was Trish's mother. And when I tell her, how will Trish react? Will she demand to see the body? Will she want to go with her grandparents?

More questions I have no way of answering, at least not yet.

Another glance at my watch confirms it's now two minutes after twelve. If I was human, I could treat myself to lunch to kill time. Or go to the gym for a workout. Two things I reluctantly had to give up. The eating thing for obvious reasons. The workout thing because one time I forgot to check how much weight was on the bar and the expression on David's face when I effortlessly bench-pressed the same three hundred pounds he had struggled with moments before is something I will never forget. I had to let the bar come crashing down and pretend it almost killed me.

I acted my way out of it that time. I doubt I'd be so lucky the next.

The one thing I can think of doing is driving downtown and arranging to have my new furniture delivered to the cottage. If the store can handle it, I might be able to move in by the end of the week. I can't wait to be back in my own home. And maybe Trish would agree to move in with me while we sort out her future. It surprises me how much I'd like that.

I'm pulling out of the parking lot when I see them. The Blues Brothers from Frey's apartment are sitting in a beige Fairlane across the street from the lab. They are looking right at me, though like cartoon characters, they turn their heads in unison when they catch me looking back at them. I let my gaze pass over them and ease into traffic. Not surprisingly, they pull out, too, and fall into place about two car lengths behind.

I have a hard time concentrating on the road. When did they start following me? Did they pick me up at Frey's? Or Carolyn's? I was too preoccupied with getting beat up by Trish's grandmother to notice. Damn. They followed me to my parent's home. They must have. The image of Carolyn's face flashes in my head. I have to get these guys before they decide to pay my folks a visit.

I slip my cell phone out of my purse and plug it into the hands-free system on the dash. As much as I hate doing it, there's only one person who can help me. I dial Chief Williams' private number. I got it from Avery a few months ago, and though I only used it once, I have no trouble remembering it. Photographic memory, another vampiric talent.

Williams' greeting is curt. "Warren Williams here."

"It's Anna."

A pause the length of a heartbeat. "This is a surprise. Are you ready to talk?"

"I'm ready to ask for a favor. Will that do for a start?"

This time there's no hesitation. "What do you need?"

The car directly behind me has turned right, giving me a clear shot at the Blues Brother's license plate. I read it off to Williams. "I need you to stop that car. I'm heading south on Sixth approaching Ash. Do you have a patrol car in the area?"

"To do what?"

"Get some identification. Find out who they are."

There's the half-muffled sound of Williams barking an order. Then he's back on the line. "Patrol car will intercept them in about two minutes, so talk fast. Does this have to do with Carolyn Delaney's death? I read the report. You were on the scene."

It didn't take him long to get that report. I fill him in on what happened this morning—most of it anyway. I have to actually *tell* him, no mental telepathy. Thought transference doesn't work through phone lines because electrical currents interfere. For once it seems that having to *speak* the words is a nuisance that takes much too long.

When I get to the part about *why* I was at Carolyn's, Trish and her relationship to my family, he interrupts by yelling in my ear. "You knew yesterday that there might be a connection between the Franco girl's death and Trish Delaney's disappearance and you didn't say anything?"

"No," I respond archly. "I didn't know for sure there was a connection. Trish's mother left a lot of details out of her story. And she asked us, my mother and me, not to say anything."

This time there's more disbelief than anger in his tone. "Your mother knew, too? Doesn't she realize that she put her career in jeopardy by withholding information from the police?"

"What information?" I'm starting to feel I made a mistake calling him. "We didn't know anything for sure. And finding Trish was what we were most concerned about. How could we predict her mother would be killed?"

Williams' tone softens. "Is there anything else I should know?"

It's not a soothing, everything is going to be fine softness, but a threatening one.

Still, as I finish the story, I omit any reference to Trish and Frey. When Williams asks if I know where Trish is, I lie and say no. I let him think I went directly to Carolyn's to ask her more questions.

Williams is suspiciously quiet when I finish. Finally, he says, "Anna, if you have evidence that these guys are implicated in Carolyn's death, you need to tell me. We can pick them up right now."

"Believe me, if I had evidence of that I *would* tell you," I reply. And it's the truth, if for no other reasons than to protect my parents. "If these guys were the one's who killed Carolyn, when the cop stops them, he'll know. Carolyn lost a lot of blood. She was beaten and tortured, which means blood spatter. No way could they have avoided getting blood on their skin or clothes."

Williams barks a short laugh. "Then I've dispatched the right car," he says.

I know immediately what he means. "There's a vampire cop in that car?"

"Yep. So even if these guys wore raincoats and rubber boots, if they got a drop of blood on them, anywhere, Patrolman Ortiz will pick up on it."

A flash of strobe lights in the rearview mirror gets my attention. "Here we go," I tell Williams. "The patrol car just pulled them over."

"Do you want me to call you on your cell when I find out who these jokers are?" he counters.

I consider it. But there's no place for me to pull over where I won't be in plain sight. I don't want them to guess I was the one who called the cops.

"No. Call me at the office. I'll head over there now."

Williams cuts the connection and I turn on Ash, then again at Pacific Coast Highway, and drive to the office. David's parking space is empty, which is a relief. He and Gloria are probably enjoying a nooner somewhere. At least they'll be out of my hair.

By the time I unlock the door, the telephone is already ringing. I snatch it up.

"Anna?" It's Williams.

"What did you find out?"

There's a moment of dead air and then he says. "You'd better get your ass down here."

I hate that tone. Especially from a big shit, old soul vampire who, in spite of having two hundred odd years on me, I actually bested once. You'd think he'd show more respect.

When I don't answer right away, he blows an irritated breath into the receiver. "Did you hear me? Or are you being pissy because I didn't say please?"

"Please would be nice."

"Yeah, well bite me. Get down here. Now. Those guys following you? Guess what? They're Feds."

CHAPTER 25

T HE BLUES BROTHERS ARE FEDS? "NO WAY," I TELL
Williams. "They can't be."

"Yeah? Tell them that. They're on their way to my office as we speak. And they want to see you. I told them
you'd be here, so get in that hot car of yours and come
down. Now."

He disconnects and I'm left listening to dead air. This
doesn't add up. If they are Feds, what were they doing
at Frey's? And why didn't they identify themselves?

Shit.

Since I hadn't had time to put my purse down or take
off my jacket, I do an about face and head back to the car.
SDPD headquarters is on Broadway between Thirteenth
and Fourteenth. Shouldn't take me longer than fifteen
minutes. For once, I'm actually hoping lunch hour traffic
will slow me down. I need time to think.

As luck will have it, I hit every green light. There's not
a trolley or train crossing to halt my progress, and I find a

parking space right in front of the big granite and blue-steel building. Since it's located across from City College, that's no mean feat. I deposit the requisite coins in the meter and go inside. The reception area has utilitarian blue plastic benches not designed for comfort, one cop behind the desk, and a line of about ten people ahead of me. I shift restlessly from foot to foot, awaiting my turn with the receptionist. Williams left word that I was expected, and the desk sergeant gives me a code to use on the elevator. Part of building security. No one accesses anything except the reception area without a code of some kind or another.

The elevator whooshes up to the top floor. Another uniformed cop greets me in another reception area. Williams has left orders to usher me right in.

It's the first time I've met Williams on his home turf. He's seated at a big mahogany desk, a manila folder open in front of him. He doesn't look up, and only acknowledges my presence with a wave of a hand toward one of three chairs across from him. He doesn't use vampire wavelengths to project a single thought or emotion. His mind is a closed, black void. I make sure mine is, too.

I take a seat and glance around. His office is impressive—big, lots of windows, with a view over the Coronado Bay Bridge. There are bookcases full of memorabilia from past and present. Lots of cop stuff, like old badges and antique guns. Only another vampire would speculate if he had personally used this stuff in past generations as a lawman. For the first time I wonder if Williams has always been a cop.

I swing my gaze back to him. His bearing is different here, his attitude toward me, colder and more professional. In his uniform, he cuts a striking figure. He's tall, six foot and lean. I expect he must have been the same age as me when he became a vampire, thirty or so, because his skin is smooth, his face unlined except for tiny laugh lines that radiate from the corners of his eyes. He once told me that to pass as a fifty-year-old human he has his dark hair professionally streaked with gray.

I run fingers through my own short-cropped hair. I suppose I'll be doing the same thing before too long.

The way you piss people off, I doubt you'll live long enough to have to worry about that.

His tone is dry. He has raised heavy-lidded eyes to peer at me across the desk. *You didn't quite tell me everything about your adventures this morning, did you?*

Ah. You're talking to me. Good. I thought you'd called me here to impress me with your digs. Or the speed at which you shuffle papers. And, I must say, both are impressive.

Williams folds his hands and leans toward me. *In about two minutes, we're going to be joined by two special agents of the FBI. Any idea why they are interested in you?*

I can honestly say, I do not. It's true. If they are indeed Feds, I don't have a clue. He looks at me so suspiciously that I can't help myself. I mimic his action, folding my hands and bending toward him. *What do you think they want with me?*

Irritation radiates out from him like the burst of a solar flare. *Damn it Anna. They told the patrol cop that you attacked them outside of Daniel Frey's condo. Is that true?*

I shrug. *Maybe. But they were breaking into Daniel Frey's house. What kind of special agent does that?*

A better question is why were you there?

To ask about Trish.

Not exactly a lie. Williams is looking at me with such intensity, it takes every bit of willpower to keep from squirming. And to keep him out of my head. It's a relief when the opening of the office door interrupts us. I turn away from Williams to watch the two men approach the desk.

I was too preoccupied with keeping them away from

Trish at the condo to get a good look at their faces. I have the chance now. Both have their eyes locked on me and neither is smiling. One is about five foot ten, one hundred seventy pounds, square bodied, square jawed. He sports a military buzz, his light brown hair almost invisible against his scalp. His suit fits well, though the tailoring isn't quite good enough to hide the bulge of the gun snugged up under his armpit.

His partner is one or two inches taller, fifty pounds heavier. He's the one who went to work on Frey's door with the picklock before I interrupted. He has dark hair and eyes, a boxer's nose and thick lips. His suit jacket is open and his Glock sits on his hip.

Their suits are almost identical, black, lightweight. Both wear white shirts under their jackets, one with a thin, dark tie, the other, with a red patterned tie that is just this side of fashionable and, maybe, real silk.

Williams rises when they enter, crosses from behind his desk and holds out his hand. "I'm Warren Williams."

The one with the nice tie returns the handshake. "Special Agent Tom Bradley." He half turns toward his partner. "This is Eric Donovan."

The men shake hands all around. No one acknowledges my presence. I'm about to stand up when the one with the good tie, Bradley, skewers me with a look that can only be described as scathing.

Is he trying to scare me? I ask Williams drily.

Williams jaw tightens as he tries to ignore my intrusion into his head and concentrate on what Bradley is saying.

"This is Ms. Strong?" Bradley asks, glowering at me.

Williams nods and makes the introductions. "Anna Strong, Special Agents Donovan and Bradley."

They don't offer to shake hands and neither do I. Instead, they take seats, one on either side of me. Williams returns to his place behind the desk.

Donovan speaks next. "I think we met earlier today, Ms. Strong. At the home of Daniel Frey."

I nod.

"What were you doing there?" he asks.

"I was there to see Mr. Frey. What were you two doing there? Besides trying to break in?"

"And later," Bradley says, ignoring my questions. "We saw you at Carolyn Delaney's apartment."

"I knew Carolyn."

"How did you know Carolyn?" It's Donovan again.

My neck is getting tired from the constant swiveling. I look over at Williams. *This tag team stuff is starting to wear thin.*

Just answer the damn questions. His tone is a warning.

I direct my gaze to Donovan. "I told Detective Harris the story this morning. I'm sure Chief Williams will let you see the police report."

"We have seen it," Bradley interjects. "We want to hear the story again. From you."

That does it. I don't handle bullying very well and my patience is at an end. I push my chair back and stand up. Williams is shooting daggers at me and trying to interject himself into my head. I shut him out. Donovan and Bradley rise, too, and press closer as if to restrain me if I try to walk out.

"Am I under arrest?" I ask.

The two Feds shake their heads. That they are sorry to have to admit that is stamped on their faces.

"Then I'm going to leave. Unless, of course, you are willing to tell me what you were doing trying to break into Daniel Frey's condo and why you're following me."

Donovan and Bradley exchange a look. I know they're humans but I could swear they're communicating with each other. Most likely they discussed how to handle various scenarios before getting to the station. It's what David and I would have done.

In any case, they finally break their eye deadlock and Donovan says, "Please sit down, Ms. Strong. We'll answer your questions."

This time I push around him and take the seat to the far right. I'm not doing the ping-pong thing again.

They arrange themselves facing me and Bradley begins. "We are agents with a special unit that investigates sex crimes—in particular, sex crimes involving children. We are here because we believe there is a ring operating out of this area that uses children to make pornographic videos that they offer for sale over the Internet."

"Kiddie porn," Donovan interjects, as if maybe I've been living in a cave for the last fifty years.

I nod that I get it.

Donovan continues, "But we've seen a horrific escalation in the last few months. Children are not only abused in these videos, but killed."

My stomach lurches. "Why did you go to Daniel Frey's? Do you think he is somehow involved?"

"We don't know," Bradley replies. "But his name came up in an earlier investigation, in Boston. Nothing was proven. No charges were filed. Now he lives here, in San Diego, and we're hearing rumors again about these snuff films."

I can't believe what I'm hearing. If this is true, and I turned Trish over to him, I delivered her to a monster. My concern is so overwhelming I forget to shelter my thoughts. Williams is in my head before I can prevent it. In a heartbeat he understands what I kept from him before.

He has Trish?

I don't have to answer, the look on my face must say it all.

Go, he tells me. *I'll take care of the Feds.*

I don't wait to see how he does it. I don't care. I bolt out the door.

CHAPTER 26

M Y HANDS ARE SHAKING SO BADLY THAT I barely get the keys into the ignition. Recriminations ring in my head. Why did I discount the rumors about Frey? The ones he so glibly denied? How could I have trusted a man I didn't know with any girl's life, let alone one who may be my niece? What the hell was I thinking?

By the time I pull into the parking lot at Valley Vista High, I'm in such a state, I know if I face Frey now, if he understands what I'm feeling, he'll be bound to either attack or flee. Either way, I will have lost Trish. There was nothing in his projected vision to give me a hint where she is being held. I have to make him take me to her. Maybe there are other girls in danger. The only way to know for sure is to see for myself.

I force myself to sit in the car, hands on the wheel, not moving a muscle until I clear my mind. The dashboard clock reads 2:45. I concentrate on it, focus on the numerals, listen for the click detectable only to a nonhuman ear as each minute ticks away. At 2:55, I draw a deep breath and hold my hands in front of my face. The trembling has stopped. My heart is no longer battering my ribs. The struggle now will be to neutralize my thoughts. I've done it before. But this time is different. I only had myself to protect when the showdown came with Avery. Now there's another life, an innocent, and if Frey sees through my deception, she will be the one to pay the price.

A bell clangs in the schoolyard, and like horses from a starting gate, the students rush from their classrooms and head for the parking lot.

I wait another five minutes. Then I climb out of the car and make my way to Frey's classroom.

He's waiting for me at the door, his coat over his arm and his briefcase clutched at his side. His eyes narrow a little when he peers into my face. "Are you all right?"

I nod. "Had a rough day."

"What happened?"

I gesture toward the car. "Can we talk on the way?"

He doesn't seem to be reading anything other than my desire to get on the road. He nods and follows me as I retrace my steps to the car.

He hesitates at the gate to the parking lot. "Do you want to see your mother before we go?" he asks.

I already have my keys in my hand. I use the remote to unlock the doors. "No. I'll talk to her later."

He lets it go without comment and settles himself into the passenger seat. Just as I put the Jag in reverse and turn to check that there's no one behind me, he lays his hand over mine on the gearshift.

His touch triggers an involuntary reaction. I jerk my hand away. Immediately, I regret the lack of control. He's really looking at me now, an enigmatic specter of doubt hardening the lines around his mouth and eyes.

"You can't keep it from me, Anna. You may as well not try."

But it seems I can. I'm doing it. For the first time, I don't feel powerless against him. But I also don't know how long I can hold him off. I forge the thought carefully. *It's Carolyn.*

Trish's mother?

Yes. She was killed last night.

That seems to distract him long enough for me to get us on the road. When he's back in my head, his tone is thoughtful, concerned.

How will you tell Trish?

He doesn't ask how it happened. He assumes it was an accident, I read that from his own projections. I don't correct him, inquiring instead, *Where are we going? You haven't told me.*

His reply is offhand, *To Balboa Park.*

Balboa Park? The idea spins around my head throwing off questions like sparks from a flare. The municipal park is a big place, but it's a public place. Where would he be hiding Trish in the park? The only answer I come up with makes me grind my teeth in frustration and concern. It would be difficult to hide a child in the park, but not a body. There would be lots of places to hide a body.

Frey grabs my arm, and the unexpected contact makes me jump. I snap my head around to look at him. *What?*

He's looking in the passenger side mirror. *I think we're being followed.*

My eyes dart to the rearview mirror. If Williams let those Feds go to follow me—But it's not the Ford Fairlane behind us. It's a Volkswagen.

Frey starts to swivel around in his seat but I grab his arm. *Don't. If someone is following us, it's best we pretend not to know.*

He rights himself in the seat. *What are we going to do?*

My eyes are on the car in the mirror. It looks familiar, though I can't place it. *What makes you think we're being followed?*

From the corner of my eye, I see Frey shrug. He answers out loud, his tone hesitant. "I noticed the car when we left school. There's a guy driving. He followed us onto the freeway. If he were a student, he'd live in the area and would have gotten off already. We're almost to College Avenue and he's right behind us."

"Doesn't necessarily mean he's following us."

"Do you want to take that chance?"

No. "We'll go to my office," I say. "Can you get the license plate number? I can't see it in my mirror."

Frey squints at the side mirror as he tries to make it out. "No. Damn it. The plate's too dirty. Maybe we should forget about going to see Trish today. Take me home. If he follows when we take the Friar's Road exit, we'll know for sure he's after us."

I stifle the urge to howl in annoyance. But then, reason takes over. Frey is right. And if I take him home, we can spend some quality time alone together.

The anxiety lifts and I nod at him. I'm on the 94 Freeway, and instead of heading downtown, when the junction with 15 North approaches, I take it. The Volkswagen does, too. At the Friar's Road exit, I don't signal but cut across three lanes of traffic to a cacophony of horns and rude gestures.

The Volkswagen is right behind me.

Is this guy arrogant or just plain stupid?

And as soon as I ask myself that question, I remember where I've seen that car before.

CHAPTER 27

"WHAT'S WRONG?" FREY ASKS.

"I know who it is," I say through gritted teeth. Why didn't I notice the little creep before? First the Feds, now him. I've been leading a fucking parade. I'm seriously pissed at myself for being so careless.

There's a stop light at Friar's and Mission Village Drive. Traffic is backed up, as it usually is in late afternoon at that intersection. I decide to use it to my advantage.

I turn to Frey. "Do you know how to drive?"

He looks surprised at the question. "Of course I know how to drive. I just choose not to."

We've inched our way toward the intersection, but the light is turning yellow again. "Then take over." I open the door.

Frey's surprise turns to anxiety. "What? What are you talking about? Where are you going?"

But I've already jumped out and started for the VW,

two cars behind. *Pull into the stadium parking lot. I'll meet you there.*

To myself, I add, *Please don't let him wreck my car.*

But Frey's reply follows me, *I'll try not to. And thanks for the vote of confidence.*

I don't bother to respond or look back. Quicker than it takes to register in No-neck's head, I'm standing at the passenger side door of his car. The door is locked, but the window is open so I reach inside and pull the door open. He does a double take as I slide into the seat.

"Well," I growl. "Fancy seeing you again."

I've startled him into speechlessness. In fact, I've startled him into a near heart attack. I can tell because his heart is pounding so hard, I can hear it. Along with the rush of his blood. That, coupled with the anger I'm feeling toward mankind in general, brings the vampire in me to the surface.

I don't know what it looks like when the animal takes over. I only know what I see in the eyes of humans when it happens. No-neck's face has gone pale, his breathing is shallow. A human who allows vampires to feed from them can still distinguish the difference between control and rage. His eyes are locked on mine, and though car horns blare at him to move as the light changes, he is frozen in place.

"Move, asshole," I snarl. "Or I'll rip your miserable throat out right here."

His Adam's apple bounces as he takes a couple of shaky breaths. "Where should I go?"

I gesture to my car just ahead of us. "Keep doing what you've been doing—follow my car."

He puts the VW in gear and we lurch forward. After we've cleared the intersection, he asks, "What are you going to do to me?"

"Depends on you," I snap. "And what kind of answers I get."

His hands are shaking as he pulls up behind the Jag. Frey starts to get out, but I wave him off. I want to do this by myself.

I notice No-neck's car registration in a plastic holder on the visor. I reach over and rip it off. "Let's see who we have here."

The registration lists the owner's name as Darryl Goodwin, his address, 3946 Quail Street in San Diego. "Are you Darryl?"

He nods.

He's wearing a tank top and a pair of shorts. I reach out a hand and lay it on his bare arm. "Okay, Darryl, we can do this the easy way or the hard way."

His eyebrows shoot up.

"The easy way is I ask you some questions and you answer." I rub his arm encouragingly. "The hard way is I bite your worthless neck and suck until you're dead. But before you die, I'll get the truth out of you. All of it. So what's it to be?"

His Adam's apple is dancing again.

"Okay, let's give this a try. We'll start with an easy question. Why are you following me?"

Darryl seems to be having a hard time getting words out. My impatience is searing. I dig my nails into his arm and open a long, ragged cut, drawing blood. I know it's risky. In my state the scent of his blood and fear are like an aphrodisiac too powerful to resist. But I don't have time to waste with him.

I scrape a fingernail deeper. He gasps and tries to pull away. My grip tightens. "Let's try harder, Darryl. Why are you following me?"

He recovers enough to whine, "I was curious, that's all. I saw you at Carolyn's this morning. With the cop." He looks at me sideways. "She's dead, isn't she?"

But this is my interrogation, not his. "What were you doing at Carolyn's?"

A little of the bravado comes back. "You know. I like getting laid, and she likes getting a break on the rent."

My fingers curl into fists. He sees the reaction, and holds his hands up. "I didn't mean any disrespect, her being dead and all."

"How long were you there, Darryl?"

A little smile twists the corner of his mouth. "Long enough to see that old lady whack you. I can't believe you let her get away with that. Who was she anyway?"

"Another question and I'll tear your arm out and beat you to death with it. Are we clear, Darryl?"

He gulps and nods.

"Good. Now, have you followed me everywhere since then?"

Another nod. "From Carolyn's to that house in La Mesa—nice place, by the way. Is that where you live?"

I yank on his arm, hard, and he yelps. "Okay, okay. Anyway, then you went to the hospital and to an office on Pacific Highway and then to the police station. Back to that school, and now, you know, here we are."

Christ. He's been on my tail every minute and I never noticed. I don't know whether I'm angrier with him or myself.

The silence stretches on while I decide what to do with him. I thought I scared him enough the first time I ran into him at Carolyn's to make him want to stay away from me. Now, it seems I've just piqued his curiosity.

I tap my fingernail against the cut on his arm, draw more blood and bring his arm to my mouth. Glaring at him, I suck ever so gently, savoring the taste, the texture. Not as sweet as from a vein, but warm, refreshing. I feel him relax a little. Then I bite down. Hard.

He utters a sharp, high-pitched cry of pain and tries to pull away.

My teeth ravage the arm. I gulp down the blood, losing myself for a moment in the hunger.

His cries of panic bring me back. When I look up, I see Frey start walking toward us.

I take one more mouthful and reluctantly release his arm. I wave Frey off, licking the blood from my fingers. "Darryl, Darryl, what am I going to do with you?"

The change in my tone and the ragged bite mark on his arm drain the remaining color from Darryl's cheeks. He cradles his arm and looks like he might finally be scared enough to cooperate.

"So let's try again. Why are you following me? Did you think if you found out where I lived you could drop by for a quickie once in a while? That we might become friends? What were you thinking, Darryl?"

His mouth twists, his tone wavers just this side of panic. "I don't know. I didn't plan to see you this morning. When I did, I acted on instinct. I just wanted to find out who you are."

His answer rings true, but it's neither comforting nor reassuring. There's only one way I can think of to keep this kid away from me and from those I love.

"You like going to Beso de la Muerte, don't you?"

The change of subject catches him off guard. He gives a jerky nod.

I lean in toward him and take his arm once again. I raise it to my mouth. At first he tries to jerk away, but when I suck at the wound this time and lick it closed, I feel him relax. I reach a hand up and pull his head close, breathe into his ear, and let my hand play with the waistband of his shorts.

He actually moans.

"Let's make a deal," I whisper. "You stay away from me here in San Diego, forget everything you saw today, and I'll meet you down there on Friday. That's two days from now. Two days and I'll give you what you want."

He takes my hand and pushes it down his stomach, shifting on the seat until I feel a stirring between his legs.

His skin is slimy and slick with sweat. I close my eyes and think of Trish to keep from gagging.

His tone is rough with desire. "How do I know I can trust you?"

I want to answer by grabbing his miserable cock and yanking until he screams. Instead, I stroke it and coo, "Hey, you know everywhere I went today. I think you could find me pretty easily if I didn't show. What do you have to lose?"

"How about a little preview?" he says, squirming on the seat.

"Uh-uh." I pull my hand away and sit back. "You'll just have to wait until Friday. Do we have a deal?"

He's got his own hand between his legs now, and his eyes are glassy and unfocused. "Fuckin-A," he says. "We have a deal."

"Okay, then, Darryl. You can play with yourself when you get home. I want you to leave now."

He sits up straight on the seat, one hand occupied while the other reaches across and starts the engine.

I can't watch this anymore. I climb out and stand there while Darryl pulls out of the parking lot. He actually waves a jaunty hand at me making me wonder how he's steering. I'm scrubbing my own hand against my jeans with such friction I feel the palm burn.

Frey steps out of the driver's side of the car and looks at me with a mixture of revulsion and disbelief.

You agreed to fuck that cretin?

I don't know what surprises me more, that Frey heard the conversation in the car or that he uses the word "fuck."

He snorts. *I'm a jungle cat, remember? I have good hearing.*

I push past him and get into the car. *I have no intention of fucking Darryl. Ever. I just wanted to buy us some time.*

Frey drops into the passenger seat and I hand him Darryl's registration. *Hold on to that. Darryl may think he knows where to find me, but I know where to find him now, too.*

He shoves it into the glove box and snaps it closed. *How do you know that guy?*

Beso de le Muerte. I glance over at him. *Do you know the place?*

He shakes his head. *You go there to feed? What's the matter with you? Don't you know that place has a bad reputation?* His condescending tone and disapproving expression are too much.

And what would you have me do? I can't pick up cans of Alpo at the pet store like some of us. I need blood, remember?

I don't eat dog food, he replies archly. *And I thought you had a human boyfriend. At least, I know you have a human you have sex with because I can smell it on you. Why don't you feed from him like a normal vamp.*

Like a normal vamp? This conversation would be ludicrous under any circumstances. But to have it now with a man I suspect may be a worse monster than any I've yet encountered sets my blood on fire. I've already wasted too much time. I want to find Trish and I want to find her now.

I reach over and grab Frey by the scruff of the neck. Snarling, I pull him from his seat and hold his head close to my mouth.

I wonder how feeding from a shape-shifter will be?

I feel his body stiffen, and his hands rise to ward me off. But before they can, I'm tearing at the collar of his shirt, exposing his neck, ripping through skin and cartilage with a ferocity that stuns him into immobility. Darryl awakened the thirst. It blazes within me. I find the artery, sink my teeth into it and drink. I will learn the truth about Daniel Frey.

Blood has interesting tastes and qualities that vary from species to species. Human blood tastes like a mineral supplement and warm salt water, rudimentary. You get no feeling for the individual from human blood, not a good thing as I'm learning from my pal Darryl. Vampire blood, on the other hand, is more complex, like a fine wine. It's full of the essence of the vampire's life, all his history reduced to stark simplicity and there for the taking. When you drink from a vampire, you ingest what he is, or at least what he lets you think he is. I know now from Avery that it is possible to hide your true nature under the guise of love.

Daniel Frey is a different creature altogether. His blood is acidic, sour, burning my throat as I drink. At first, I feel nothing except the rush of energy that flows from his life force into mine. I need more. I worry at his throat, sucking harder, ignoring his groans and hands that make a feeble attempt to push me away.

I open my mind to him. *Tell me. What have you done to Trish?*

His thoughts are muddled, lethargic. *I don't understand. I showed you that she is safe.*

A trick. I know about your past. I know about Boston.

I let him hear the conversation at the police station. There is a shift in his consciousness, an understanding of what I know to be true. And in the rush of his blood, Daniel Frey lets me see into his soul.

CHAPTER 28

I LET MY HEAD FALL BACK ONTO THE HEADREST and lick the blood from the corners of my mouth. I'm embarrassed and ashamed. I was wrong about Frey. Still, my body tingles with the infusion of his blood. When I glance over at him, he is leaning back on his seat, too, and his hand is on his neck. From his expression, though, I don't think he's feeling quite the same things I am.

"Don't worry," I say, sounding sheepish even to my own ears. "I haven't left a mark."

For the first time, I notice the claws retracting as I watch. "Why didn't you stop me?"

A brittle smile twists the corners of his own mouth but his eyes are cold. "Believe me, if you had kept at it a moment longer, I would have." He tugs again at the torn collar of his shirt. "And it's not my neck I'm thinking about. You've ruined my favorite Perry Ellis shirt."

"I'll buy you a new one."

There is a protracted silence which is finally broken

when he swivels on the seat to face me. "Why didn't you just ask me about Boston?"

I feel color flood my face. "I should have. I'm sorry."

I blow out a breath. "It just seemed too coincidental—the killings in Boston and now here." But before I voice any other concerns, I'm hit with a realization that sends shock waves rippling along my spine.

I'm not hearing Frey in my head anymore. *What's happening?*

But he just sits there, an expression of anger, irritation and disappointment stamped on his face. Then the expression changes. "Oh, you get it now, huh? We can't communicate that way anymore. You've ingested my blood. You've broken the link. Now we have to communicate this way. You are such a pain in the ass."

"Broken the link? What does that mean?" I look down at my hands. "Jesus. Am I part shape-shifter now?"

"Don't you think you should have asked that question before you attacked me?"

His tone is scalding. My face must betray the anxiety I'm feeling because he relents with an abrupt wave of his hand. "No. You are not part shape-shifter. Vampires only consume the essence of their supernatural victims, not the physical manifestations. But in some cases, like this one, it creates a barrier that prohibits thought transference. I don't know why. It just happens."

"Does that mean I won't be able to communicate with all shape-shifters?" I'm thinking of Culebra now.

"No." His look is pointed. "Only those you feed from."

Is that a relief? I'm not sure. I crank the engine and look around. I can't believe I lost control so completely that I attacked Frey in the middle of a parking lot in broad daylight. Granted, it is a lower lot and we don't seem to have attracted anyone's attention, but it was a stupid thing to do.

I pull out and head back for the freeway. This time I

make sure no one is following. In fact, I don't take a direct route to Balboa Park, but a circuitous one. From the stadium, I take I-15 to I-8, get off at Rosecrans, switch to Sports Arena Boulevard, take Nimitz south to Harbor Drive, Market to Sixth. No one car is behind us the entire drive.

When I turn into the park, Frey speaks for the first time since we left the stadium.

"I think you should let Trish stay here," he says.

"You trust these people?"

He nods. "Yes. With my life."

I'm approaching the parking lot in front of the museums that line the El Prado. As usual, there are no spaces right in front, and I have to wind my way down toward the organ pavilion to find a place to park. Once we do, I turn in the seat to face Frey.

"Who are these people you work with? What are they?"

"Humans, mostly."

"Humans?"

He rolls his shoulders. "You'll see. There are also shape-shifters, seers, vampires." He raises an eyebrow. "You'll no doubt recognize one in particular."

"Because he's a vampire?"

But Frey has opened the door and is standing with an impatient scowl beside the car. "Let's go. I thought you were anxious to see Trish."

I am.

And I'm not. How am I going to tell her about her mother?

Frey has already started down the sidewalk so I rush to catch up with him. The park is full of people, families, students, artists with their easels set to catch the play of sun and shadow on buildings that shouldn't exist. Balboa Park was a temporary shell built to accommodate the Panama-California Exposition held in 1915. But the beauty of the place was far from temporary and restoration followed restoration. Now the park houses an impressive array of galleries, museums, restaurants and a world-class zoo. I've been to the park too many times to count and I never suspected that what is visible to the human eye is only a fraction of what actually is.

Frey doesn't explain where we are going. He simply leads me down the El Prado toward the fountain in front of the Space Theater. On the right is the railroad museum, and the various gallery exhibits and visitor centers. On this side, doors open to administrative offices, some open, some closed to the public. When we reach the end, across from the huge Natural History Museum, he veers off the sidewalk, following a path that snakes back through shrubbery.

"Won't someone see us?" I ask, suddenly conscious of how easily I had been tailed today not just by the Feds, but also by that idiot Darryl.

Frey motions for me to stop. "Watch," he says.

He takes another step toward the building and—

Vanishes.

I actually jump. "Frey?"

No answer and no Frey.

I take a timid step forward myself, then another. There's a rippling, like silk being moved by the wind, and a feeling of stepping through a heavy mist, and suddenly, I'm standing beside Frey.

His expression is the impatient scowl of one annoyed at being kept waiting. "It took you long enough."

I ignore him and look back at the sidewalk, at the people passing back and forth, and feel a tingle of excitement. The one or two who actually appear to be looking right at us, act like they see nothing. I touch my hand to my face.

"Are we invisible?"

He shakes his head. "No. This place is protected."

"Protected? How?"

He's moving toward a door I hadn't seen from the sidewalk. "A spell, of course. Only those invited can enter."

A spell? Like Beso de la Muerte? I don't remember any kind of portal there, though. And here, there are hundreds of people who pass by everyday. "But what if someone decided to take a walk back here? Wouldn't they pass through the portal or spell or whatever the hell it is?"

"What part of needing to be invited didn't you understand?"

"Well, what would happen?"

He blows out an irritated breath. "Nothing would happen. They'd find grass and shrubs and a maintenance man asking them to get back on the sidewalk."

Frey's attitude has certainly cooled since I bit him. I guess I should have expected it, but I felt I had no choice at the time and I'm not going to apologize again.

He's turned his back on me to face the door. He's withdrawn a long, slender key, the old-fashioned brass kind, from the pocket of his jacket and is inserting it into the lock.

I swallow back the rest of my questions. And carefully neutralize my thoughts. I don't know what I'm going to see inside or who.

The door is heavy metal and actually groans when Frey thrusts it open. His body blocks my view and I push past him, anxious to see what's inside and get to Trish.

At first, it looks just like the reception area in a hundred other business offices. The walls are white stucco, striped with the patterns of sun and shadow cast by trees outside and funneled into the room through a row of small, high windows. There's a single metal desk with a computer and telephone, but no person, human or otherwise, in sight. It's very quiet—spooky quiet. And I realize that unlike other reception areas, there are no couches or chairs or racks of out of date magazines to occupy your time while you wait.

Wait for what?

Frey has gone around the desk. He punches some keys on the computer keyboard. There is a whir, a flash of light, and then the screen goes dark again.

He returns to stand beside me.

I'm suddenly aware of something else—there are no other doors in this room except the one we came in through.

I glance up at Frey, uneasiness causing a chilly edge to creep into my voice. "Where are we?"

He keeps his eyes straight ahead. "Don't worry. You'll see Trish soon enough."

"But what is this place? How do we get—"

A rumbling beneath my feet chokes off the words. At first, I don't trust, don't believe, the sensation. The floor is vibrating, falling away. The feeling is like being on a high-speed express elevator. I touch a hand to the desk to steady myself, though the descent doesn't seem to faze Frey. He eyes my hand on the desk and looks down at it with a tight little smile. I snatch my hand back and straighten up.

It seems as if we fall for a long time. I get a flashback to when I was a kid and Steve and my parents and I went to Disneyland for the first time. The entrance to the Haunted Mansion. That delicious, scary plunge that had me gripping Steve's hand so hard he finally yelped in complaint.

In the time it takes for the memory to ebb and fade, we've come to a stop. Frey turns around and faces the door we came in through. With a hand on the knob, he glances back at me. "Are you ready?" he says, not unkindly this time.

I nod, though I'm not sure it's true.

But Trish is here. And that means I must be here, too.

CHAPTER 29

I DON'T KNOW WHAT I EXPECTED THE UNDER-
ground headquarters of all things that go bump in the
night to look like, but as I pass inside I do know it's not
what I see in front of me now.

It's a big square room, lit from above by high intensity
lights so bright it's hard to believe we're underground.
Whitewashed stucco, windowless walls stretch ten feet to
the ceiling. There are people. Lots of people who look
and "feel" normal. They're milling about, sitting at desks,
talking into telephones with headsets as their fingers
bang away at computer keyboards.

It looks for all the world like a telemarketing center.

I shake my head. "What are they selling? Penny stocks
or junk bonds?"

Frey shakes his head, too, but in a way that indicates
he thinks I'm an idiot. He ignores the question, and with
a hand at my elbow, steers me to the back of the room.

In this room, there are other doors. Substantial looking

wooden doors with no windows or peepholes. He leads me to one, knocks quietly. Then waits.

"Come in, Daniel," says a cheery voice.

I glance up at him and start to ask how anyone could possibly know who was out here, then stop myself. After all I've seen today, why would I question that?

Once inside, two impressions hit me immediately. One is that there is a feeling of tranquility in this room unlike anything I've ever experienced. The second is that it emanates from a woman who is one of the most exotic creatures I've ever seen.

She reminds me of a fairy-tale princess, tall, graceful, slender of form and fair of face. She's dressed in a long rose-colored smock of some silky fabric that molds to her body and moves like mist around her. Her hair is golden in color, framing her face with tendrils that reach to her shoulders. I couldn't begin to guess at her age. Her face is the perfect oval, seamless, set off by Wedgwood blue eyes, elegant cheekbones and lush lips. I'm staring at those eyes, unable to pull my own away, when she begins to laugh softly.

"You're staring at me, Anna," she says.

That pulls me back. "You know my name? Has Frey told you about me?"

"No," she crosses to stand in front of me. One hand reaches toward my face, but she stops herself. "Do you mind?" she asks.

"Mind?"

"If I touch your face?"

"I don't understand."

"I'd like to get an idea of what you look like."

It takes an instant for me to comprehend. "You're blind?"

"Quite."

"But how did you know I was staring at you?"

Frey moves to her side. "She's an empath, Anna. She feels what you feel, but she only sees through touch."

She's standing in front of me, those wide eyes calm, expectant.

"Can you project what you see?" I ask her. "Would I see it, too?"

"Ah," she says. "It's been awhile since you've seen your reflection." She tilts her head. "But not that long, I suspect. It's your first visit here."

It would be interesting to get an idea of how I've changed since I've become vampire. I know what my parents and David say. But to actually see an image is tempting.

I take a step back. "Later, maybe," I say.

I expect a flicker of disappointment or irritation to ruffle the perfect serenity of her face, but the only irritation comes from Frey.

"What's the matter, Anna? Afraid of what you'll see?"

I'm getting tired of his attitude. I've already apologized for biting him. What more can I do? Bitterness and a tinge of warning creep into my tone. "I'm here to see Trish. Not play mind games."

Frey ignores me. He touches the empath's arm very gently, drawing her attention to him. "I'm sorry, Sorrel. Anna hasn't been otherworldly very long. She doesn't easily accept what is."

Sorrel? An empath named Sorrel? I'm trapped in a Star Trek episode. A small bubble of laughter escapes before I can stop it.

Frey rounds on me. This time he says it. "You *are* an idiot, Anna."

But Sorrel places a hand on his arm. "No, Daniel. Anna is right. She is here to see her niece and assure herself that the girl is unharmed."

My attention snaps to Sorrel. "My niece?"

Sorrel smiles and her hand brushes mine. The smile and the touch wash over me in a golden wave that warms my blood and calms my agitation. "Yes."

And with that single word, the irritation I've felt for Frey, the anxiety over Trish, the rage directed at what's been done to her melts away like ice in the desert. It's just gone. And with it all desire to seek retribution fades into nothingness. All I feel is peace.

A trick? I shake my head to clear it. Nothing happens. I remain trapped in a vapor lock of serenity.

"Stop." It takes tremendous energy to form the word.

Sorrel quirks an eyebrow. "Stop?"

"Yes." My voice doesn't sound right. The edge is gone. I want it back. "Don't do this. I expect you mean well. But I want you to remove whatever spell you've cast on me."

Frey takes a step toward me. "It's not a spell, Anna. It's Sorrel. Her presence. Her gift is to draw pain and replace it with serenity."

"Then make her go away."

I expect Frey to argue, tell me that I've lost my mind. But he doesn't.

He looks instead at Sorrel.

And she looks at me. "I understand, Anna. There are things you must feel in order to do what you do. I will leave you to your visit. But later, if you change your mind—"

She lets the words hang in the air between us like a promise between lovers, freely given and open-ended. I believe her. I also know the kind of tranquility she offers has no place in my world. I think she knows it, too.

She starts to leave, but I stop her. "Wait. Before you go, how do you know about Trish? How can you be sure she is my niece?"

The empath raises a hand as if to touch my cheek, but draws it away before making contact. "You'll know soon, too," she says softly. "It's in the blood."

The blood? Is she talking about the DNA test? I want to call her back but Frey has followed Sorrel out the door, and with her departure, my head clears. Just like that. I'm myself again and all the pent-up emotion of the last few days comes surging back. It should be cause for dismay. Instead, it feels . . . good.

Alone for the first time, I notice the room. It's not very large, maybe ten by ten, furnished only with two big buff-colored leather chairs placed facing each other. That's it as far as furniture. No tables or lamps. I glance up at the ceiling. The same powerful overhead lights as the room outside fill what I imagine would be a pretty dark space without artificial sunlight. But where I expect to hear the hum of fluorescent or incandescent bulbs, there's only silence. Strange from so powerful a light source. But maybe it's some kind of solar thing, funneling energy from the outside. There's also an odor—not unpleasant—like a subtle perfume. A hint of lavender, a hint of citrus.

I have only an instant to consider this before the door opens again and I prepare myself for what is sure to be another rant from Frey.

But it's not Frey.

It's Trish. She grins when she sees me and waves a hand.

"Isn't this place cool?" she says. "I can't wait for my mom to see it."

CHAPTER 30

I BARELY RECOGNIZE THE GIRL STANDING IN FRONT of me. Trish is smiling, her eyes bright and her face radiant. Gone is the aura of sadness and fear that surrounded her before. She's wearing a clean pair of jeans with a crisp white blouse and a pair of sneakers on her feet. Her hair is brushed back from her face and shines with a healthy glow. She smells faintly of the room's scent—lavender and lemon. Could it be soap or shampoo?

She looks happy.

Sorrel again?

I take a step toward her. "Are you all right?"

She nods. "Of course. Everyone is so nice. Mr. Frey was right when he said I'd be safe here." She lowers her voice in a conspiratorial whisper though the smile never wavers. "I'm not sure what this place is exactly. Mr. Frey said it was some kind of secret headquarters, like you see in movies. But I'm not supposed to know any more than that or he'll have to kill me."

She giggles at a joke I don't find the least bit funny. Just as I wonder about Trish's demeanor.

I motion to one of the two chairs and beckon Trish to take a seat. She does. I follow suit, facing her, feeling like a counselor in a therapy session. Maybe that's what this room is used for.

But I don't know how to begin this session.

Trish is looking at me, an amused half smile touching the corners of her mouth. "I figure you're here because things are better now, right? You've caught those men and it's safe for me to go home. Ryan must be going crazy. I wasn't allowed to call him from here. Mr. Frey said he would let him know that I was all right. Ryan wouldn't believe him, though. He'd want to talk to me himself, so we'd better stop by his house on the way home."

Her words run together in a bubbling torrent of joyful speculation. She seems to have completely forgotten her mother's part in what happened to her—or to have excused it. I can't believe that one any more than I can understand the other.

"You want to go home?" I ask her gently.

She nods. Something in my expression must trigger doubt then, because the smile falters, a flicker of uncertainty dims the brightness in her eyes. "What's wrong?"

I wait a heartbeat too long to answer.

Trish jumps to her feet. "Has something happened to my mother?"

I wish I could come up with some way to make this easier for her. I actually consider reminding her of the reason she's here, but that would be replacing one horror with another. I push myself up out of the chair.

"Trish, I'm sorry. Something has happened. Your mother was killed last night. The police are looking into it. And I will, too, of course."

I realize I'm rambling, the same way Trish did moments before. But Trish is staring at me, empty eyed and slack jawed, all traces of life gone from her face. I take a step toward her, but she backs away.

"I'm really sorry, Trish. I wish I could make this easier for you. Your grandmother is here from Boston. She doesn't know where you are. If you'd like, I can get a message to her."

As I speak the words, I want to bite them back. Why did I say that? I can't imagine that cold, arrogant bitch being of any comfort to Trish. I just don't know what else to offer. Trish doesn't know about the relationship she has to my family. I'm afraid telling her will only add to her confusion about her mother.

Trish is staring at me, but with the shocked, glazed expression of one whose thoughts are turned inward. I can only imagine what terrible images are projecting themselves inside her head.

"Trish? Talk to me, honey."

Comprehension creeps into her eyes. Like a drowning man who has been pulled from the sea, she draws a deep, ragged breath. Her chest heaves, but there are no tears. She begins to shake. I slip out of my jacket and hold it out to her. But once again, she draws back.

"How did it happen?" she asks.

The picture of Carolyn's battered face and the knowledge of what had been done to her comes rushing back. But I could no more tell Trish any of that than I could remind her of why she is here. I lay the jacket on the back of a chair, using the time to gather my thoughts before answering.

"The police aren't sure." It seems the least painful response.

But she grasps the ambiguity and it sparks a flash of anger. "Don't," she snaps. "Don't treat me like a child. You know what happened to me. You know the part my mother played in it. Was she killed like Barbara? Was she killed because of me?"

I realize now that the image Trish projected when she first walked into this room was only partly due to Sorrel's presence. Trish wanted desperately to believe the things that happened to her were a nightmare from which she had finally awakened. Twenty-four hours in a safe environment and the possibility that her life might be her own again had made her giddy with youthful optimism.

God, I do not want to be the one to shatter the illusion. And yet, this is the second time I've been the bearer of bad news. Telling her about Barbara was bad enough. How on earth can I explain to her about her mother?

I've never felt so helpless. I'm the adult. I should have instincts about this sort of thing. But seeing the distress in her face and the dread in her eyes renders me speechless.

I wish my own mother were here.

The door opens, and for just an instant I irrationally think maybe it is my mother come to rescue us.

But of course, it's not. Frey comes in and his expression softens when he looks at Trish.

"Anna told you about your mother? I'm so sorry."

Trish goes to him, letting him put his arms around her, leaning against him and accepting from him the kind of solace she refused from me.

It's a bitter rebuff. If I'm to believe Sorrel, Trish is my niece. I should be the one comforting her. I take a step toward them.

I look into Frey's eyes and he seems to be reading my reaction. He shakes his head gently in a warning to respect Trish's feelings.

It stops me. I know he's right. Trish needs to have someone she can open up to. I'd hoped it would be me. But we've only known each other one day. Frey is a teacher she likes and respects. It's natural she would choose him.

I don't have to like it, though.

Frey guides Trish over to one of the chairs and gently

lowers her into it. She sits, clutching one of his hands as if afraid to let go. He smiles down at her and then turns to me.

"There's someone outside who wants to talk to you," he says.

"To me?" I ask, surprised. "Who knows I'm here?"

He shakes his head, sitting down beside Trish. "Don't worry. It's someone you know. He's waiting for you outside the door."

His words are a subtle push for me to leave the two of them alone. I bend down to look at Trish, to engage her eyes. "I'll be right outside, Trish. If you need me, Frey will come get me."

She is looking at me, but I can't tell whether my words are registering. All I see in her eyes is a dreadful void.

I straighten up. "Frey, can I talk to you outside a minute?"

He seems hesitant, but the expression on my face must convey the meaning behind my words. I'm not asking. He opens his hand, freeing himself from Trish's grasp. She gives a little gasp and reaches for him again, but he strokes her hair and says softly, "It's all right. I'll be right outside the door."

She doesn't look reassured but she lets her hand drop into her lap and offers no objection.

Frey follows me out of the room. As soon as the door is closed behind us, I round on him.

"What are you going to say to her?" I snap. "You don't know what happened to Carolyn."

Frey is looking past me.

I turn, too, and at the same time a familiar voice interjects itself into my head. *He knows, Anna, I filled him in.*

And there is Chief Williams, out of uniform now, but looking as clearly at home in these surroundings as he did an hour or so ago in his office.

CHAPTER 31

WHY DOES IT NOT SURPRISE ME THAT YOU'RE here?

Before he can answer me, Frey must send him a telepathic message, because he says, *Yes, go back to the girl. Anna and I will talk in my office.*

I put a hand on Frey's arm to stop him. "Wait a minute. I'm not leaving."

Williams motions Frey to go on. "My office *here*. We're not going anywhere."

Frey obviously says something else, but since I cut our psychic link by biting him, I'm not privy to it. By the weary expression on Williams' face, I can guess it's about me.

When Frey leaves us, Williams' temper erupts. "You *bit* Frey? What were you thinking?"

"What was *I* thinking? You let me leave your office this afternoon thinking he was a monster. He wouldn't answer my questions. What the fuck did you expect me to do?"

"And if I had told you that Trish was safe with him, would you have believed me?"

Of course not. I don't say it aloud or project it, but it's the obvious answer and Williams knows it.

He lowers his head and peers at me. "Besides, you should thank me for getting you out of there. Otherwise, you'd have Frick and Frack from the FBI on your tail as we speak." He jerks a thumb. "My office is right down the hall. We can talk there."

With a glance at the door behind which Frey and Trish are no doubt discussing her mother's death, I reluctantly follow Williams. Disappointment and a feeling of inadequacy squeeze at my heart. I want to be there for Trish, to be the one she turns to for comfort and healing. I'm family. Frey is a stranger.

She doesn't know that, Anna.

Williams' tone is not harsh, it is laced with a kind of sympathy. Not typical in his dealings with me. He's stopped in front of another of those nondescript doors that line the back of the great room. He holds it open. *Come in. Please.*

Please? A courtesy? You must be feeling guilty about letting me think the worst of Frey.

He reads the disdain in my tone but shrugs it off. *Frey is the one who should be angry about that. After all, he's the one you attacked because of it.*

Contempt isn't fazing Williams. He must have something really important to discuss.

Unlike his spacious quarters at police headquarters, this office is small, nondescript, austere. It looks to be the same size as the one I shared with Trish. The only furnishings are a metal desk and two straight-backed chairs—one behind the desk and one in front of it. There is nothing on the desk, not a telephone or computer.

Williams pulls the chair from behind the desk and positions it beside the other. He motions for me to sit.

"Why not?" I respond. "I'm sure you have a lot to explain. Might as well get comfortable." But as my butt hits the cold, hard seat, I amend that. "Well, at least as comfortable as possible. I take it you're not such a big shit here, huh? Don't warrant padded chairs."

But Williams seems impervious to my insults. His expression never wavers from polite concern, and his eyes don't spark or flash with anger or annoyance. Sorrel, again? Or something else?

What's going on?

Williams sits back in his chair, looking hard at me, keeping his thoughts to himself. I let it go on for a moment before I repeat, "What's going on? What did you get me in here for?"

His eyes study me for another moment, then clear and his gaze sharpens. "Trish's grandmother is raising hell. She called for an appointment to speak with me directly this afternoon. She's already contacted the FBI. She knows there was a connection between Trish and Barbara Franco. Now with Carolyn's murder, she's convinced Trish is—" He blows out an angry breath. "That Trish is involved in both murders."

The words should send me into another spasm of rage. Instead, only a great sadness descends. "Like daughter, like mother," I whisper.

Williams raises an eyebrow. "What?"

"The first night I met Carolyn, when she came to my parent's house, she tried to convince us Trish may have had a hand in Barbara's murder. Now Carolyn's mother is spouting the same garbage."

He gives me another one of those you-should-have-told-me-this-before looks. But says, "Unfortunately, that 'garbage' makes for great headlines. She's called a press conference for this evening." He glances at his watch. "Five o'clock, right after our meeting, and on the steps of the mayor's office."

"The mayor is in on this?"

"Not yet. But this is an election year. The Bernards don't live in San Diego but they are wealthy people with a lot of influence. The mayor will align herself with them if it proves expedient."

"And you know this how?" But the answer flashes through my head before he can reply. "I forgot. The deputy mayor. A fellow vamp. Great."

"You remember her from Avery's?"

He asks the question with hesitancy. The first night I saw Williams was the first night I was introduced to life as a vampire. My mentor, Avery, invited me to a party at his home. Williams was there, as was Isabel Santos, the deputy mayor of San Diego, along with four or five other luminaries, all vampires, all high on the social register. I wasn't formally introduced to any of them, though intervening circumstances threw Williams and me together soon afterward.

I feel Williams' sharp eyes watching me, just as I feel his mind prodding for the emotion those memories evoke. He has other issues with me. I raise my eyes to meet his.

Why would she do this? I ask. *Why would she want to accuse her granddaughter of murder?*

The corners of his mouth turn down. *I don't know. I thought I'd ask her that very question when I see her this afternoon.*

I want to be there.

This produces a short bark of laughter. *Right. And let her take another shot at you.*

I can see Detective Harris was thorough in his report, and I can read in Williams' reaction that he would have liked to have been there to see it. I grip the sides of the chair and lean forward. *It's not bloody likely that she'll get a chance like that again.*

Williams holds up a hand. *Hey, I'm not being critical. I think you showed remarkable restraint.*

Then what do you suggest we do? How do we protect Trish?

The only way we can, he replies. *We find the real killer and expose Carolyn.*

That will not make Mrs. Bernard happy. Or the mayor.

Williams smiles. *Not my problem. I'm not the one up for reelection.* Then he gets the same cop look that I've seen on Max's face when he's about to tell me something I'm not going to like. *You need to be prepared for what's going to happen after the press conference.*

What does that mean?

Listen, Anna, I know what Trish has been through. None of it is her fault, but right now, the official investigation is focused on Trish's disappearance. Carolyn told her neighbors that Trish was using drugs. The motive that's being put forward is that Carolyn was killed for refusing to give Trish money. No one knows about the abuse or Carolyn's part in it. If we're going to crack the kiddie porn ring, it has to stay that way.

It's not hard to grasp the meaning behind his words. *Trish's disappearance is going to make it look as if she's guilty.*

Yes. She needs to stay here. If she leaves, I can't guarantee she won't be arrested.

What if she wants to attend her mother's funeral? What do we tell her?

He waves a hand. *It's a murder investigation. I can hold the body for a while. But the important thing is that we work fast.* His eyes flash with a knowing gleam. *Do what you need to get these guys. I'll do what I can to stall.*

What makes you think I can do this?

Are you telling me you can't?

Our eyes lock a moment. It's the first real vote of confidence I've gotten from him. *What about Frey and the FBI?*

Frey will do what he needs to do—keep Agents Bradley

*and Donovan busy. I've managed to convince them that
you are of no consequence in their investigation. They
think your appearance at his condo was because the two
of you are lovers. You were at Carolyn's this morning at
the behest of your mother, who has asked for your help
in the Barbara Franco case. Now that there has been
another crime, the police have warned you off. You've
agreed to let the professionals take over.*

I shake my head and stand. *Great. You couldn't come
up with a better reason for me to be at Frey's? You had to
say we were lovers?*

Funny, he retorts. *That's the same thing Frey said.*

Williams rises from his chair to stand beside me. "I'll
walk you out."

We start back down the hall and I pause in front of the
door where Trish and Frey are talking. "I need to get my
jacket and I'd like to say good-bye to Trish."

He shakes his head. "They've left."

"Left?" I push open the door. The room is empty. My
jacket hanging from the back of the chair is the only indication we were here at all.

"Frey has taken her to the living quarters." Williams
explains from the hall.

I rejoin him, looking around. There is a steady murmur of voices coming from the thirty or so people seated
at computer terminals. Besides that, there is nothing but
silence coming from the dozen or so doors that line the
back wall. "Where are the living quarters?"

He waves a hand toward the last door at the end of the
hall. "That way."

"How big is this place?"

"Big enough. I'll give you a tour if you like."

I debate whether to press Williams into taking me to
Trish. I can tell from his demeanor and the neutrality of
his thoughts that he will acquiesce to my demands. He's
waiting for me to make the decision.

"Let's go," I say after a moment. "When I come back here again it will be to take Trish home."

Williams hasn't asked or probed to find out what I plan to do. I find that reassuring, since at this point *I* don't know what I'm going to do. He leads me back toward the entrance, nodding acknowledgment to the greetings he gets along the way. As far as I can tell, everyone in this strange telephone center is human.

Who are these humans? What are they doing here?

His lips quirk in a tight little smile. *They are our fundraisers.*

I snort. *I told Frey that's what I thought. He just called me an idiot. So what do they sell?*

The future.

What?

Williams laughs. *They're psychics. All of them.*

But they're human.

Of course. All psychics are human. All humans have the ability to become psychics. It involves learning to focus and tap into the part of the brain that interprets more than what is.

I thought psychic hotlines were a scam.

Most are. These, however, are not. They service a very special clientele.

Special how?

He shrugs. *People important to the future of the world.*

You mean like heads of state? Religious leaders?

Williams stops near one of the consoles and turns to face me. *No. The real power behind what the world is to become. You, Anna. You are one of those people. Would you like to see?*

My heart flutters and then begins to pound in my ears. I don't understand or believe any of this. I don't want to. I force the fear out of my thoughts and replace it with resolve. *Don't do this, Williams. Not now.*

I brace myself, expecting him to seize the opportunity

to force whatever the hell he sees as my future down my throat. He's tried before.

But instead he smiles. *I know. You have Trish to think about. Take care of it. Then we'll talk.*

The softening of his attitude is more disturbing than what I'm used to. I think I prefer the acerbic Williams.

He's pushed a button on a panel beside the elevator "door." There is a whir as the cage descends. The little reception area appears as the doors slide open.

Williams touches my arm before I step inside. *God speed.*

I see his face as the doors close, hopeful, confident.

What God is he referring to? I'm not sure I want to know.

CHAPTER 32

W HEN I STEP THROUGH THE MYSTIC WATER-
fall shielding the entrance to whatever that was
I'm relieved to be back outside. Frey and Williams
seemed very much at home in those strange surroundings. I'm much more comfortable in this one.

But I'm also struck with the painful awareness that I
don't have a plan. I hardly know more than I did when I
found Trish hiding in my garage. But I do have one un-
tapped resource. Ryan.

And the instant I think it, I realize I've left his number
in the pocket of the jeans I was wearing yesterday. On the
way back to the apartment, the fact that I seem to be going in circles, literally as well as figuratively, is frustrat-
ing enough to make me laugh out loud.

When I get off the elevator, I am greeted by a couple
of burly construction types hanging my new door. I don't
see the building manager around and I really don't like
the fact that strangers have access to my apartment. My

discomfort, however, is nothing compared to the awkwardness of the two guys when they watch me approach and realize that I'm the occupant.

The guy holding the door clears his throat. Loudly.

The second guy shoots a nervous glance into the apartment.

It's at that moment I know.

I put a finger to my lips and shake my head.

They nod in comprehension, obviously bright enough to recognize it's my favor they need to curry.

I slip inside and pause to listen. There's a rustling of fabric, a slide of wood against wood as drawers are opened and closed.

Someone is going through my things.

I catch Burdick, the building maintenance supervisor, in the bathroom, at my hamper. He sifts through the clothes inside, selects a pair of panties and shoves them into a pocket. His malevolent little face is scrunched up in a smile.

"You should have taken the black ones, Burdick. Pink is not your color."

Burdick's breath catches in his throat. His eyes squeeze shut. He reminds me of an ostrich who thinks because his head is buried, the rest of his body has disappeared, too.

I cross over to him, clucking my tongue.

He doesn't open his eyes.

I put a hand on his shoulder. He jumps.

I take his shoulders and turn him to face me, away from the mirrors.

"But, you know what they say? Lemonade from lemons. I think we can work this out."

He grunts.

"I want to move out. This weekend. But, gee, that means I can't give the proper notice. That won't be a problem, though, will it?"

At that, he opens one eye and moves his head slowly from right to left. As far as I can tell, he has yet to draw a breath.

"And as for the deposit, I want it back. First and last month's rent and my security deposit. All of it. In a check on Saturday. That's three days from now. Think you can arrange it?"

That at last provokes a reaction. "All of it? I don't think I can do that—"

"Of course you can, Burdick. It will be a lot less expensive than defending yourself against the charges I could bring against you for this. Especially since I have two witnesses right outside. They seem like smart guys. They aren't going to jeopardize their own skins for you."

He opens the other eye, his lips press into a thin line, and his brows scrunch together. "How do I know you won't press charges anyway?"

"You don't," I respond cheerfully. "Guess you'll just have to trust me."

There's a timid knock from outside and an anxious voice calls in, "Burdick, we're done here. Should we wait for you?"

I answer for him. "Yeah. He's on his way out."

Burdick manages to gather his wits about him enough to straighten his shoulders and steady his voice as he prepares to leave. "Okay. You'll get your check. I don't want any trouble." He starts to pull the panties out of his pocket.

I stop him with an upturned hand. "Keep them." As if I could ever imagine wearing them again. There isn't a disinfectant strong enough. "Consider them payment for the door."

I follow him out and close and deadbolt the door with a decisive click. When I'm alone, I realize my hands are shaking.

How many assholes am I going to have to deal with in

my immortal life? How many monsters like the creeps who hurt Trish, and how many insignificant insects like Burdick? Is this what I have to look forward to for all eternity?

I return to the bathroom to splash water on my face. The towel I grab to dry off has a scent clinging to it—Max's. I bring it to my face and inhale. It's a reminder that there are good men out there.

Good *men*.

Another complication I can't face right now.

My jeans are in a pile on the living room floor. I fish Ryan's number out of the pocket. The idea that Burdick might have touched them, too, or the underwear tucked inside when I pulled them off, makes me cringe. But hopefully he wouldn't have been depraved enough to touch things in full view of his workmen.

I can only hope.

To be on the safe side, I handle the jeans with two fingers and dump them into the hamper. Maybe I should burn them.

Then I focus on the number, written in precise, uniform numerals. The stamp of a budding engineer. I dial it and he picks up on the first ring.

"Where is she?" he demands in a rough whisper.

"Why are you whispering?"

I can hear his teeth grind. "I'm in school. We aren't supposed to have our cell phones on. Tell me. What have you done with Trish?"

I glance at my watch. I never gave a thought to the time. "When is school over?"

"In about an hour. Damn it. Where is Trish?"

"What school?"

There is a voice in the background calling Ryan's name impatiently. He snaps back at me, "Mission Bay High."

"I'll be out front. Look for a red Jag."

He doesn't have a chance to answer. The connection is cut, probably by some angry teacher. Hopefully, I didn't get him into too much trouble. How am I going to convince him that Trish is safe and that it's in her best interest that he give me that computer? He certainly isn't easily frightened or intimidated—not by me anyway.

I blow out a lungful of air, trying to expel the negative energy that darkens my mood. I look around the apartment. At least I'll be getting out of here and back to my own house soon. That triggers the thought that I never did get around to having my furniture delivered. That number is in my purse and after calling the store and arranging delivery on Saturday, I actually feel a little better. Saturday. Three days from now. I'll be moving back into my own place. The DNA test results will be back and I'll find out just how good Sorrel is.

Three days.

CHAPTER 33

M ISSION BAY HIGH SCHOOL IS LOCATED ON Grand Avenue, one of the busiest thoroughfares in San Diego. When it was built, however, it wasn't so busy. MBH is one of the oldest schools in the county and it looks it. The buildings are sun bleached and badly in need of paint. The meager landscaping shows signs of giving in to the constant onslaught of salt air and the annual pounding of seventeen hundred pairs of student feet. The grass is brown, and a few scruffy bushes cling to life. But the school has a surfing team and that makes it one of the most popular among teens and assures parental support.

I pull up about five minutes before the end of the school day and Ryan is already at the curb, pacing and frowning with the intensity of a pit bull. He barely lets me come to a stop before he yanks open the door and jumps in.

"Let's go," he says in tight voice.

I look pointedly at my watch. "I thought school wasn't over for another five minutes."

"It's over for me. Has been since you called. Now take me to Trish."

His face is so implacably hostile it almost trips an outburst of my own temper—until I remind myself that this is the kid who helped Trish and protected her when she had no one else. He deserves some respect for that.

Act like an adult, I tell myself. Say something meaningful.

I turn in the seat to face him. "Would you like to get something to eat?"

"Are you crazy? I want to see Trish. If you don't take me to her, I'll jump out of this car and start yelling that you're a pervert trying to molest me. I can be very persuasive. Do you want to see?"

His response is explosive and full of rage. But under the rage blazes fear. He's scared to death for Trish. And he now sees me as the enemy—another adult out to take advantage of her.

I hold up a hand. "Ryan, listen to me. Trish is all right. She's safe. I'm sorry I can't take you to her. You must have heard what happened to her mother. The police are looking for Trish. They think she's involved. We had to take her to a place where no one can find her."

"We?"

"Mr. Frey and I."

Ryan's expression is a mask of dark skepticism. "You told me I'd be able to talk to her. Mr. Frey never answers his phone anymore. And if Trish was really all right, she'd call me. I think you're lying."

His voice shakes a little at the end, as if he's fighting tears. He has turned his face away from me so I won't see if he loses the battle.

I place a hand on his arm. His whole body stiffens, but he doesn't jerk away. I take that as a good sign. "Let me tell you why I came to you. I have a friend in the police department. He knows where Trish is and he's not going to tell anyone. He's giving us a chance to help her."

His eyes narrow and slide toward mine. "Us?"

"Yes. You and I. We have to figure out who hurt Trish. I know they are behind what's happened to Barbara and to Trish's mother. If we can do that, we will go to the police with the information. The police will believe it when they see the videos from the computer."

A spark of suspicion flares in his eyes. "I won't turn it over to anybody. It's the only proof we have that those men did what they did to Trish."

"I'm not asking you to. At least not yet. But, Ryan, the police have experts who might be able to trace where the videos come from. Or to identify the men in the pictures."

He shakes his head. "You never see a face." His voice cracks again.

A woman pulls beside me and rolls down her window. "Can you move your car?" she huffs. "You're in a loading zone."

For the first time I notice that school has let out, and the line of cars forming with parents here to pick up their kids is backing up traffic on the busy street. I smile an apologetic smile and start the car.

"Are your folks expecting you home right away?" I ask Ryan when we're back on the road.

He shakes his head. "They'll be at work until six or so."

"Is the computer at home?"

"Do you think I'm that stupid?"

Anger again. I guess that's better than fear. I eye the backpack he has clutched between both hands. "Okay. I take it that means you have it with you. I want to see the videos. Maybe I can catch something you didn't. Do you want to go back to my place at the beach?"

"Will we be alone? I don't want anyone else to see this. At least not yet."

I nod. "We'll be alone."

"Okay. But I won't let you touch it. It took me hours to fix it after the last time."

I agree with a bob of my head. "If we can't identify anyone from the video, maybe we can find out where it is broadcast from. I heard once that if you determine that, there's a way to backtrack—"

"By cross referencing with a cell tower location to get the Electronic Serial Number." Ryan finishes with a flourish of his right hand. "I *know* that. The only problem is that we need someone with access to telephone company records."

It's my turn to shoot him a sideways glance. "I know someone who can get those records for us."

He doesn't ask who. "Then we've got them," he says. "Because I know where the videos are broadcast from."

"You do? Where?"

"From Trish's house."

"Are you sure?"

Ryan nods. "Trish told me the guys would make the videos and send them out to a website. They get sold on the Internet through an underground site called 'Sexual Freedom For All.' Catchy name, huh? They claim the videos come from overseas, not that anyone bothers to check."

"You know a lot about this."

He sniffs. "I learned. I've been trying to hack into the telephone company myself. I'm good, but not that good yet. And I've had to be careful so I wouldn't get caught. But if you know someone who has access to the records, we can track down who owns the computer."

For the first time, his voice has a touch of hopeful optimism. He's quiet for a minute, and then he asks softly, "Is Trish really all right? How did she take the news of her mom's death? It's been all over the TV."

And that reminds me of the news conference Carolyn's mother has scheduled for this afternoon. I glance at my watch. "Trish is fine, but, Ryan, we're going back to my apartment. Trish's grandmother is holding a news conference in about fifteen minutes. I don't want to miss it."

I hang a U-turn and head downtown. It's tight, but we manage to make it to the apartment with five minutes to spare. I try to prepare Ryan for what he's likely to hear. But I suspect his natural, youthful skepticism isn't deep-seated enough to accept that Trish's grandmother could possibly believe her capable of murder.

Mrs. Bernard's television persona is quite different than the one she presented to Detective Harris and me. Her face is composed but drawn in a frown of anxious concern. She's wearing a quiet dark suit, an open-collared cream blouse, and a pearl necklace at her throat. She's alone at the microphone, although there is someone standing behind her and to the left. If I had to guess, I'd bet the guy is her lawyer. He looks the part with carefully slicked back hair and an expensive suit. We missed any introduction and tune in just as she starts to speak.

"Thank you for coming on such short notice. I appreciate the mayor's allowing me this forum. This is a very sad day for my family. My daughter, Carolyn Delaney, was viciously murdered last night. She led a troubled life, but she had a pure, sweet spirit. That spirit allowed her to be taken advantage of. I believe it led to her death. Her daughter, Trish Delaney, is only thirteen. But, unlike her mother, she is a hard, desperate soul. Carolyn, as a single mother determined to make it on her own, did the best she could to raise Trish. She refused help from us, her parents. She put herself through school and became a nurse. She wanted to give Trish the kind of life any child deserves. But some children cannot, or will not, respond to the most basic parent-child relationship. Trish ran away, got involved in drugs and now, this."

Her voice falters. She pauses, recomposes herself, and continues. "You will never know how it breaks my heart to come before you and admit that I believe my own granddaughter had a part in her mother's death. But sorrowfully, I do. And the plea I'm making now is to you, Trish. Please, please give yourself up. You need help. We, your family, will see that you get it. Come forward. Don't let the nightmare drag on."

She steps back from the microphone and the man behind her comes to the front, holding up a hand to stem the barrage of questions hurled at them from the reporters gathered below. "Mrs. Bernard will not take questions at this time. You have copies of the prepared remarks. Thank you for your time."

Then the two of them are hustled back up the steps by uniformed policemen and into the City Administration Building. I snap off the television and turn to Ryan.

His face is so blighted with disbelief that it breaks my heart. "She thinks Trish did it? What kind of grandmother would say things like that?"

I could answer that question for Ryan, but calling her a "fucking bitch" doesn't seem appropriate. Instead, I roll my shoulders and exercise a modicum of adult restraint.

"She's not a very nice lady, Ryan. We can't do anything about that. What we can do is find out who that computer belongs to and get those men. You and I both know they are the ones who killed Carolyn and probably Barbara Franco."

His jaw sets. "But what will happen to Trish? She can't be made to go live with that woman, can she? There has to be somebody else who can help her."

There is. But I can't tell Ryan, yet. I have to have the DNA test for my family to legally make a claim for Trish's guardianship. In my heart, though, it gives me a little peace to know we will be able to protect Trish from her grandmother. I also realize I've accepted what Sorrel told me.

She'd better be right.

But, unable to share any of that, I point to the back-pack. "First things first, Ryan. Let me see those files. Maybe I can catch something you didn't."

He looks skeptical, but he doesn't voice any objection. He pulls the laptop out of his backpack and sets it up on the coffee table in front of the couch. He cues it up and swivels it around to face me.

"I can't watch this again. There are ten files. Each was released and sold separately. The first one is the most recent. They are in reverse chronological order. Hit 'enter' to start and hit the 'next' icon on the bottom of the screen to go from one to the other." He throws me a narrow-eyed look of warning. "Just those buttons. Nothing else."

His tone is dry and detached, but his face betrays grim condemnation. I scour my head for something to offer him as a distraction while I go through the files. "Would you like to watch television?" It's the only thing I can come up with.

He shakes his head. "No. I have homework. I can do that. I would like a drink, though."

"Great. There's Coke in the fridge. Help yourself." I jab a thumb in the direction of the kitchen.

He disappears while I steel myself to start the most despicable chore I have ever had to face. Before I can bring myself to hit the key, though, he's back. He has a can in his hand and a frown on his face.

"You don't have any food in there. Don't you ever eat?"

CHAPTER 34

RYAN ACCEPTS THE EXPLANATION THAT I HAVEN'T any food in the house because I eat out. A lot. It's a light moment in what I expect to be a very dark afternoon. He settles himself into a chair and pulls a textbook, a battered notebook and a well-chewed pencil out of his backpack. In a moment, he's mercifully lost in his homework and I force myself to begin my own.

Ryan said the files were in reverse chronological order. I hit the button and the picture snaps into focus. They've been taken with a digital camera and the sound quality is not very good. But the pictures don't need sound. There are no identifying characteristics. They are all hands and limbs and Trish's young, scared face.

I don't realize how tense I am until the picture fades into blackout. My hands are bunched into fists at my side. My eyes burn with tears of rage. Ryan's voice makes me jump.

"It's pretty awful, isn't it?"

He's been watching me and I didn't realize it. I can't bring myself to look at him.

"It's worse than awful." I lower the screen on the laptop. "I'm not sure I can watch anymore."

He heaves a deep sigh. "That last one is the worst. It's the reason Trish decided she had to leave. That spanking stuff? It was the first time they did that. The guy hurt her. She knew it wasn't going to get better."

I press the palms of my hands against my eyes. "And Carolyn was always there?"

He nods.

I nearly choke on the fury that's rising in my throat. What happened to Carolyn wasn't nearly bad enough. Ryan's calm, watchful eyes bring me back. He expects me to do something about this. I know I have to watch the video again. I was so drawn in by the horror of what was being done to Trish, I neglected to focus in on the monster who was doing it.

"I have to watch it again. To see if there is anything we can use to identify the guy who hurt Trish."

Ryan rolls his shoulders. "There won't be. When I watched it, I looked really, really hard. He makes sure his face is always off camera."

I suspect he's right. But I reopen the laptop and let the video repeat. This time I concentrate on the scenes with the man. When he first appears to lift Trish off the bed, the camera is kept waist high. He's wearing jeans and a T-shirt tucked into a leather belt. His hands are large, his arms tanned and well developed. No tattoos. No scars. He isn't wearing any jewelry, either, no rings or watch.

When he lays Trish back down on the bed, only the back of his head is visible. His hair is dark brown, long, almost shoulder length, hiding his neck and shoulders. It doesn't move naturally and it only takes an instant to recognize that it's a wig. It falls down around his face so that not even a profile is caught on the tape.

I let the video play out, and then I sink back on the couch.

The guy was smart. It would be nearly impossible to make any kind of identification from what I saw. His clothes, jeans, blue T-shirt, leather belt. Nothing distinctive.

I feel Ryan looking at me again. "I was right, wasn't I?"

"You'd make a good detective. It's the same way in the others?"

"Yes. There is more than one guy, though, so maybe you'd better watch one of the others. Just to make sure."

I'm not sure I have the stomach for it, but I know Ryan is right. I cue up the next most recent video and let it play out. I'm physically ill.

I close the laptop and try to concentrate on something else until the nausea passes. I sort through what I know. The two videos I saw were twenty minutes long. There are ten of them. Trish ran away after they started to get rough. I found her on Tuesday.

"Ryan, what day did Trish run away?"

He puts his book down and rejoins me on the couch. "She left on Sunday. She wanted to be gone before her mother came home from work early Monday. The men always came on Monday afternoon, after school."

"They came once a week?"

He nods.

So Trish has had to endure this for almost three months. "Do you know how Trish's mom came to know about me? How she found out where I lived?"

Ryan shrugs. "I'm not sure. She saw you on television, I know that. Once when you and that big guy you work with were interviewed on the news. About a month ago, I think."

I remember. David and I had just brought in a fugitive wanted in a murder case. It was big news for about fifteen minutes. That must be when she started threatening Trish to send me after her if she ran away again. Trish was her meal ticket.

Did she connect me with Steve then? With my mother?

Questions I may never get answered.

I gather my thoughts back to the present. "Well, did Trish ever mention how her mother came to know the men who made the videos? Carolyn said she worked at a hospital. Did she meet them there maybe?"

Again, the shoulders roll, and his brow wrinkles with concentration. "I don't know. Maybe. I know it started not too long after Carolyn's last boyfriend left. She was having trouble at work. I think she was worried she would lose her job. But after Trish started doing those— things—her mother didn't seem so worried anymore. And she didn't have to work as much. She only went in two or three times a week."

A knock at the front door startles us both. I glance over at Ryan and he's watching me, a look of concern on his face.

I motion toward the laptop. "Take your things into the bedroom. I'll see who it is."

He gathers up the computer, his books and backpack and disappears through the door without a word. I look through the peephole and see two familiar faces. With a frown, I pull open the door.

"Well, Agents Bradley and Donovan. What a surprise."

Bradley is eyeing the unpainted front door. "What happened to your door?"

I don't answer so he does it for me. "You have a little trouble? Throw someone through it maybe? I can't figure out how you pulled that stunt with us at Frey's, but I'm working on it."

I flex my right arm. "I'm stronger than I look."

He snickers and he and Donovan push past me.

"I don't remember inviting you in," I say.

Bradley smoothes his tie with the palm of his hand. "Really? Cause I could have sworn I heard you say come in. Eric, you heard it, too, didn't you?"

Donovan smiles. "Yep. I heard it plain as day."

Bradley looks around the apartment. "Not much here. You a minimalist, Ms. Strong?"

My back teeth grind together in aggravation, but I manage to smile. "Why are you here? Can't be to get decorating tips. Anybody who dresses as spiffy as you two wouldn't need them."

They both force grins and again, with no invitation from me, lower themselves onto the couch.

"Sure," I snap. "Have a seat why don't you?"

I refuse to give them the impression that I expect their stay to be anything but short. I cross my arms and peer down at them. "What do you want?"

Bradley crosses one leg over the other and leans back. "Your boyfriend seems to have pulled a disappearing act. He hasn't gone back to his condo and he's not at school." He glances around the apartment. "He's not here, is he?"

"Boyfriend?"

He raises an eyebrow. "Daniel Frey."

"Oh."

Donovan takes up the refrain. "Well, is he here?"

"No."

"So, if I was to take a stroll into your bedroom, I wouldn't find him. Is that what you're telling me?"

"I'm telling you that if you were to take a stroll into my bedroom, I'd bring charges against you for unlawful search. Then I'd sue both your asses for harassment."

Bradley's posture stiffens, the playful mannerisms drop. "You are not helping yourself, Ms. Strong."

"I didn't know I needed help, Mr. Bradley."

The two exchange the same kind of meaningful look they exchanged in Williams's office a few hours ago. Donovan gives his head a shake and turns to look up at me.

"Do you have any idea what he's involved in?"

When I don't respond, he continues. "Do you know how many kids are victims of sexual exploitation every year? How many are raped, sodomized, forced into prostitution, beaten, strangled, and shot? We find their bodies in garbage cans and alleyways, on the bottoms of lakes and rivers, and in the middle of nowhere. Like the place they found Barbara Franco. Daniel Frey is a monster. And he has access to children everyday. He has to be stopped. Your mother is a school principal, for god's sake. I can't believe you wouldn't want to help us bring him to justice."

I think of what I just saw on Ryan's computer. No one wants to get the men who did that to Trish more than I do. And if they are also responsible for Barbara's death, I want them to pay for that, too.

But Daniel Frey is not the monster. I look into Donovan's face and know there is nothing I can say to convince him or his partner. The only way I will ever do that is to find those responsible myself.

The silence lengthens between the three of us, broken finally when Bradley hauls himself to his feet. "We haven't made an impression on you, have we, Ms. Strong?"

Donovan rises, too, but pauses for a parting shot. His curt tone rakes me with contempt. "If we find out that you harbor the slightest suspicion that we are right about Frey and you don't help us, we'll arrest you as an accessory. And just so I'm clear, that is an accessory to child endangerment, aggravated assault, pimping a child and murder." He watches as his partner starts for the door.

"Better think about that." He takes a business card out of the pocket of his jacket and flips it onto the coffee table in front of the couch. "By the time you get out of jail, you'll be an old lady."

Well, not quite.

I watch the two of them let themselves out the same way they let themselves in. If I thought for one minute telling them about Carolyn or giving them the videos would change their minds about Frey, I'd call them back. But the videos don't prove a thing. They have it in their heads that Frey is behind the ring and the only way I'm going to fix that is to produce the ones who are.

CHAPTER 35

I LOCK THE DOOR BEFORE CALLING RYAN OUT OF the bedroom.

"Who were those guys?" he asks. "And why were they saying those things about Mr. Frey?"

He looks confused and a little frightened. "They're federal agents. They think Mr. Frey has something to do with what's happened to Trish's mother and to Barbara."

He frowns. "Why would they think that?"

"It's a long story, Ryan. And not important because I know he isn't involved in any of it. The trick is going to be proving it."

There's another trick, too. Getting Ryan home without those two following us. "I'd better get you home. We'll have to take the stairs. They'll be watching the elevator and the front door, I'm sure."

"But your car is parked out front."

I smile at him. "I have another car. One I use for work, mostly. It's in the garage downstairs. I think we can scrunch you down in the back seat and get out without them knowing."

He slips the laptop into his backpack and slings it over his shoulder while I grab a denim jacket from the coat closet and slip it on over my T-shirt.

"I wish I could talk to Trish," he says softly.

I pick up my purse and fish car keys out of its depths. "You will, Ryan. Soon. I promise. Now I'm going to take you home and call my friend on the police force. He'll tell us what we need to do to find out who owns that computer. He may need you to bring it in. Will you be okay with that?"

Ryan's mouth draws into a firm resolute line. "If it will get Trish back, yes. But I won't let him keep it. I won't let anybody keep it. When we get these guys, I'm going to destroy it so no one will ever again see what they made Trish do."

I don't have the heart to remind him that the videos are already out there. The best we can hope for is that they will get lost in the sea of porno available on the Net and eventually fade away. And that the scumbags who download this crap get caught and thrown into a cell with a giant named Bubba.

The hallway is empty when we leave the apartment. I lead Ryan to the stairway at the end of the hall. We make it to the garage without incident.

My "other" car is a Ford Crown Vic. It's the same model most cops use. Ryan climbs into the back and I throw an old blanket over him. I keep a few tricks of the trade in the trunk, a long blond wig, a pair of oversized glasses with tinted frames, a straw sun hat. I put them all on. Instant disguise.

When we exit the garage, the Blues Brothers are parked right across from the Jag in that same old Fairlane. I should have asked them what kind of budget their department has to make them drive an old car like that. Or maybe driving something so unorthodox is their clever idea of concealment. It certainly isn't your typical cop car.

I'll have to ask them the next time we run into each other. This time, however, the car is the only clever thing they have going. They don't give me more than a passing glance when I cruise by.

When we're safely away from the apartment, I ask Ryan for his address. He doesn't live very far from the cottage. In fact, he lives on the bay side of Mission, maybe two miles away. I drop him off about a block from home, in front of the Mission Café.

When he scuttles out from under the blanket, he does a double take at the way I look. Then he grins. "Pretty good disguise. You must have to sneak away from guys a lot."

Since I'm not sure what he means, and I'm very sure I don't want to, I let it pass.

"Remember to be careful, Ryan," I tell him as he gets out of the car. "Keep those dogs of yours close."

The grin vanishes. "Don't worry. I'll be home all night. With the dogs. Be sure to call after you talk with your friend."

I nod that I will and watch until he's turned the corner. Then I reach for my phone.

When I try to contact Williams at his office, I'm told he's already left for the day. Probably tired of being hounded by reporters after Mrs. Bernard's press conference. There's no answer at Frey's, either.

I'm debating whether I should check in with my mother when the phone rings. I glance at the caller ID.

"Good timing, Mom. I was just about to call you."

"I've been trying to call you all afternoon. Your phone has been off. The police were here, Anna."

Her tone is accusatory and her speech clipped, as if she's biting off each word to control her anger.

I try to diffuse the hostility with curiosity. "About Barbara?"

"And about Carolyn. Why didn't you tell me Trish's mother was killed?"

I close my eyes in exasperation. "I should have, Mom. I'm sorry."

"The police think you are involved. You and Daniel Frey. And a teacher told me he saw you and Frey leave school together this afternoon. Was he right?"

There's something about my mother's disapproving tone that makes it impossible for me to lie to her—at least to lie to her about this. "Yes, I was with Frey this afternoon."

She sucks in a breath. "Does he know where Trish is? Do you?"

God, now what? If I tell her the truth, she'll make me go to the police. If I don't, she'll detect it with her mother's intuition and I'll be in worse shit with her than I am now.

"Mom, I can't answer that. Not yet. You have to give me a little time to work this out."

"Work *what* out?"

"Please. Just trust me. You know I would never put a child's life at risk. I've talked to the police. They don't believe I'm involved anymore." A half truth. The Feds think I'm involved big time. Which makes me add, "You may hear from a couple of federal agents."

Another quick intake of breath. "You mean the two from the FBI?" She says it more like a statement than a question.

I grit my teeth. "They've already been in touch with you?"

"Oh yes. Agents Donovan and Bradley visited me at school. They have the impression that you and Frey are lovers. Want to clarify that for me?"

I rub a hand over my face. "I'm sorry, Mom."

"I'm sorry, too, Anna. I'm beginning to regret letting you get involved in this at all."

The disappointment in her voice makes me cringe. There's a long moment of silence before she speaks again.

"I'm giving you twenty-four hours. Get Trish back by then, Anna. I don't care how you do it. But I want to see that child safe and in our home where she belongs. Do I make myself clear?"

She doesn't wait for an answer. She doesn't have to. She breaks the connection and leaves me scalded by the heat of her command.

CHAPTER 36

MY LIFE HAS BEEN REDUCED TO A STRING OF deadlines, the latest imposed by my own mother. The fact that she didn't ask about whether or not I started the DNA testing attests to how angry she is with me.

It's a little after six, and foot traffic is picking up on Mission. From my parking space, I watch people drift into the Mission Café, mostly couples holding hands and smiling at each other in quiet contentment. Loneliness settles around me like the shadows from the dying sun. I've never had a typical boy-girl relationship. When I was younger, I never wanted one. And being around David and Gloria and seeing how crazy they make each other confirms that I certainly don't need that kind of aggravation now. My motto has always been when you have the itch, find a guy and scratch it. Max fills the bill. He drops in, we fuck like bunnies for a day or two, and he's gone.

Perfect for both of us.

Or so I thought.

When did Max start wanting more? What did I miss?

Or did I just assume because of our jobs, our relationship would always be the same? Short sighted even for the human Anna. And selfish. The blare of a horn snaps me back. I glance over my shoulder and a guy in a FedEx van holds up two hands in a "what gives?" pantomime. I'd forgotten that I'd pulled into a loading zone.

Good timing, I say to myself, steering away from the curb. These are not thoughts I need to be having.

Time to weigh my options. I could go back to the apartment and call it a night. God knows I'm weary enough. Or I could go to a bar for a beer. But that would mean getting hit on, or worse, *not* getting hit on. I couldn't handle it either way.

That leaves only one other choice. I hang a U and head for the office. I'll check telephone messages and mail and pretend I still have a day job. If I'm lucky, there'll be beer in the fridge and I can sit on the little deck outside our office and watch the sunset. If I try hard, I might be able to remember how it was when all I had to contend with were human concerns.

David's Hummer is not parked in his designated space. I didn't expect that it would be at six thirty, and yet I feel a pinprick of disappointment. I can't believe it's only been a couple of days since I've seen him. It feels much longer than that.

I toy with the idea of calling him, of asking him to join me for a beer.

But if Gloria is still with him, he'll insist she come, too.

That I can't face. No matter how lonely I feel.

I lock the Ford and pocket the keys, slinging my purse over my shoulder. At the horizon, low clouds hover just over the water. There are a lot of people on the boardwalk, normal, human, strolling south toward Seaport Village, the lilt of music and the rich smell of grilling fish and barbecue drawing them as powerfully as the promise of a spectacular sunset.

For an instant, I'm tempted to join them, to lose myself in the crowd and pretend I'm one of them. But only for an instant. I'm not one of them and it's no use to pretend. I heave a sigh and head for the door.

I have the key out and ready. Since our office is located on the water side, I make my way around to the back, steps muffled by rubber soles on the wooden deck. As I round the corner, an electric jolt of warning brings me to an abrupt stop. The door to our office yawns open.

The hackles at the back of my neck stand straight up and I'm instantly alert. The vampire swallows up the human side of my nature in one gulp. With a low growl, I give the door a gentle push and let it swing open.

There are no lights on inside. In the half twilight, I see a solitary figure standing at the slider on the far side of the office. His back is to me, and he seems lost in the play of light on water. The glare from the sun on the window blurs his image. Soundlessly, I approach, mind probing gently to determine who or what he is. I get no response.

Human? The vampire side of my nature draws back a little. I can easily overpower a human without resorting to fangs. I cast no reflection in the window so I'm at his side before his quiet voice breaks the silence.

"Hello, Anna. I've been waiting for you."

"Frey?" I grit my teeth and scowl at him. "Are you crazy? I almost—"

"What? Bit me? Been there, done that."

He turns to look at me and starts to laugh. "You look like Malibu Barbie."

I snatch off the glasses and hat with one hand and peel off the wig with the other. "What are you doing here?"

He has a can of beer in his right hand and he waves it at the window. "Enjoying the view. You must do very well to be able to afford an office here."

"We get a break on the rent."

He raises an eyebrow. "Boyfriend?"

"No. Father. Any other questions?"

He takes a last swig from the can and tosses it into the wastebasket beside the desk. "No."

I let my shoulders slump and try to ease the knots out of the muscles in my neck. Adrenaline pumps with unrelenting force through my veins. "Why didn't you say something? You must have known I was here. You know, with this"— I lay a finger alongside my nose.

He smiles. "It was more fun to see what you'd do."

"How did you get in?"

"Your partner. He was just leaving when I arrived."

"And he said you could wait? Alone in our office?" It didn't sound like David.

Frey shrugs. "He was with this great looking woman. Looked familiar, though I don't know why. Anyway, I told him you were meeting me. That you were supposed to have left him a message. He seemed irritated but not surprised that you hadn't. The woman mumbled something like, it figures, and they left."

Great. Another piece of kindling to add to Gloria's growing pile. Any minute now, she'll strike the match and my partnership with David will go up in smoke. If it isn't already. I drop into the chair on my side of the desk. "How is Trish? I thought you'd be staying close to her tonight."

He lowers himself into David's chair. "She's got Sorrel to look after her."

"So, you haven't answered my question. What are you doing here?"

Frey leans back and tents his fingers. "Where else would I go? The Feds are watching my place. Probably yours, too. I took a chance they wouldn't be watching the office. At least not tonight."

I nod that I, too, suspect he's right. "I hope you've

arranged a substitute for school tomorrow. Mom is up in arms about everything that's happened. She's already had a visit from the Feds."

"No surprise there. Those jackals leave no stone unturned."

He has a peculiar inflection in his voice. In the gathering dusk, his eyes glow. He turns those eyes on me and a shiver runs up my spine.

"What's going on, Frey? You look—*weird*."

He holds a hand up and turns the palm back to front. "I thought you might want company. Did you know that there is a full moon tonight?"

I give my head a shake. "No. Am I supposed to?"

"I suppose not. The moon doesn't affect you."

"I thought it didn't affect you, either."

He pushes himself out of the chair and begins pacing in front of the sliding glass door. He seems restless, agitated.

"Frey?"

He stops abruptly and whirls to face me. "Did you find out anything today?"

"Nothing we can use." A video image flashes in my head and I pass a hand over my face to erase it.

"Nothing?" He starts pacing again. "Where did you go after you left the park?"

I'd forgotten that he doesn't know about Ryan and the computer. "Has Trish told you anything about her friend?"

But he doesn't seem to be listening. He's pulling at the neck of his T-shirt, as if the collar is too tight. Sweat glistens on his face.

"What's wrong with you?" I ask.

He grimaces. "I didn't tell you the entire truth about the moon. The moon, the tides, and the alignment of certain planets, all have an effect on me. I can change anytime I want. But there are certain nights when I don't have a choice. Under normal circumstances, I'd lock myself inside my condo and ride it out. But these aren't normal circumstances, are they?"

He says it as though it's taking every bit of effort to keep some terrible primal urge in check. Maybe it is. I'm glad I'm no longer privy to his thoughts.

"You're creeping me out," I say. "Should I leave you alone? I could lock you in."

He jabs a thumb toward the slider. "Except for that."

"Yeah, but that leads to a deck over the water. Panthers can't swim, can they?"

"*I* can swim," he says.

Good point.

"Is there anything I can do?"

His answer is to resume pacing. The shadow of night and a low creeping fog bank have swallowed up any remaining daylight. The office is plunged into darkness. Though I can see as well in the dark as I can in the light, the idea of being alone with him like this is unsettling. I reach to turn on a desk lamp.

I'm stopped by a low growl.

"Don't."

The voice doesn't sound like Frey's. I pull my hand back and peer at him. He's standing upright, but his face is changing. The features grow blunter, the nose flattens, and the ears elongate and shift to the top of his head. His eyes become sullen yellow orbs, the pupils split into onyx diamonds that flash silver with the movement of his head.

Those eyes watch me now with an intensity that sends fear skittering along my spine.

When he opens his mouth to speak again, it's with a guttural hiss. "I'm sorry. I didn't know where else to go."

"Why didn't you stay at that place in the park?"

"I couldn't trust myself. There are humans who work there who have never seen a transformation. I didn't want to scare them. And Trish is there. She's been insulated from the true nature of that place, but if she should see me like this—"

Frey is moving his head in little circles, as if working kinks out of his neck and shoulders. He rips at his T-shirt with hands that are morphing into claws. The fabric shreds and drops away.

"I won't be able to talk much longer," he says. The tips of needle sharp teeth protrude from blackened gums. He's crouching now, clumsily pulling at his slacks until he's worked them off. His legs are covered with a fine mat of dark hair.

I watch, transfixed at a sight the best Hollywood special effects man couldn't duplicate. The panther is emerging from the shell of Frey's human form, a perfect cat face, silky fur about two or three inches long and black as the night outside our window. Only it's not quite a complete transformation. Frey is standing upright, and his eyes retain a spark of intelligence beyond that of an animal. The only sounds he's making are rumbling growls that seem to come from the center of his chest. And he's watching me. I feel like a rat in a cobra cage. One sudden move and he'll pounce.

He's moving around the desk, upright, but with a fluid grace. A quick and disturbing thought sends my pulse into race mode. I don't know what shape-shifters do when they take on their animal characteristics. Do I look like dinner to Frey?

I push back from the desk but remain seated, ready to defend myself. Great. A fight to the death with a panther. The perfect end to the perfect day. Frey comes closer, his gums curling back as he continues to emit those deep, rasping snarls. I'm prepared to jump to my feet, to fight him with every ounce of strength and cunning I have at my disposal. One animal against another. I know I'm strong enough to beat him. I just have to stay out of reach of those claws. Get behind him and—

Frey has dropped to all fours. His head is even with mine as we continue to watch each other. I plant my feet, draw strength, and center my thoughts.

"Come on kitty," I whisper. "Make your move."

There's a flicker of recognition in those almond eyes. And I swear, he's smiling. He lowers his head and pushes it against my chest. The sounds from his throat are louder now, but the timbre is different.

He pushes again against my chest and gently nuzzles my hand.

I stare at him in disbelief.

The purr is almost deafening.

I lay a hand on his head. "Jesus, Frey," I mumble. "Am I ever going to get used to this crap?"

CHAPTER 37

THURSDAY

IT'S ABOUT MIDNIGHT WHEN I CAN'T KEEP MY EYES open any longer. I fall asleep, my head on the desk, Frey's furry head on my lap. I'm jerked awake by the blare of a cruise ship horn as it pulls out of the harbor. I sit straight up, heart pounding, eyes blinded by the glare of sun on water. The desk clock reads 6:15.

Frey is gone. So are his clothes.

I let my head fall back on the desktop and groan. I just spent the night babysitting an overgrown pussycat. I don't know how he got himself to wherever he went. Hopefully, he waited until he had transformed back to human, but at this moment, I don't much care.

It's time to get Williams and Ryan together and find out who that computer belongs to. With another groan, I hoist my sad butt out of the chair and look around for the wig and glasses. I wonder if Bradley and Donovan have realized yet that I gave them the slip. If they have and they're any kind of detectives at all, they will have checked DMV to see how many cars I have registered in my name. And while the Ford is registered under the name of our company, I'm assuming that, by this time, they'll know that, too.

I reach for the desk phone and call a taxi. I tell them to pick me up in the parking lot in front of Seaport Village on Pacific Coast Highway. I put the wig back on and the glasses and swap my denim jacket for a ratty leather trench coat I leave in the office for just such emergencies. I put the hat in a desk drawer and jot a note to David telling him I'll call him tonight. I optimistically add that I'll have Trish back home by then and will report to work tomorrow morning.

The power of positive thinking.

Now to get out of here without anyone seeing me— just in case anyone is looking. I peer out and around the door. At this time of morning, there's not much traffic on the boardwalk. A few joggers and dog walkers from the condos nearby. But I can't see into the parking lot and I can't exit that way without taking the chance of getting caught. A low wooden railing separates the decks along the waterside offices. I could easily climb over the railings and work my way to the front. The only problem will be if a startled tenant getting an early start on the day mistakes me for a prowler and calls the police.

A chance I'll have to take.

For once, luck is on my side. I get to the end office without incident. I'm just about to venture out onto the boardwalk when a familiar voice brings me up short.

It's Special Agent Bradley and from the proximity of his voice, I take it that he's standing out of sight just around the corner. He must be talking into a cell phone because I only hear one side of the conversation.

"Yes. I know. We just got here. Her car is in the parking lot." Pause. "I don't know if Frey is with her or not." Pause. "If he isn't, we have people at his house, at school." Pause. "Yes, I realize he gave us the slip. But we tracked her down, and we'll catch up to him, too. And it's the computer we want, right? Frey is just the excuse we—"

Bradley's voice is drowned out by the approach of a garbage truck. Even with vampire superhearing, I can't distinguish any more of the conversation.

And I very much want to.

He mentioned a computer. *Ryan's* computer? How could he possibly know about that.

By the time the garbage truck has moved on, so evidently has Bradley. It's quiet again in the parking lot.

It's either make a break for it now or be trapped here until the occupant of this office shows up and starts yelling.

Not much of a choice.

I put my head down and venture around the corner. The Fairlane is parked in front of the ferry landing, maybe half a block away. Bradley is leaning against the trunk, looking out at the water. I turn my back and stagger stoop shouldered toward the bushes that line the pedestrian walkway. If by chance he does glance this way, he'll see an osteoporotic woman, clad in a filthy, torn and patched leather coat, stumbling with intoxicated resolve toward the bushes. A homeless woman. And that will render me invisible to anyone not wanting to risk being touched or asked for a handout.

I've seen it a hundred times.

I make it to the bushes and beyond to the parking lot where my cab sits waiting. The driver, a dark-haired, olive-hued Hispanic, eyes me when he watches me approach. But I pull my purse out from under my coat and flash a couple of twenties at him. The uncertainty vanishes.

"Where to?" he asks.

I tell him to take me to SDPD headquarters.

That brings a smile. "Ah. You're undercover."

I smile back. "Something like that."

I relax into the seat. I rehearse what I'm going to tell Williams and how I'm going to spin the fact that I've known about the computer all this time and it brings me back to Bradley's phone conversation.

How could Bradley know about the computer?

The implications make my head swim. By the time we pull up in front of police headquarters, I'm so anxious to run this by Williams that I forget to remove the coat and wig. The sergeant behind the desk actually holds up a warning hand to stop me when I approach.

"Whoa, there, ma'am," he says. "What can I do for you?"

I look at the nametag on his shirt pocket. "Sergeant Harvey, I'm here to see Chief Williams."

He's a good-looking black guy with short clipped hair and wide shoulders, but he's looking at me like he's not sure whether to try to placate me or haul my ass out of the building. "Chief Williams is not here yet, ma'am," he says.

"I know he's here," I snap back. "He comes in every morning at six. Call him. Tell him it's Anna Strong. He'll see me."

Sergeant Harvey hesitates. He's probably thinking he should frisk me before turning away for the brief moment it will take to make a call. I try to make the decision easier for him. I remove the sunglasses and shrug out of the coat. As I do, his hand travels to the gun on his hip, but his eyes never leave my face. He watches carefully as I let the coat drop to the floor. I'm wearing the same outfit from yesterday, jeans and a short-cropped cotton sweater that falls to just below my waist. The sweater is not form-fitting, but it's tight enough that if I were carrying a gun, it would certainly show. I raise the cuffs on my jeans. No ankle holsters.

"To go any further," I tell him, "I require a red light and music."

That almost brings a smile. His shoulders relax and he reaches for the phone. But he's watching me, and I have no doubt he'd have his gun out in a heartbeat if I made any quick moves.

I don't.

He speaks quietly into the receiver. I can hear him, though, and it appears Williams has answered the phone himself. Sergeant Harvey starts to give a brief description and I remember the wig. I pull it off and run a finger through my hair. He amends the description. That seems to do it. He replaces the receiver and gives me a code for the elevator.

"The chief is waiting for you."

I gather up my things, head up and put a lock on my thoughts. I want to be careful what I reveal. At least at first.

Williams is waiting when the elevator door opens. He's looking at the coat. "You need a better tailor," he says. "That coat almost got you arrested for vagrancy."

He turns and heads for his office. The enticing smell of fresh brewed coffee greets us at the door. He doesn't seem to be probing my head, nor is his manner anything other than mildly curious.

I eye the pot enthusiastically. "Any chance I can have a cup of that?"

He looks at me, a quizzical half smile playing at the corners of his mouth, and makes a go-ahead motion with his hand. "What did you do?" he asks as I pour a mug. "Spend the night on the streets?"

"Why would you ask that?"

"You have the same outfit on as yesterday."

I take a deep, satisfying pull of the coffee before replying. "You must be a detective. But no, I didn't spend the night on the streets. Actually, I spent the night in my office. With Frey. You ever see him make the change?"

He shakes his head. "But I've seen similar. Don't see any claw or bite marks, though, so I assume he behaved himself." He settles himself into the chair behind his desk and waits for me to sit, too. "So why did you spend the night at the office? Why not your apartment?"

"Bradley and Donovan. They paid me a visit yesterday afternoon to convince me that Frey was a menace to society. They pulled out all the stops, including threatening to charge me as an accessory. Then they set up surveillance outside my building. Figured I'd run straight to Frey, I suppose, and warn him."

Only maybe that wasn't the reason, at least not for Bradley. I flash back on his phone conversation. He's looking for the computer, not Frey. And he knows I can lead him to it.

How does he know that?

In the second I let those thoughts filter through, Williams is in my head.

What computer?

I tell him. All of it. Then ready myself for what will come because I've withheld important evidence.

Like in the park, though, Williams surprises me. His demeanor is more thoughtful than angry. He inclines his head and says, *Predators use computers to lure children into meeting them. They keep their records on them. Getting our hands on it is a good first step.*

I nod. *Max explained that. The trail left on a hard drive.*

Now a flash of aggravation. *Max knows about this?*

I shake my head. *Not specifically. I just asked him some general questions. But what about Bradley and the computer? How does he know?*

We'll have to ask him the next time we see him. But what we need to do now is get that computer and start a trace. Call Ryan. The sooner we do it the better it is for Trish.

He swivels the phone on his desk toward me and I dial Ryan's number. He picks up, and I ask if he can meet me before school. He agrees.

Williams' voice interposes itself in my head, telling me that he'll send me in a squad car to pick Ryan up. I pass the information on to Ryan and ask, "Will your parents be home?"

"Yeah," he answers. "They don't leave for work until eight or so."

"Good. It will give me a chance to meet them and tell them what's going on. It's time they know."

There's a brief pause, then he says, "Okay. But they're probably going to be pissed."

I can't help smiling. "Probably. I'll try to smooth things over."

There's a pause, then Ryan adds softly, "They don't know what's on the computer. I just told them it has to do with Trish's running away. I couldn't let them see—"

"I understand, Ryan. You've been a good friend to Trish. I'll make sure they know that."

We hang up and Williams again reaches for the phone. He dials a two-digit number and tells dispatch to send a squad car around to the back. He's specific as to which squad car he wants. He's just replaced the receiver when the phone rings. He listens, throws me a nod and says into the phone, "Thanks, Sergeant Harvey. Give me five minutes and send them up."

"Better take the stairs out of here," he says. "Our favorite special agents are on their way up. Probably to lodge a complaint against you." He glances at his watch. "I'll meet you and Ryan at the Mission Café in a half hour."

CHAPTER 38

Donovan and Bradley are beginning to seriously piss me off. I'm getting tired of sneaking down stairways and hiding in bushes. I grab the coat and the long, blond wig and head for the exit. It's time we got this thing settled.

The squad car is waiting for me right outside the underground entrance in back. The cop is leaning against the passenger side door, smoking a cigarette. He flips it away when he sees me approach.

I know what he is before he sends out a probe.

You must be Ortiz, I say, figuring Williams would pick a vampire cop to drive me. I extend a hand.

He grins and takes it. His handshake is firm and dry. He follows my glance to the smoldering cigarette. *That's the best thing about being immortal. I'll never have to give up smoking.*

I raise an eyebrow in reply. Not something I've given much thought to. He opens the door and I get in. Then I watch as he passes in front of the car to claim his place in the driver's seat. In human years, he looks to be in his late twenties, five foot ten, 160 lean pounds. He's cute more than handsome, with an aquiline nose, dark hair and eyes and olive skin stretched over high cheekbones. He pulls away from the curb and throws me a rueful smile.

Cute? No man likes to be called cute.

His tone makes me laugh. Something I haven't done much of in the last couple of days. He asks me where we're going and I give him Ryan's address. He lapses into silence, both external and internal. I haven't met too many vampires and wonder fleetingly if I should ask him about how he came to be. But instead, I sink back on the seat and close my eyes. I need to clear my mind. I have a feeling that meeting Ryan's parents and telling them what we've kept from them is not going to be pleasant.

When we pull up in front of Ryan's house, he's waiting at the door. Behind him, a couple stands watch with the worried look of concerned parents. I tell Ortiz to wait for us in the car and walk up alone, feeling curiously like I'm walking into a lion's den.

Ryan is frowning with anxious impatience. He introduces me to his folks in a perfunctory manner, clearly eager to be on our way.

Unfortunately, his parents have questions, and when they invite me inside, I follow them in.

Mr. and Mrs. North are in their late forties, both tall and tan and dressed in his and her versions of the power suit. The living room they lead me into is furnished with Pottery Barn essentials—canvas covered couch and chairs, whitewashed occasional tables with wicker basket storage, ladder display units tucked beside windows with an impressive view of the city beyond the bay. The shelves are full of white-framed photographs of the family at play, artfully comingled with an impressive collection of seashells.

I barely have time to take it all in before Mr. North starts in. "We are not pleased with Ryan, Ms. Strong," he says. "Nor are we pleased with you. You have put a child in danger. He has information that should have been given to the police immediately. Instead, you told him to keep it to himself. Now that girl is missing and her mother is dead."

At least they're not blaming Trish for her mother's death. Maybe they missed the press conference. "Did you know Trish well?" I ask.

Mrs. North waves a hand as if understanding the real meaning behind my question. "If you're asking if we believe she had anything to do with her mother's death, the answer is no. Trish's mother was not a nice woman. We were sorry when she took Trish out of school here and moved to East County. I think Trish felt safe with us. We were sorry to see her go."

Ryan is shifting from one foot to the other, his eyes on me and his fingers clutching the book bag with white-knuckled intensity.

I'm not the only one who notices. "Clearly, my son is anxious to get this over with, Detective Strong," Mr. North says. "But I want your assurance he is not putting himself in any danger."

I don't correct the "Detective" Strong. Instead I run with it. "Police Chief Williams has taken a personal interest in the case. He is meeting with us himself this morning. He is very impressed with Ryan. I can assure you, Ryan will be safe."

I offer my hand to his parents. Mrs. North takes it first.

"Find Trish, Detective Strong," she says. "She deserves better than she's been given."

Mr. North shakes my hand in turn, and then he gives his son a brief hug. "Take care of him, Detective Strong," he says to me.

Ryan squirms away self-consciously, embarrassed at

the display of parental concern. I think it's sweet, though telling Ryan that would no doubt add to his humiliation.

I feel their gaze on our backs as we make our way to the sidewalk and the waiting squad car. That wasn't so bad, though I hook an eyebrow at Ryan. "*Detective* Strong?"

His mouth curves into a grim, tight-lipped smile. "When you said you would be picking me up in a police car, I kind of let them think you were a detective. It just seemed easier."

If that gets back to Williams, I'll never hear the end of it.

Ortiz takes us to the Mission Café and drops us in front. Williams' orders were for him to wait with us until he showed up, but I see no reason to keep him. Williams will be here in ten minutes, so I thank Ortiz and tell him I'll explain to the chief that I let him go.

At first, he balks. But I remind him that I'm a vamp and can take care of myself, and that he probably has more pressing matters to attend to—like keeping the streets safe for those who aren't and can't.

We have this conversation without speaking, Ryan standing outside the car waiting for me to join him. Ortiz finally agrees and I climb out, spying the coat and wig I'd rolled up and thrown into the back seat. I took them to prevent Bradley and Donovan from seeing them in Williams' office. But I certainly don't need to be hauling them around with me now. "Take those with you, will you?" I ask, motioning toward the bundle. "Leave them with Sergeant Harvey and I'll pick them up later."

He gives me a two-finger salute and pulls away.

Ryan looks toward the café. "What are we doing here?"

I usher him inside with a hand on his elbow. "Chief Williams thought it best to meet at a safe location."

One of the waiters indicates that we should seat

ourselves. I steer Ryan to the back wall and we take a table with a clear view of the front. "Want something to eat?" I ask Ryan. "Great French toast."

He looks at me like I'm slow witted. "I know," he says. "I practically live next door to this place, remember?"

"Sorry. You're right."

But when the waiter comes to take our orders, he only asks for a glass of orange juice and I order coffee. The waiter looks a little surprised. Nobody comes to the Mission Café for just coffee and juice. It's the best breakfast place in town and one of the eating places I miss the most. This and Luigi's near the cottage. Oh well. Those days are gone.

I tell him that we're waiting for someone and that eases the uncertainty from his expression, however temporarily. Williams is sure to disappoint him, too.

Ryan hasn't let go of the book bag since we left the house. "You can put that on the seat next to you," I suggest.

But he shakes his head. "No. It wouldn't be safe."

"Ryan, we're in a public place. I'm here. I wouldn't let anyone take it."

"You're a girl," he says. "You might not be able to stop it."

I start to smile, to crack a remark about how he seems to have forgotten how I handled Cujo, but I don't. He's far more agitated than I've ever seen him. "Has something happened?"

He leans across the table. "I think someone's been following me," he whispers.

"What?"

"There was a guy outside my house last night. He stood across the boardwalk, by the dock on the bay. He thought no one noticed, but I saw him. He was looking at my house."

"Are you sure? Until this morning, I don't think anyone

knew about you, Ryan. I didn't tell anyone and I'm pretty sure Trish didn't. Mr. Frey knew nothing except your name and that you helped Trish run away."

Ryan shakes his head stubbornly. "I didn't imagine it. He was there."

"Can you tell me what he looked like?"

Ryan looks around as if to assure himself that we can't be overheard. He glances over his shoulder, toward the door and freezes. "That's him."

I follow his gaze.

Special Agent Bradley is standing at the door to the café. He's talking to the waiter, his eyes sweeping the interior. When he spots us, he smiles and points.

"There they are," he tells the waiter in a low voice.

I listen carefully for the rest.

"My family is right there."

I can hear Ryan's heart pounding in his chest. My own heart is doing the same thing. His family? I have a very bad feeling as I glance at my watch. Williams is ten minutes late. When I left him, Donovan and Bradley were on their way up. What's Bradley doing here now?

I look over at Ryan and motion for him to come sit beside me, leaving the opposite chair for Bradley.

Ryan gets up and moves stiffly around the table. I put my arm over his shoulder and squeeze. "It's all right. I know who this is." It's only half a lie.

But Ryan hears the unease in my voice. He lowers the book bag so it's out of sight under the table.

Bradley approaches. I figure his wide smile of greeting is deceptive, aimed more at anyone who might be watching than Ryan and me. I'm proven right when he takes the seat opposite me at the table and the smile vanishes. He reaches across and takes my hand.

"We should be going, Anna," he says, squeezing. "I have a car waiting out front."

I pull my hand back. "I don't think so. Chief Williams

is joining us. He would be upset if we left before he got here."

The waiter approaches with a coffee pot and an extra cup. Bradley waves him off with a frown that leaves no question as to its meaning—leave us alone. The waiter backs off.

Bradley leans toward me again. "Williams isn't coming," he says. "He sent me. I'm supposed to bring you and the boy back to his office. He and Donovan are waiting for us there."

Ryan is watching Bradley. "Who is he?" he asks me.

Bradley answers the question himself by producing his badge and ID. "FBI, son," he says. "Special Agent Bradley. I understand you have evidence we can use to put some very bad men behind bars. Anna, here, has been helping us. Now it's time you showed us what you have."

Ryan shifts in the seat, hands out of sight under the table. "Why were you at my house last night?"

Bradley nods, a smile of approval touching his lips. "You'd make a good field officer, Ryan," he says. "I didn't think anyone saw me."

"You haven't answered his question," I interject. "Why were you at his house?"

The smile evaporates when he looks at me. "Routine investigation. We found out where Trish went to school before she moved. We got a list of her friends. When you gave us the slip yesterday, we spent some time checking names on the list. I got Ryan. When I was convinced Trish wasn't with him, I moved on."

It sounds so simple. And logical. I feel Ryan relax as he slumps a little, tension draining from his shoulders and neck.

I feel no such relief. Something is wrong. Williams would never have sent Bradley to meet us without getting in touch first. Especially after our conversation this morning.

I pull out my handbag and wallet, extracting a twenty. "Ryan, will you please go pay our bill?" I put my hand on his under the table and gently pull the book bag out of his grasp. "Then we'll go with Agent Bradley."

Bradley straightens in his seat and reaches across to pluck the money out of Ryan's hand. "I'll take care of the bill," he says quickly. "You two stay here."

He jumps up and makes his way to the cashier. I turn to Ryan and put as much intensity as I can into my voice and expression. "You have to get out of here. Now."

His face colors and his mouth opens.

"Don't ask questions and don't argue." I'm grasping his arm to emphasize how serious I am. He tries to pull away, but I squeeze harder. "I'm not kidding, Ryan. Something is wrong. Get up now and go out the back, through the kitchen. Don't go home or to school. Go to the cottage. Don't call anyone and don't answer the door. Just stay there until I come for you."

I've got the keys out and I thrust them at him. He looks close to tears, but he swallows hard and takes them. He starts to reach for the bag.

"No. I should have done this before now. I'll keep the computer. As long as I have it, you should be safe."

Ryan's eyes grow big and I turn to see Bradley finishing up with the cashier.

"Go. Now."

For once, Ryan doesn't hesitate or argue. He jumps up and disappears into the kitchen. I know the back door leads to an alley, and Ryan knows his way around the neighborhood well enough to get to the cottage without having to travel the main road.

I take the computer out of the bag and lay it on the table. It's the first thing Bradley sees when he comes back. He looks around for Ryan, but his expression shows neither concern nor anger at his disappearance.

"You sent the kid away?"

I nod, running a finger over the laptop. "This is really what you want, isn't it?"

He smiles and picks it up. "And I know where he lives, don't I? Just in case it becomes necessary to question him in the future."

He motions for me to get up and grasps my arm as we walk outside. The Fairlane is parked at the curb. I could easily get away, grab the computer, and be off before he realizes what happened.

But the chill in his voice when he talked about Ryan sounded a warning. His meaning was clear. If I'm to protect Ryan and save Trish, there's a lot more I have to learn. And Bradley appears to be the man with answers.

CHAPTER 39

BRADLEY PUTS THE COMPUTER INTO THE TRUNK of the car. He opens the passenger side door. "Get in."

I slide onto red leather tuck-and-roll upholstery. "Nice car," I say. "Your dad know you have it?"

He doesn't respond. His face is a neutral mask. He acts as if he's lost all interest in me now that he has the computer. He puts the car in gear and pulls into traffic.

"Where are we going?"

He doesn't answer that question either, so I try another. "How did you keep Williams from coming to meet Ryan and me?"

That one provokes a reaction. A smug smile. He glances at me. "*I* didn't have to do anything. Seems Williams was called to a command performance at the mayor's office. He figured you'd be safe since you had Ortiz with you. You'd just sit tight and wait for him. But when I saw Ortiz back at headquarters, I guessed that you'd sent him away. I guessed right. Patrolman Ortiz didn't think it was a problem to tell the FBI where he'd left you."

"How did you know about Ortiz anyway?"

"We were leaving when Ortiz got back to headquarters. I recognized the wig and coat he handed to the desk sergeant. Saw them this very morning on a stoop-shouldered old drunk down by the harbor. "So, where's your partner?"

"Accompanying the chief to the mayor's office. Didn't see any point in both of us going. After all, Donovan knows everything I do about the investigation."

His tone is mocking.

We're headed south on Mission Boulevard, back toward town. Bradley lapses into cold silence. We take Pacific Coast Highway past the airport, and for a brief minute, I think we're going to my office. But then he turns east on Broadway, toward SDPD headquarters.

Which makes no sense at all.

"Where are we going?" I ask again.

This time he answers. "We're going to visit a friend of yours."

I frown at him. "What friend?"

We pass police headquarters and continue on Broadway into southeast San Diego. Now I've traced a lot of skips into this neighborhood, but not one I'd call a "friend."

Southeast is the "bad" side of town. It sits up on a bluff with a view over Highway 94, and once you cross that freeway bridge, you're in another world.

In the daylight, the neighborhood looks benign. Little stucco ranch-style houses in various states of disrepair on big lots. But when you look more closely, you see those little houses are surrounded by big fences. Concrete bunkers three to five feet high topped with ornamental wrought iron. And like bunkers in wartime, their purpose is to keep what's inside protected from whatever or whoever is outside, whether that might be the police, the drug dealing competition or a determined bounty hunter.

David and I don't relish our forays into this neighborhood. I can't imagine why Bradley is bringing me here now. But I know it can't be for any good reason.

In the early morning, the streets are deserted. The business conducted here is done at night. The Escalades and Hummers are as secure in their driveways behind padlocked gates as their owners are secure in their beds behind security bars. There are a few young children playing in yards, accompanied by some nasty looking dogs, but for the most part, it's eerily quiet. There's a feeling of uneasiness, like tiptoeing around a sleeping giant you don't want to waken.

Bradley seems to know the area well. He navigates the maze of streets south of Market easily, finally pulling to a stop at the curb in front of a pink stucco house. The ironwork on the fence matches the bars on the doors, a sign of an "upscale" residence. The grass is cut in the yard, and it's actually green.

Someone must be watching for us because as soon as Bradley opens his car door, the garage door at the end of the driveway slides open, too.

That's when I see it.

A blue VW.

I look at the numbers on the mailbox.

3946.

And the street sign on the corner.

Quail Street.

This is Darryl Goodman's house. No-neck.

I can't believe I didn't guess it.

Darryl is approaching the gate, smiling as if he's greeting a lover, excited, eager, his eyes bright with pleasure. "You're a day early," he says. "We aren't supposed to meet until tomorrow."

He looks over my head to Bradley. "You got it?"

Bradley moves to the back of the car and opens the trunk. Darryl watches as he removes the laptop and holds it for him to see. He claps like a satisfied little kid.

Then he turns to me. "And where are our little friends?"

"What little friends?"

"Don't be coy, Anna," he fires back. "It doesn't suit you."

Bradley slams the trunk closed and grabs my arm, propelling me toward the gate. "She let the boy go," he says. "But I know where to find him."

Darryl nods and unlocks the gate. He swings it open for Bradley and me to enter. The closer I get, the more I'm assailed by an odor emanating from Darryl's body. It's sickening sweet and pungent. Too late, I realize what it is. Bradley is behind me, blocking any escape as my legs go suddenly weak.

Darryl puts out a hand to steady me. "What's the matter, Anna? Don't like my aftershave?"

CHAPTER 40

BUT IT ISN'T AFTERSHAVE.

Garlic. Darryl reeks of garlic.

Bradley watches us with a puzzled frown. "What's going on? What's the matter with her?"

Darryl's smile is self-satisfied and arrogant. "You don't know about Anna, do you?"

"Know what about Anna?"

"I have such a surprise for you." He grips my arm tighter and pulls me toward him. "And for you, too, Anna. Come on, let's go inside."

My legs tremble from the mere effort of walking. He holds me against his side with an arm around my shoulders so I can't escape the smell. One of the old myths about vampires is undeniably and irrevocably true. We can't abide garlic. Avery tried to explain it once—something about garlic containing a compound that affects our energy source. Drains it is more accurate. I've experienced it in a small way when I've been exposed to food laced with garlic. But this is beyond mild queasiness. And there is something else happening. An overwhelming feeling of lethargy. I'm powerless and too overcome with exhaustion to care.

Darryl opens the door and shoves me inside. Relief to be out of his grasp washes over me. But the relief is temporary. I'm in a living room—small, cramped, almost pitch black because of heavy drapes covering the windows. I stumble over an ottoman, straighten up, and immediately lose balance as the nausea hits. Wreaths of garlic are hung on the walls and festooned over furniture like macabre party decorations. I double over and start to retch.

Darryl laughs.

Bradley's puzzled voice seems very far away. "What the hell did you do? God, the smell in here is awful. Open a window."

"Oh no," Darryl says. "Couldn't do that. Anna would like it. And for once, Anna is not going to get what she wants."

Bradley moves into my line of sight. He's looking at me, confusion casting a shadow on his face. "Is she allergic to garlic? I don't get this, Darryl."

Darryl comes close, grabs my arm, and flings me toward the couch. I land on my side, fighting to clear my head, still retching.

Darryl sits on the ottoman facing me. "I'm going to tell you what's wrong with Anna," he says. He's watching me as he directs his words to Bradley. "She's a vampire."

Bradley laughs. "Yeah. Right. Whatever you've been smoking, I'd like a hit."

"I'm serious," Darryl says. He reaches out a hand and smoothes a lock of my hair away from my face, as if to get a better view.

I snarl and snap at the hand, but he's too fast. I'm snapping at air. It takes all the strength I can muster to get a few words out. "I'm going to kill you," I say.

He raises an eyebrow. "Yeah? Well, then, go for it. I'm right here."

Bradley's voice cuts in. "Whatever delusions you two share, I'll leave you to them. I'm out of here. You've got the computer. I've got to get back to my partner and the chief."

Darryl never takes his eyes from mine. "You going to take care of that other little problem?"

"As soon as I can find her. That girl seems to have vanished off the face of the Earth. But I'll stay on Frey. He's the key; I'm sure of it."

Bradley leans down so that his eyes lock into mine. "Are you going to need a trash pickup?" His expression makes it clear who the "trash" is. "We don't want to make the same mistake we made with Carolyn."

Darryl grins. "I told you, Anna's a vampire. Won't be anything left but a pile of dust."

Bradley exhales with a huff. "Whatever." He straightens up. "Well, Anna, it's been a pleasure. I'll let Darryl answer any questions you may have about our partnership. I have a feeling he'll be eager to share. You've made quite an impression on him."

He starts toward the front door and I realize my only hope is to follow him outside. If I don't get out of this room now, while I can muster a rational thought, I'll be at Darryl's mercy.

But Darryl seems to be anticipating what I'll try to do. He reaches out an arm and just the mere pressure of his hand on my shoulder keeps me from moving. He remains like that until we hear the door shut behind Bradley. Then he lets the arm drop.

I collapse back against the cushions. "Tell me." I can barely form the words. "About Carolyn."

He shrugs. "We wanted to know where Trish was. She wouldn't tell us. She gave you up, though. She didn't like you very much."

He reaches behind, to the coffee table where he's placed the computer, and pulls it onto his lap. He opens it, powers it up, and from the audio, I know it's one of Trish's videos that he's watching.

His eyes are riveted on the screen, and lust, like oily sweat, glistens on his face. When it's over, he closes his eyes and smiles.

"She's great, isn't she? So young. So pretty. She feels shame. Well, that will change. We'll have to take her to the next step. Her fans are growing impatient. The video of her cherry-popping will bring big bucks. I'm thinking of participating in that one myself. The spanking is a new twist. We can milk that for a while."

He talks as if to himself. My gut twists with rage. I have to get out of here.

Darryl continues, lost in the swampland of his own thoughts. "My dad started this business. Years ago when we lived in Boston. Of course, then there was more risk involved. You actually had to get out there and find the talent. That was my dad's downfall. In fact, it was how I came to know Bradley and Donovan. They arrested my dad. Couldn't do anything for him, but when Bradley saw the money we were making . . . Well, let's just say he underwent an attitude adjustment."

He gets up from the ottoman and moves to a chair opposite me. "It was Bradley's suggestion I move west. He made sure I wasn't indicted with my father, for a price, of course, and a cut of any future business. I had some money the Feds didn't find, so I bought this place and a few apartment houses in areas I thought might prove fertile hunting ground. I was right. Carolyn Delaney moved in with her daughter. She had lousy taste in men, and she had expensive habits. She was always behind in the rent, always short of money. And she had a kid. In short, she was perfect. We'd fuck once in a while for credit. But Trish was the real reason I hung around."

As he talks, I take mental stock of my condition. Now that he's moved to the other side of the room, my head seems to be clearing. He must have ingested a shit load of garlic. It's impregnated his system and exudes through his pores with such intensity, his touch renders me immobile. The garlic cloves on the wreaths in front of me are not peeled, however, which blunts their potency. At least a little.

I shift, raising my head and drawing my legs up, testing my range of movement. He sees it and wags a finger.

"Don't try to get up. You won't make it." He reaches behind the chair and pulls out a three-foot length of some dark wood that's been chiseled to a point at one end. "I don't want to rush this, but I will if I have to."

I nod. My best chance is to keep him talking long enough to gather strength. I can't fight him, but if I can make it outside, I can get away.

"How does Frey figure in all this?" I ask, letting my head fall back on the couch.

He nods approvingly and places the stake at his feet. "Frey had a hard-on for my father. It started in Boston when Dad enlisted one of his students to star in a specialty video. Much like the one we envision for Trish. But the girl got a streak of conscience afterward and attempted to kill herself."

He waves a hand. "Such a waste. Anyway, one of her friends went to Frey and he set the Feds on us. But Frey was almost too clever. He couldn't explain how he knew so much, and he wouldn't reveal the girl's name. He came under suspicion himself. There wasn't enough evidence to charge him with anything, but he had to leave the state just the same. School districts are funny about things like that."

He barks a short, brittle laugh. "Can you believe it? He showed up here. We'd just gotten this thing started with Trish and he shows up here. Good thing Bradley was keeping track. He made sure he and Donovan were assigned to investigate Frey."

The tips of my fingers and toes are tingling. There's an eerie feeling of energy being restored. Cell by cell, my system is repairing itself, releasing the poison through my pores.

But it's not enough. Not yet. I need a few minutes more.

Darryl is watching me with keen eyes. Best to keep him talking.

"What about Barbara Franco? Did you know her in Boston?"

He looks puzzled. "In Boston?" He grins. "Well, how about that? She's from Boston, too?"

He doesn't pursue it so I do. "If you didn't know her, why did you kill her?"

There's a pause while uncertainty casts a shadow over his face. But his need to brag wins out over caution. It's what I'm counting on.

He shakes his head, frowning. "I know what you're asking. Did we kill her for a snuff film? That's the kind of thing that gives our business a bad name. In the first place, snuff films are urban legend. They don't exist. They don't have to. Technology makes it unnecessary to take that kind of risk. Special effects nowadays—"

He's ramping up for a lecture. Jesus. "I don't care about special effects. What happened to Barbara?"

The irritation in my voice sends a second flash of doubt across Darryl's face. He reaches for the stake and starts to get up. "You wouldn't be trying to fool me with all these questions, would you?" he asks.

It's now or never. I heave myself up and leap as far away from Darryl as I can. He comes after me, lunging across the room. I can't make the door. The only other way out is the window, shrouded in heavy drapery. I run at it full speed and clutching the drape, plunge headfirst through the glass.

I strike the ground and roll. Glass fragments shower around me, but the curtain protects my face and head. The fresh air hits me with the clarifying force of a douse of cold water. I let the curtain fall and run.

Darryl is howling at the window. I glance back once to see him trying to follow me, blood seeping from wounds on his arms and legs as he snags himself on broken glass. Too bad it's not his neck.

Then I'm off, racing the wind.

CHAPTER 41

I KEEP RUNNING, AWAY FROM DARRYL AND HIS carefully prepared, poisoned lair. Once I get across the freeway bridge, I stop. I don't have my purse; it's in Bradley's car. Which means I don't have my cell phone to call for a ride or to alert Williams to what's transpired. The only thing I can do is continue to police headquarters on foot.

The run is actually restorative. I pump my arms to the rhythm of my stride, and by the time I've reached my destination, I feel as if I've worked all the toxin out of my system. I feel strong and alert and very, very angry.

And as luck would have it, what should I see parked in front of police headquarters but the Fairlane. I peer inside, but as I suspect, Bradley has either ditched my purse somewhere or put it in the trunk. Since I have an overwhelming urge to do violence, I decide to check the trunk. I grip the ridge with both hands and peel back the metal until the trunk is doubled back on itself. I want to rip the thing right off, but somebody might be watching.

My purse is inside, tossed into a corner, to be planted somewhere incriminating, no doubt, when the time is right. I snatch it up, wondering whether to alert Williams that I'm on my way up, or to just appear and watch Bradley squirm.

You can't go up, Anna.

I whirl around. *Casper?*

You have to get to Ryan. Bradley suspects he's at the cottage. He's on his way there now with two of Darryl's friends.

Casper's voice is different somehow. There's an urgency I've never heard before. *I have no way to get there.*

From the corner across the street, a car engine sparks to life. I turn again, toward the sound.

Anna, remember what I told you before. You are at a crossroads. The path you choose now determines what you are to become.

For a fleeting moment, excitement overshadows my concerns. I'm going to meet Casper. I must be.

I wait for the car to pull away from the curb.

It doesn't.

Impatience flares. *Damn it, Casper. Come on.*

There's no answer, and no movement from the car. Furious now, I cross the street and jerk the car door open.

The engine is running, the keys dangling from the ignition. The driver's seat is vacant.

Shit. You can't keep doing this.

But I know I'll get no answer. And no satisfaction. I slam into the front seat and peel away from the curb with a screech of tires. I hope this is his car. And that I burn every bit of rubber off the damned tires.

The car is a little Miata, responsive, fast. I dodge morning traffic and head for Mission Beach. When I get to the cottage, I use the alley in back to scope things out. There is a car parked in front of my garage, a black

Chevy Suburban with tinted windows. I pull behind it, blocking the escape route.

I test the back door. It's locked. I can't see much through the windows, just into the kitchen and a hallway beyond. I also can't hear any voices. I'm just about to make my way around the house to the front when the brush of a hand on my arm makes me jump.

I've got his throat in my hands before my brain registers that he is no threat and reason takes over. "Jesus, Ryan." I squeeze him against my chest in a hug of relief and apology. "What are you doing?"

He puts a finger to his lips and gestures toward the house. "That FBI man is here," he whispers. "He's got people with him. He said I should go with them, but I don't trust him. I told him I had to get my stuff and snuck out the back. I've been hiding in the garage, waiting for you."

An almost parental impulse to remind him that I told him not to let anyone in flares, but it dissipates just as quickly. This is not the time for scolding. Instead, I turn his shoulders and push him toward the gate. "Your instincts are good. Let's get out of here."

We duck away from the door and are almost at the car when a shout from above snaps our attention to the balcony outside my bedroom. Bradley is there, his expression one of mingled confusion and rage.

"Stop." His voice bellows across the yard. He's fumbling for something under his jacket.

I push Ryan toward the car and we dive inside. A bullet hits just below the windshield and is deflected onto the glass. The safety glass morphs into a starburst, the pattern radiating outward like an intricate spiderweb.

I shove Ryan down and crank the engine.

The second shot passes through the glass and slams into the console. It's almost impossible to see through the windshield now. I put the car in reverse and use the side mirrors to back out of the alley. Once on the street, I punch at the glass until the windshield falls away. People passing on the sidewalk stop and stare. From the corner of my eye, I see Bradley and a second man running down the alley toward us.

My foot slams the accelerator and we're gone before they reach the road.

For a kid, Ryan keeps his cool. He's holding onto the panic handle on the car door with a grip that's turning his knuckles white, but he's not cowering in the seat or yelling distracting questions or demanding to go home.

I like him more and more.

But what am I going to do with him?

It will be only a matter of minutes before Bradley comes after us. I have to ditch the car. Straight ahead is Belmont Park, home of the Giant Dipper Coaster and the Plunge, a huge saltwater pool. It's either an eighty-year-old treasure or a past-its-prime eyesore, depending on your point of view. But it's a busy, crowded amusement park and just what I need.

I pull into the parking lot and look for the right spot. I find it between two big SUVs. Perfect concealment for the tiny Miata. Ryan and I jump out and I herd him toward the entrance. We don't go inside, but rather watch from a protected vantage point beside the box office and wait for the black SUV to appear.

It does, almost immediately. But to my relief, instead of pulling into the parking lot, it veers toward Mission Bay Drive and downtown.

To Darryl's, probably. If I'm lucky, the little shit will have bled to death.

Now that the immediate danger has passed, Ryan's eyes are big with delayed panic. "Where's the computer?" he asks. "You don't have it anymore, do you?"

"It's okay, Ryan." I put my arm around his shoulder reassuringly. "We don't need it anymore. I know who's responsible for the videos."

"Who is it?"

"I don't think you ever met him. He was a friend of Trish's mom."

His shoulders tense. "It wasn't Trish's stepfather, was it?"

There's a tone in his voice that hasn't been there before. It's bitter and full of recrimination. "Stepfather?"

He narrows his eyes. "Trish called him her dad. But I knew he wasn't. I overheard her mother talking to him once when she didn't know I was around."

"What did you hear?"

"Trish's mom was warning him to stay away from her and he laughed and said why? Since they weren't blood, what was the problem? It made me sick."

It makes me sick, too. And angry all over again. What Trish has gone through is loathsome. Carolyn is dead, and I have no idea who the stepfather is. But Bradley and Darryl are very much alive and I make a silent oath that they will pay.

CHAPTER 42

B UT RIGHT NOW, I HAVE A PROBLEM. I CAN'T LET Ryan go home and I can't keep him with me. That leaves one alternative.

The cab picks us up in front of Belmont Park. Ryan looks surprised when I tell the driver where we want to go, but once again, he doesn't ask questions. His faith in me touches my heart.

When we approach the door to Frey's magical headquarters, I touch Ryan's arm. "Follow me," I say. "You might feel something funny, like passing through damp spiderwebs, but it's okay."

His eyes widen. He's looking past me to the garden. "There isn't anything back there. Where are we going?"

I answer by stepping through the barrier. His expression stills and he holds out a hand toward the invisible curtain, unable to believe what has happened. At the feel of the curtain on his skin, he yanks his hand away. I hear his voice as if from a great distance. "Anna?"

I step back through.

"What happened? Where did you go?"

I smile. "It's all right, Ryan. I can't explain it. I don't know how it works. But I'm taking you to Trish. You just have to trust me."

His eyes dart over my shoulder. "Trish is in there?"

I nod.

He looks around at the people passing by on the sidewalk and leans toward me. "And they won't see us?"

"No." I remember how Frey explained it to Trish. "It's a secret government facility."

Ryan's expression brightens. "Wow. This is really cool."

And this time, he doesn't wait for me to go first.

TRISH AND RYAN HAVE THEIR HEADS TOGETHER, talking in excited whispers, while Frey and I stand outside the little office.

"Are you sure it was a good idea to bring him here?" Frey asks, watching.

I shake my head. "I'm not sure of anything except that Ryan needs to be protected."

He motions for me to follow him and I do. We end up in Williams' office down the hall. When he hears about everything that happened in the hours since he left me, he frowns.

"I should have stayed with you. I'm sorry."

I shrug. "You can make it up to me. I'm going after Bradley and Darryl. I need your help."

"What do you want me to do?"

I shoot him a hard look. "I want you to turn yourself into a panther."

He lets a growl escape his throat. A very convincing growl. "No problem. What else?"

"Garlic. You're not affected by it, are you?"

* * *

I ASK FREY TO BORROW A CAR FROM ONE OF THE psychics on duty. Preferably, I tell him, an old one. I can't be sure what condition it will be in when we return it.

He has no trouble securing one, which I take as a good sign. After all, a psychic should know whether lending her car to a stranger is a good idea or not, shouldn't she?

Once we're on the road, Frey asks about the plan.

"Plan?"

His lips pucker with annoyance. "You don't have one?"

"Oh, you bet I do," I snap. "We go in, tear Darryl's heart out, destroy the computer and anything else we find that has any link to Trish. Then we burn down the scumbag's house and go after Bradley."

He grins. "Works for me."

I glance over at him. "You know I never suspected Darryl to be a part of this. He's different on his home turf. Either that or he's a damn good actor. Is he the reason you came to San Diego? You suspected he was taking over his dad's business?"

Frey shakes his head. "I never met Darryl in Boston. If I had, I damn sure would have recognized him the other day. His last name is different from his father's, too. Probably changed it when he moved here."

I wait a moment. "Things became uncomfortable for you in Boston? Darryl mentioned something about your coming under suspicion there because you seemed to know too much."

He sniffs. "That was Bradley's doing, I'm sure. But yes, a rumor went around that I had made a deal to extricate myself by turning on Darryl's father. The truth was, one of his father's victims was a student at my school. She attempted suicide. Her best friend came to me and told me why. I did some investigating, contacted the Feds and they got him."

The same story I heard from Darryl. I glance at Frey; his expression is harsh. "But you left Boston."

"Our school board was very conservative. I didn't have much of a future there once the rumors started flying. It didn't matter that they were unsubstantiated. But the one concession they made was to let me resign with the promise of a good recommendation. It's how I got my job here."

He lapses into silence, but after a moment, he adds softly. "You know this is not going to be the end of it for Trish. Her videos are already out there."

I know it. I just don't want to hear myself say that I know it. I shrug. "I just hope Darryl kept good records. I'll track every scumbag customer if it takes the rest of my life."

The absurdity of that remark makes Frey laugh. And I know why.

Sometimes I forget what I am.

We're approaching Darryl's street. Frey starts to undress, pulling his shirt over his head, skimming out of his slacks. He sees me watching and grins.

"It's easier on my wardrobe to do this now. And I'll need something to change into later, right?"

Last night I didn't really pay attention to Frey's body, I was too busy wondering if I was about to become dinner. Today, it's different. I take a quick, involuntary appraisal. Frey's chest and shoulders are broad, powerful looking, his arms and thighs well muscled and firm.

"Damn, Frey. I'm impressed."

He slips Gucci loafers off his feet and flips them into the back seat. The only thing he has on now is a pair of very brief briefs. When he looks at me, an intense physical awareness prickles my skin.

I arch an eyebrow and wait.

"This is as far as I go on a first date," he says.

I blow out a puff of air and wait for my heartbeat to return to normal and the heat to dissipate from my skin.

What the hell am I thinking?

I pull over at the corner of Darryl's block, dragging my thoughts back from the abyss, and tell Frey which house is his. "I'll go in through the front, get him to come outside so you can sneak in the back."

If he caught my momentary lapse into sexual fantasyland, he doesn't show it. He simply nods and looks around. "I won't make the change until I get into his yard. It's pretty quiet around here. I shouldn't have any trouble."

"You can get over these fences?"

"Like a cat."

He steps out of the car and disappears faster than I would have anticipated. In a moment, I hear the frantic barking of a dog a few doors down. Then a yelp of pain and silence. I don't want to know what made it stop.

CHAPTER 43

I PARK A FEW HOUSES DOWN FROM DARRYL'S AND
climb out of the car, pocketing the keys. It's oddly
quiet in the neighborhood for a weekday morning. No
commuters on their way to work, no children waiting for
school busses on the corner. I see the edge of a drape in a
living room window rise and fall as I pass by on the sidewalk, but as long as I keep moving, I don't seem to be attracting any undue attention.

It's quiet in front of Darryl's place, too. I expect to see
the Chevy Suburban from the cottage parked in front, but
it's not here. Darryl's garage door remains open, though,
and the VW is inside. I'm pleased that we'll find him at
home.

I glance at the gate. It's secured by a heavy chain and
an industrial-sized padlock. It doesn't take much effort to
kick it free. And the noise produced when the gate
crashes onto the driveway has the desired effect.

Darryl steps out of the front door.

He stares at me. His face reflects neither surprise nor anger, but rather mild curiosity. His shirt and jeans are damp with blood. I smell it even from this distance. Ordinarily, that would be enough to trigger the hunger. But the cloying stink of garlic still overpowers the scent of blood.

Until I see Frey, I know I will have to keep as far away from Darryl as I can.

He moves, finally, a small half turn, as though preparing to go back inside. But instead, when he faces me again, he has a gun in his hand. He looks at it, then at me.

"I know this can't kill you," he says thoughtfully, as if speaking more to himself than to me. "But I imagine it hurts to get shot." He chambers a round and aims for my chest.

I dive for the ground as the bullet rips into the concrete. I roll away as the second shot slams into the ground inches from my head. I'm up and at him before he gets the third shot off.

It's a weak hit, the garlic stops me like an invisible force field. But it's enough to knock him off balance and into the living room. Unfortunately, it's not enough to dislodge the gun from his hand. I jump away from him, back into a corner and crouch to await his next move.

He gets up slowly, smiling. "I heard from Bradley a few minutes ago. He was surprised to see you. Said it was bad luck for me that I let you get away. Well, maybe I've got a second chance to make it right. I bet I can shoot you in a lot of painful places. You might just become cooperative enough to tell us where you took Trish and that friend of hers."

He raises the gun and takes aim. I tense, ready to leap out of range. Where the hell is Frey?

The shot reverberates like a cannon in the small room. But the bullet goes wide and high, raining a dust storm of ceiling plaster down on my head. Darryl starts to scream. The dust is thick enough to prevent me from seeing what's happening, but the sound of bones snapping makes it clear.

"Don't kill him," I tell Frey. "At least not yet."

The dust is settling a little, so I step around to the windows and throw back the drapes. I open the windows, too. There are two besides the one I dove through earlier. Sunlight and fresh air stream in. There's a ceiling fan dangling precariously overhead, Darryl's shot loosened the plaster around it. Can't flip that one on. But there's also a fan sitting on the floor in the next room. I bring it into the living room, plug it in, and let a flow of cool air clear away the last of the dust.

Frey, in his panther form, is snarling into Darryl's frightened face. He's knocked him on his back, and the sound I heard must have been the snapping of an arm that Darryl now cradles against his chest. The gun has slid somewhere out of sight.

Darryl is whimpering and trying to scoot backward, away from Frey. But like a cat stalking a mouse, the panther moves with him, not making a sound, watching with quiet intensity, waiting for the right moment to pounce.

"I wouldn't make any sudden moves if I were you," I tell Darryl. "He'll bite your head right off."

As if to prove the point, Frey snaps his jaws.

Darryl yelps and cringes back.

I put a hand on Frey's head. "I'm going to take a look around. If he moves, kill him."

Frey nuzzles my palm and resumes his vigil.

I find what I'm looking for in one of the back bedrooms—three computers with all the necessary hardware and software to turn out the stack of DVDs and VHS tapes that line the floor. Some are already packaged for mailing, others sit in their jackets. There are a dozen piles. Just about the number of videos they forced Trish to make.

I kick at the stuff on the floor, scattering and stomping

until I've reduced as much as possible to shards of plastic and ribbons of tape.

But my rage is far from satisfied.

I return to the living room.

"Bite him," I tell Frey. "His leg."

Darryl starts to scream before Frey sinks fangs into the calf muscle of his right leg. I watch as Frey closes his jaw and shakes his head, worrying at the leg as a cat would a bird. I let it go on for a full minute, before I call him off.

Frey backs away just a little, eyes bright, sniffing and lapping at the blood pooling under Darryl.

I squat down beside Frey, lay a gentle hand on his head, and turn my attention to Darryl. "You remember how this works, don't you, Darryl? I ask you a question, and you give me an answer. Only this time, it won't be me biting you if I don't like what I hear. It will be my little friend here."

Darryl's eyes are dull with fear. They're locked on the jungle cat, never shifting away, when he asks, "What do you want to know?"

"Were there other girls besides Trish?"

He shakes his head, and at the movement, Frey tenses and growls. Darryl freezes, his voice barely a whisper when he answers, "No. Just Trish."

"Who are the men with Trish in the video?"

Darryl closes his eyes. When he doesn't respond, I wave a hand. "The other leg."

His eyes pop open, "No. Please. I'll tell you."

I stop Frey with a nod.

Darryl wipes at his face with his good hand. "I met them at a bar. They're college students. They go with me sometimes to Beso de la Muerte. They were there the last time. You know, when I was with you."

I do remember. The two at the bar. "Names."

He spouts them off, and I sort them away, conjuring

up their faces in my head. I know I'll recognize them when I see them again.

"Where do they live?"

"An apartment near SDSU. 6300 Montezuma Road."

"Good." I pat his leg, the good one. "So far, so good. Now, what happened with Barbara Franco? Who killed her?"

Darryl's voice becomes a whine. "It was a mistake. We only wanted to scare her into keeping quiet."

"We?"

"Me and the guys on the video. We picked her up on the way to school and took her out to the desert. But she wouldn't listen. She kept fighting. One of the guys took off his belt and started hitting her. Then he put it around her neck. It was over so fast. She just died."

"And then the sick fucks had their fun with her, didn't they?" It's my own voice but from a place I don't recognize. The fury is back.

Frey hears it, too, and muscles ripple under the dark fur as a low growl emanates from his chest. He bares his teeth and growls.

I want to let him finish it. But there is one more thing.

"The people who buy your videos. I want to know who they are."

"It's all on the computer. I can get it for you."

The answer comes too quickly.

"I'm not stupid, Darryl. What did you do, fix the computer so you could delete everything if you needed to?"

He lapses into silence.

I think about my conversation with Max. "I think I have the solution. I'll take the computers with me and turn them over to Chief Williams. His experts will get what we need."

Darryl's eyes narrow. "But if you do that, they'll get the videos, too. It's all there. Everything that we did with

Trish. Do you want to take the chance that somebody might make a copy?"

No. I don't. The idea that the scum who bought those tapes would get away with it and move on to other victims turns my blood to ice. On the other hand, exposing Trish to more humiliation if she's made to go to court to testify against any of them is just as bad.

Darryl smiles at my distress, knowing the reason for it. The smug expression on his face is too much. It makes me angry enough to forget about the garlic infusing his blood. I don't know what kind of effect drinking from him will have, but in a flash of anger, I don't care. I bend over him, growling, and actually have the skin of his neck in my teeth when Frey lashes out with a paw. The blow sends me tumbling off Darryl. In a flash, I'm back.

Like animals fighting over a bone, Frey and I face off. I want to finish Darryl. Drain him. Make him die screaming. I want it so badly I'm willing to fight Frey for him. Every muscle in my body, every cell prepares to do battle. I'm on all fours, like the panther, and the sounds coming from my throat are as ferocious as the ones coming from his.

A spark of something human flashes in Frey's eyes. He is snarling, lips curled back to expose fangs as long and sharp as daggers, but he doesn't advance. He watches me, motionless. His breathing becomes a soft susurration, the only sound in the room. Next to us, Darryl lies frozen in terror, his heartbeat so frenetic it echoes in my ear as if it were my own.

A voice I barely recognize erupts from my own mouth. "I want to end it."

Frey moves so fast, I have no time to react. He breaks Darryl's neck with one snap of powerful jaws.

And for Darryl, it's over.

CHAPTER 44

I'M NOT SORRY HE'S DEAD.

I'm sorry I didn't get to kill him.

And I'm angry with Frey for stopping me.

Frey remains crouched over the body. He's watching me.

The fury and the bloodlust still sing in my veins. I can't let go of either. I don't want to. I need some release. If not from the human, then from the panther.

But he either knows or senses what's raging inside me. He remains motionless, liquid gold eyes locked on mine. Muscles tense and ripple under the fur. He waits for me to decide.

Something breaks inside me. The red haze lifts from my mind. This is Frey. My friend. Trish's protector.

When I back off, he turns away, too. He slinks toward the window and, without looking back, leaps through. When I look outside, I see him lying under the canopy of a shade tree, head resting on front paws like a pet tired after a long day of play.

I rest my cheek against the glass. The coolness is a balm on my feverish skin. I'm waiting for the vampire to retreat and the human Anna to reappear. It takes longer than it should. Is this an indication that I'm becoming more animal—if that's in fact what being a vampire is all about—and less human? Not a comfort.

Finally, my pulse slows and my blood cools. I return to Darryl's body and stand over it. He has a look of surprise on his face. I try to dredge up pity or compassion. I can't. He was a child pornographer, he killed Trish's mother and admitted being an accomplice to Barbara Franco's murder. He deserved what he got.

But I have to clear my head and decide what to do next. Bradley is out there as well as the two who killed Barbara and molested Trish. My original thought to torch the place would be the easiest way to destroy the computers and the videos, not to mention a way to explain Darryl's death. But there may be evidence on those computers to tie Bradley in with Darryl—bank records or e-mails, maybe. As it stands now, my word is all that I have to offer as proof that Bradley is involved.

I have to take the computers. I trudge back to the bedroom. Besides the laptop Darryl took from me earlier, there are three computer systems and a digital camera. I also find a box of disks and some files in a cabinet in the closet. I bring everything into the living room and pile it on the coffee table. I'll pull the car around to load up.

When I look for Frey, to let him know what I'm doing, he's no longer under the tree in the backyard. No matter. If he's not waiting for me at the car, I'm sure he's somewhere nearby. How far can a panther get in broad daylight? Or a near naked man, for that matter?

I reach into my pocket for the car keys.

The pocket is empty.

Shit.

I glance around the living room.

They could have fallen out of my pocket in here, or outside when I was dodging bullets.

I don't find them near Darryl's body or in the bedroom. That leaves only one alternative. I yank open the front door—and find myself face-to-face with Bradley. He's not alone.

"Well, well," I say. "Special Agent Bradley." I look past him to the two young thugs at his side—thugs I recognize from Beso de la Muerte. "And you're Darryl's friends. Come on in. He's inside."

The expression on Bradley's face is part confusion and part distrust. He looks past me, but from this vantage point, Darryl's body is hidden.

I step back. "Come in."

Bradley steps around me, carefully, as if afraid physical contact might have an unpleasant effect.

He has no idea.

He hasn't uttered a word. And neither have his companions. They stand awkwardly outside, not moving to join Bradley. I don't know whether they're shocked because they didn't expect to see me at Darryl's or afraid because they know what I am.

I hear a sharp intake of breath behind me and know Bradley has found Darryl.

"You two better wait out here," I say, shutting the door before they can react. I snap the deadbolt in place. Let them run. I know where they live.

I rejoin Bradley in the living room. He's knelt down beside Darryl, his fingers probing for a pulse. When he hears me behind him, he makes a fumbling move to get up, at the same time reaching for the gun under his jacket.

But I stop his hand with my own, forcing his arm up and back.

He resists at first, but all I have to do is lean into him to get the desired result. If he continues to fight, I'll snap his arm at the shoulder.

He's a fast learner. He stops fighting and sags against me to relieve the pressure. His breaths become sharp, shallow gasps of protest. "You're breaking my arm."

I use my free hand to slip his gun out of its holster and toss it out of reach. Only then do I let him go, shoving him so hard he stumbles backward. He lands in an awkward heap on the couch.

He straightens up, grabs his shoulder and tries to knead away the pain. His eyes travel to Darryl's body. "Who killed him? It looks like he's got a broken neck."

"You want me to show you how it was done?"

His expression alters from unsure to calculating as he looks over the stuff on the coffee table. "You plan to turn this over to the police?"

"Does that make you nervous?"

He smiles. "Why should it? There's nothing to connect me to Darryl. I came here to serve a warrant."

Now it's my turn to smile. "Right. Without your partner. And those two outside are undercover cops, I suppose."

He shrugs and then winces. His hand goes again to his shoulder. "I have no idea who those two are. They were here when I arrived."

He's too smooth. I have nothing to use as leverage against him, and if he did confess, with no witnesses, how would I prove it?

The only chance is the one I'm going to have to take—turn the computers over to the police. Maybe Darryl wasn't as careful to shield Bradley as he thinks.

I roll my shoulders. "Guess we'd better call Chief Williams, then, huh? Let him sort it out."

He tilts his brow and looks up at me. "How are you going to explain that?" His gaze drifts to Darryl and returns to me. "It's no secret you've been protecting that kid, Trish. What's to stop the cops from deciding that you killed Darryl, especially when they see what's on those computers?"

He seems to be gearing up for something. I stay quiet and wait for him to continue.

He leans toward me. "I can fix this. You could walk out of here right now. I'll get rid of the computers. Darryl's body, too. I'll go back to Boston. It will be as if none of this happened."

"What about Trish? She's suspected of killing her mother. Can you fix that?"

He jerks a thumb toward the front door. "Those two outside. They killed Barbara. We can fix it so they're blamed for Carolyn, too. In fact, I can set everything up. Get them to confess and then arrange an accident."

"Confess to whom?"

"To you, of course. With me as witness. It's perfect."

It is. Almost. The only thing that's missing is Bradley at my feet with his throat torn out.

"Why am I supposed to believe you'll do all this?"

"Darryl let things get out of hand," he replies. "I didn't sign on for murder."

"No, you just signed on for the sexual exploitation of a young girl. An underage girl, in case you forgot."

The edge in my voice takes some of the eagerness out of Bradley's expression. "No one got hurt. Not really. If you saw the videos, you know. She liked it and—"

That's as far as he gets. I grab him by the scruff of the neck and heave him off the couch and down to the floor.

"Well," I whisper, my teeth at his jugular. "At least you'll die knowing that Darryl wasn't lying when he told you what I was."

Bradley tries to wriggle out of my grasp. I pin him down with one hand and grab his face with the other. I hear him screaming, but it's from far away. I wrench his head to the side and kiss his neck with my lips. Then I bite down. Hard.

The first lush, warm mouthful of his blood sends fire raging through mine. I push against him, my body moving to the rhythm of his heartbeat. The blood drive. I've never felt so alive.

An arm encircles my waist.

I rip it off.

It comes back, forceful, strong. Stronger than I. I'm torn away from Bradley and flung down on the couch.

Like a cat, I land on all fours, then spring to my feet. Rage, unrelenting in its intensity, propels me back toward my prize. Bradley is trying to get up. He has a hand pressed against his neck, but blood oozes between his fingers.

I smell it. I feel it.

It belongs to me.

Only one thing stands between us.

Again.

Frey.

CHAPTER 45

"Get away. You denied me once. Not again."

"Anna." He whispers my name, over and over. And words I don't recognize or understand.

Words that root me to the spot. Make it impossible to move.

He's in human form. His voice rises and falls in the litany of a chant.

I fight it, but he's holding me immobile with his voice, casting a spell that binds me as surely as chains of steel.

He repeats the words like a mantra. On and on until he sees—something. Then, he stops.

Released, the fury drains from my limbs in a rush that leaves me weak and disoriented. He steps toward me, catching me before I fall, and lowers me to the couch.

"What the hell was that?" Bradley's voice is shaky, hesitant.

I blink up at Frey. He's fully dressed. He must have gone to the car and come back. I don't know yet if I'm glad that he did or not. My body reverberates with the hunger, and my voice rattles in my throat. "That's a good question. What the hell *was* that?"

Bradley pushes Frey to one side. "You crazy bitch. You bit me." He looks at Frey. "You saw her attack me. I'm going to press charges. She must have killed Darryl, too. It's a good thing you got here when you did. You're my witness."

He stops, frowning, maybe wondering for the first time just how Frey came to be here. And how much he heard before making his appearance.

Frey smiles. "You're right to be worried. I'm a witness all right. But not for you."

Bradley takes a step back, and his eyes sweep the room, looking, no doubt, for his gun.

"Don't bother," Frey says. "The gun is gone."

I glance at the door. "Did you see the two outside?"

Frey nods. "They're secured. I happened to mention how Bradley here said that they were responsible for all the murders. I also pointed out that when Williams gets here, it would be to their advantage to speak with him first."

Bradley narrows his eyes. "Williams is on the way?"

"And your partner is with him." Frey glances at his watch. "You have about five minutes to come up with a better story than the one you concocted against Anna."

"Well," he says. "You're full of surprises, aren't you?"

"Let's just say I was motivated. Because of Boston."

Bradley ignores the comment. From the expression on his face, it looks as if he's weighing his options, deciding which story paints him in the best light.

I'm watching all this from the couch, fighting the compulsive desire to launch myself again at Bradley. Only the knowledge that my limbs will not respond, that my legs will not support my weight, keeps me from trying. I'm panting, shaking all over, unable to stop the wild fluttering in the center of my chest. The fluttering echoes in my head. I look at Frey and his eyes are on me. Whatever is happening to me, he is doing it.

"Damn it, Frey." It comes out like a croak. "Stop it."

Frey responds by tilting his head a little to the side. "They're here."

And as soon as the door opens and Donovan walks in, I'm released. The shaking stops, my heartbeat slows. I can sit up.

Donovan goes to Darryl first. He bends over the body and checks for a pulse. He turns Darryl's head gently. "Bruising from perforated blood vessels in the neck, soft structure crushed. His neck is broken." He stands up and faces his partner. "Looks like he was attacked by a big dog."

Bradley points to me. "Ask her what happened. She was here. Jesus, look what she did to me?" He drops his hand from his neck and shows the wound. "She must be on some crazy shit."

"You saying she killed him?"

"Who else? I got here and found him like that. She was the only one here."

"Why?" Donovan asks softly.

"Why what?"

"Why were you here?"

Bradley sucks in a breath. "I followed her."

"In what? Your car is at the police station."

Donovan is moving away from Darryl and toward his partner. "The two guys outside. Who are they?"

"I don't know. They got here the same time I did."

"That's not what they said. You brought them here. To see Darryl." He glances at the body. "I recognize him, Tom. He's the kid of that guy we busted in Boston. The one you said had nothing to do with his dad's business. The one you let off."

He looks around, awareness and disappointment creeping into his expression. He picks up one of the tapes from the pile on the coffee table and holds it up. "You went into business with him. Christ. You went into business with him."

Bradley spreads his hands. "How can you think that? I came here for the same reason you did, to shut the scumbag down. I don't know what those two kids told you, but whose word are you going to accept? They raped and murdered a fourteen-year-old girl. Probably killed Carolyn Delaney, too. There isn't anything to connect me to—"

"The laptop." I'm not sure I've spoken the words aloud. Both men turn to me.

"What?" Donovan says.

"The laptop. He took it from me in the café this morning. His prints will be on it. He brought me here while you were at that meeting with Williams and the mayor."

Bradley waves my words away with the brush of a hand. "That's ridiculous."

Donovan pulls latex gloves from the pocket of his jacket. "Where is it?" he asks me.

I point to the pile of videos on the table. "Under there."

He pulls it out and holds it carefully at the edges.

Bradley takes a step back. "If my fingerprints are on it, it doesn't mean a thing. I touched it when I got here and found her with the body."

"Then shoved it under this pile of crap?" Donovan shakes his head. "I don't fucking believe this, Tom."

"It's going to take more than fingerprints—"

But before he can finish, the front door opens. Williams and two cops in uniform walk in. "I just had an interesting conversation with your buddies outside, Bradley. I think it's time we head downtown." He motions to the cops, who step to Bradley's side. "I'm sure you won't mind if these gentlemen take your weapon."

Frey has been standing quietly beside the couch. Now he speaks up. "I have his gun," he says. "He dropped it."

He holds it out butt first. Williams nods and takes it. For the first time, he looks at me. "The medical examiner is on the way. Maybe you and Frey should go."

Bradley stiffens. "You're letting her go? She attacked me. She probably killed Darryl. You're arresting me, and you're letting her go?"

Williams waves a hand. "About now, I'd be worrying about saving my own ass, Special Agent Bradley. As we speak, the DA is contacting the Feds. They'll be examining your financial records. And Darryl's. I bet the two of you weren't as clever as you think."

One of the cops produces a pair of cuffs. Bradley pulls away, but the other cop closes in on him and he sees he has no choice. When he's secured, they prod Bradley toward the door. Donovan follows, holding the laptop.

Neither says good-bye.

Williams waits until they're gone to turn his attention to me. "Are you all right? You look a little pale."

I start to say of course, I'm all right. It's a reflex action. But Frey's eyes stop me. In an instant, I'm watching what happened with Darryl, and then with Bradley. He's projecting it into my head exactly the way he showed me Trish in the park. And I'm overcome with the same rage and desire to kill that renders everything else inconsequential. I would have killed both of them. I wanted to.

I wanted to.

Williams touches my arm. He is sitting beside me on the couch. I realize then that I was seeing through Williams, not Frey.

You saw it?

Frey showed me, I showed you.

The broken psychic connection. I pass a hand over my face. *What is happening to me?*

Nothing that you can't learn to control. But you have to start now. What you did to Bradley will take some explaining. I'll take care of it, but it can't happen again.

I exposed myself as a vampire.

He nods. *You have great powers, Anna. You can use those powers for good. But it takes training to learn to control the hunger. You have fought so hard to retain your humanity. You must fight to control the other side of your nature, too, or it will turn you into what you fear most.*

I thought I could control it.

Frey saw. He stopped you from killing. Twice.

Then he killed. Darryl.

In his animal form. He feared he could not stop you with Darryl. The fire was in your blood. He did it so that you would not.

And what if I had killed him?

Then you would have been lost.

I don't understand.

Williams stands and takes a step away. When he turns to look at me, his eyes are flat, cold. *Settle things with Trish. And your parents. It's time your training began. Don't wait too long, Anna.*

He looks at Frey. Frey takes my arm. "The medical examiner is here. We'll leave through the back."

I push myself off the couch. When I glance back at Williams, he's already heading for the front door.

"Wait."

He turns.

"What about Trish and the videos on those computers? What will happen to them?"

"They're evidence, Anna. I can't promise they won't be used in court."

He must read the distress on my face because he adds, "If we can get Bradley and those two outside to deal, it's possible there'll be no trial. I'll speak to the DA. It's all I can do."

CHAPTER 46

FREY AND I SLIP OVER THE FENCE INTO THE neighbor's yard. The presence of police cars assures us that even if the neighbor is at home, he isn't likely to come outside to see what's going on. We wait until we see the crime scene techs and medical examiner disappear into Darryl's house, and then we quietly make our way to the car. He takes the keys from me and opens the passenger side door.

"I'll drive. You look beat."

I don't argue. I feel as if I'm at the end of an endurance race, too tired to care if I make it to the finish line. I just want it to be over. I know that in spite of everything, I may not be able to protect Trish from the videos being used in court. And Williams' words about me have left me shaken and confused. They remind me what Casper told me. Twice. I'm losing the human Anna to the vampire.

"Do you want me to take you to your apartment?"

I shake my head. "We need to get Ryan home and take Trish to my parents."

"What about Trish's grandmother?"

"We'll deal with her tomorrow. I promised my mother I would take Trish home tonight. It's a promise I intend to keep."

Frey is silent for a moment, eyes on the road as he drives. "What will you tell Trish?"

I don't know. "I won't have DNA results back until tomorrow." I let a stream of consciousness flow. "I'll just tell her my mother offered to put her up for the night. That the press will be watching her grandmother after news of Bradley's arrest, and we thought it would be best to shield her from that."

Frey nods.

"Can we swing by the office? I'll pick up my car."

Frey does as I ask. David's Hummer is in its spot in front. I really want to go inside, touch the face of my very human partner and tell him I'll be back at work tomorrow.

But I don't because I'm not sure I will be.

I follow Frey to the park. On the way, I call my mother and tell her to expect us. I give her a quick rundown of all that's happened. I remind her that the DNA test results will be in tomorrow. It's a subtle hint not to give anything away to Trish until we know.

To that, she doesn't respond. Her excitement at having Trish safe and in her home is all that's important to her. But she's angry with me; it's evident in her tone. When she thanks me before saying good-bye, it's with a rigid formality.

When we get the kids, in spite of the circumstances that brought them here, both are hesitant to end what they see as a great adventure. It is a testimonial to the resilience of teenagers. Only Frey's promise that he will bring them back again assuages their reluctance.

Frey offers to take Ryan home, so Trish and I leave together.

"Where are we going?" she asks. Now that she and I are alone, her voice has lost its sparkle. The haunted, scared little girl is back.

I reach out a hand and touch her shoulder. "We're going to somewhere you'll be safe. My parents have offered to put you up for the night."

"Why would they do that?"

"Well, actually it was my mother's idea. She knows the press will be looking for you. They'll want your reaction to all that's happened. They won't think to look for you at the home of your school principal."

Trish blinks. "Your mother is *that* Mrs. Strong?"

I laugh at her expression. "You'll get to see another side of her. She's a great mom."

As soon as I say that, I wish I hadn't. The mention of my mother makes Trish think of hers. She slumps down on the seat. "You haven't told me what happened to my mom."

I pause, thinking of what Darryl said, and knowing that what I tell Trish now will be forever how she remembers her mother. I begin haltingly.

"Your mother died protecting you, Trish. The man who killed her thought she knew where you had gone."

"Because he was looking for the computer."

I nod. "Yes. But your mother wouldn't tell him anything."

Trish hiccups a bitter little laugh. "That's because she didn't know anything."

From the corner of my eye, I see her wipe the back of her hand across her eyes. She draws a shaky breath and asks, "Who was it?"

"His name is Darryl Goodman."

"Darryl?" She sits up straighter in the seat. "That creep? He wasn't part of the video thing. Was he?"

"He was the one who set it all up. It's not surprising that you didn't know. He was careful to stay away when those other men"—I don't know how to say it so I finish with a lame—"were with you."

There's a long moment of silence. "What will happen to him?" Her voice is small and afraid.

"He can't hurt you, Trish, if that's what you're worried about. He's dead."

She lowers her head and looks at me. "Did you kill him?"

Her voice suggests that she believes I did. Is it that apparent? How does she know? Can she sense the rage?

Do other humans feel it, too, when they look at me?

When I don't answer, she shrugs. "It doesn't matter. What about the men?"

She doesn't need to clarify to whom she's referring.

"They're under arrest. They admitted killing Barbara."

"Under arrest?" There's no mistaking the distress in her tone. "Does that mean there'll be a trial?"

"The district attorney will do everything she can to try to get the men to plead out. They're up for murder and a lot of other terrible crimes. But there is always the chance, Trish, that they will ask for a trial. No one wants to put you through that. But it's a possibility."

She rounds on me in the seat. "Then why didn't you kill them, too? Then it would be over."

The heat in her tone vibrates the air around us. When I look over at her, stunned at the ferocity of her response, her eyes flash and then darken.

"I'm sorry," she says.

For a moment, I'm too conflicted by my own feelings to respond. Part of me agrees with Trish. I should have killed them. I wanted to. I could have taken the computers or burned the house down. It would have been easy and Trish would be free. Frey stopped me.

What if he hadn't? Is that why I asked him to come

with me? Did I know instinctively that I couldn't trust myself? And Frey agreed because he knew. Williams, too.

Only now am I beginning to understand.

I'm not as strong as the blood drive. I never was.

Trish stirs on the seat beside me. I've waited too long to respond and her uneasiness is growing.

"It's all right, Trish. The way you feel is natural. I feel it, too. I didn't kill Darryl. But I wanted to. I wanted to kill those men for what they did to you, too. I might have if the police hadn't arrived when they did. I expect we both need time and a little help to get through this."

She's quiet for a moment. "Help? You mean like a shrink?"

For her, yes. For me, a different kind of therapy. But I smile and nod. "My mom will know what to do. She's a very bright lady. You can trust her."

Trish lapses into silence. When we pull into the driveway of my parent's home, my mother is on the front porch, watching, waiting. Some instinct must be at play because Trish goes to her without reservation. Mom smiles at me but doesn't ask me to stay. I only hang around long enough to make sure they're both all right.

Then I go home, alone, to call Williams.

CHAPTER 47

I FEEL HIS PRESENCE BEFORE I SEE HIM. BEFORE the elevator door opens. Frey. He's leaning against the doorjamb, feet crossed at the ankles, eyes closed.

"Don't tell me," I say, brushing past him to unlock the door. "Another full moon."

He laughs, opens his eyes, and straightens up. "No. It only happens like that once a month. Well, twice if there's a blue moon."

He follows me inside.

I toss my purse and keys on the coffee table. "Want a beer?"

"I'd prefer wine if you have it."

I shake my head. "Sorry. I'm not a wine drinker." Gave it up after Avery. He actually had vineyards in France. Which I guess I own now.

Frey is watching me. "Where did you go just then?"

"It's not important. What are you doing here?"

In a deliberately casual movement, he spreads his hands. "I thought you might want company."

"Company?"

"You seemed a little lost when I left you this afternoon. You don't seem much better now. Did things go well with Trish and your mother?"

"Peachy." I hear the sarcasm in my voice.

So does Frey. He raises an eyebrow.

"Mom will give Trish everything her own mother didn't. She'll finally have a chance to be a kid."

He shakes his head. "Trish will never be a kid. Not with what she's gone through. Can your mother accept that?"

It's my turn to raise an eyebrow. "Are you a psychologist, too? I don't remember seeing that on your résumé." There's tension building in the room that's making me edgy. "Listen, Frey, thanks for stopping by, but I think you should go. I'm tired. I need sleep."

He doesn't move toward the door, but rather takes a step closer to me. This time there's no mistaking the tension. It's arcing between us, scorching my skin.

"What are you doing?"

His hands rest on my shoulders, and where his fingers come in contact with my flesh, it begins to tingle. Heat courses down the length of my body. I remember how he looked in the car, the intense physical awareness that passed between us.

"Frey?"

I'm shivering with a searing need that's been building all day. He's responding to it. His hands pull me closer.

"What are you doing?"

His mouth is at my ear. "You need to feed. It's the only thing that will release the fury in you. I'm here. For you."

The hardness of his thigh brushing against mine floods me with desire.

And then we're on the floor, freeing ourselves from

the bonds of our clothing. I straddle him, holding him captive beneath me with thighs and calves. He moans, his hands gripping my waist, and moves, forcing himself deeper inside.

I open his neck to drink. The tempo builds until both hungers are satisfied, and only then does a great peace descend over me.

CHAPTER 48

FRIDAY

IT'S WELL PAST MIDNIGHT WHEN FREY LEAVES. I feel a little guilty about asking him to go home after hours of lovemaking that, with and without feeding, were nothing short of miraculous. But I know that the day ahead will be full and I want at least a few uninterrupted hours of sleep. His sexual pull is strong and my defenses are weak. If he stays, I don't know if I'll have the strength to face what awaits me in the morning.

When he does go, I fall immediately into a blessed, restorative sleep, freed from the anxiety that's plagued me the last few days. Only when I open my eyes and remember what happened with Frey does it hit.

Not once last night did I think of Max.

It was the same when I was with Avery.

The realization wipes away doubt and clarifies what I must have suspected all along.

I must end it with Max. Frey was right when he said feeding would release me. It did. It released my mind.

The sex released my body. I needed both. If Max had been here, it wouldn't have been the same. I can't pretend it ever would. I need to free Max to find a woman who can be as honest with him about who she is and what she needs as he has been with me.

The thought fills me with unexpected sadness. For all my bravado about being satisfied with our casual relationship, Max has been a constant in my life. Even when he suspected something more than a fight occurred the night Donaldson attacked me, he didn't push, didn't demand explanations.

Now, alone, it's easy to say I will cut Max free.

I wonder if I'll be as firm in my resolve when I face him.

I force my thoughts elsewhere, busying myself around the apartment waiting for the clock to read 9:00 a.m.— the time the DNA lab opens—throwing clothes in boxes for the move back into the cottage. The kitchen things take less time to pack. I have only the bare essentials— coffeepot, a few mugs, flatware. Pots and pans have become an unnecessary encumbrance. The furniture came with the apartment. In two hours, I'm finished.

Williams calls at 8:45, just as I'm on my way out the door.

"How are you?" he asks.

"Busy," I respond. "I was just leaving, but I'm glad you called. You sent Frey to see me last night, didn't you?"

"Yes."

No hesitation, no apology or explanation. Not that I needed any.

"An object lesson?"

"Yes."

I blow out a breath. "Well, the point is taken. I'll call you next week. We can talk then, all right?"

"Good luck today," he says then.

"Thanks. Williams, what has Trish's grandmother been up to the last couple of days, do you know?"

He is quiet for a moment. "I talked with her last night. The mayor wanted me to fill her in on what happened. She almost seemed disappointed to find out Trish was a victim. And she certainly wasn't happy to hear what Carolyn had done to her. I don't think she'll give your parents any trouble as far as custody is concerned. In fact, I'd say she wants to distance herself as far away from Trish as she can. Having a daughter who pimped out her own child to pornographers won't sit well with her country club friends back home."

"If it gets out."

He chuckles. "I sort of implied it would most certainly make her hometown papers if she gave your parents any trouble. And this way she gets to play the bereaved parent of a murdered daughter instead of a mother who created a monster."

"She accepted that?"

"She had no choice. If I was to guess, I'd bet Mrs. Joseph Bernard is on a jet headed home as we speak."

Relief washes over me. The specter of a trial still hangs over Trish, but until then, her identity as a victim of sexual assault is protected. I ring off with the promise that I'll call Williams midweek. I want a few days to see that Trish is settled, get the cottage in order, and reconnect with David.

David.

Another loose mortal end. Can I continue my business relationship with him? A decision I may not have to make. He may not want me to.

CHAPTER 49

THE SAME WOMAN WHO HELPED ME WITH THE forms on Wednesday is behind the reception counter again this morning. I give her my name, produce identification and wait while she shuffles through a file on a desk behind her. She hands me a legal-sized manila envelope and gestures to one of two cubicles to the left of the reception area.

"If you'd like some privacy," she explains.

I guess it's a good idea, having a place away from prying eyes where you can examine the results of something as potentially devastating as a paternity test.

Also makes it easier to contain the fallout.

I nod at her and slip into one of the booths, closing the door behind me. My hand is shaking so badly I'm not sure I can tear open the damned envelope without destroying the page inside. But I manage somehow.

The next moment, I wish I hadn't.

* * *

TRISH IS SEATED ON THE COUCH WITH MY DAD. They're looking at a scrapbook and neither notices that I'm in the room. Trish's face is serious, puzzled. Dad's is radiant.

Mom is standing behind me and she touches my arm and crooks a finger. I follow her into the kitchen, swallowing back the panic because I understand the significance of what I've just witnessed.

"You told Trish?" I ask when we're out of earshot.

She doesn't meet my eyes, pretending instead that her attention has been drawn to some imagined spot on a perfectly clean counter. She picks up a sponge and starts to wipe at it.

I stop her hand with my own. "Mom, what did you and Dad tell her?"

She looks at me finally, her eyes bright. "We told her that she was our granddaughter. We told her that we loved her from the moment her mother came to us and that she has a home here. We told her we would help her face whatever comes. We told her she was safe."

There is so much emotion in her voice, it sucks whatever furious response I might have leveled at her right out of my head. I realize as much as I wanted Trish to be Steve's child, my mother wanted it even more.

I know what I should say. I know what I should do. I should tell Mom about the results of the test. I should call my father in here and the three of us should try to come up with some way to explain to Trish that what we thought, that what her mother told us, was a mistake.

A sound from the living room stops me.

A sound as sweet as wind chimes on a summer breeze. Trish and my father.

Laughing.

* * *

DAVID IS SEATED AT HIS SIDE OF THE DESK WHEN I
peek in the door.

"Is it safe?" I ask.

He has a flyer in his hand and when he looks up,
though I expect a frown, he actually smiles. "If by 'safe'
you mean is Gloria here, the answer is no. She's back in
L.A. Left yesterday." He drops the flyer on the desk and
his expression sobers. "I read about what happened in the
paper. Quite a story. Is Trish all right?"

I'm so grateful for not being greeted with vitriol that I
have to restrain myself from throwing my arms around
his neck. "She's with my folks. I just came from the
house."

I toss the envelope from the clinic on the desk and
head for the coffeepot.

He glances at the envelope then up at me. "How is that
going?"

I bring a cup of coffee back to the desk and sink
wearily into my chair. "You should see the three of them.
It's like they've known each other for years. Trish is confused, of course. She has a lot of questions. But I've never
seen my parents happier. You can almost feel . . ." My
voice falters, breaks off.

David frowns. "Then why the long face?"

I pick at the envelope and instantly he understands.

"Those are the DNA results. She isn't Steve's."

I raise my eyes to meet his. "I wanted Trish to be
Steve's more than I've wanted anything in my life. I'm so
angry with Carolyn, I can hardly stand it. Why would she
do this? Why would she come to us with such an elabo-
rate story? She offered Trish's hair for a DNA test, for
god's sake. She must have known, or at least suspected
that Steve wasn't the father."

David leans back, pushing away the papers he had

spread before him. "Maybe not. Maybe she really thought Steve was Trish's father. Maybe she didn't expect you'd have anything of Steve's after all this time to prove paternity one way or the other. It doesn't matter, does it? And you weren't the only one she told that story to. Carolyn's own mother believed it."

David is silent for a moment. "What are you going to do?"

I squeeze my hands together. "I don't know. Even if Trish's real grandmother wasn't such a witch, I don't think I could turn her over to her. And I can't stand the thought of putting Trish in foster care. Jesus. I don't know."

"But your parents want her, right? And they'd be the best family she could ever have. They'll love her. What's more important?"

David picks up the envelope. "You didn't tell them?"

I shake my head. "I couldn't."

He carries the envelope over to our file cabinet. He pushes folders to the back, shoves the envelope to the bottom of the drawer, and rearranges the files to cover it.

"Your parents are the best thing that could happen to that kid. If there's any medical reason to make this report known later, it's right here. Otherwise, just because you know, doesn't mean anyone else has to."

I remember how Trish looked with my parents. How I felt the energy of hearts mending. It's why I couldn't bring myself to share the DNA results. I couldn't bear to break the bond. And neither of my parents even asked about the tests. It didn't matter to them.

And just like that, Sorrel's words are in my head. *It's in the blood.* I know what she meant.

Love.

Nothing matters more. She hadn't made a mistake.

I had.

I meet David's eyes. So calm, so sure. He saw it before I did. Love is stronger than any blood tie.

Trish and my parents will take care of each other.

Freeing me.

It's so clear. David doesn't understand, of course. He sees only the obvious. That a young girl has a future now with a family that will do what families are supposed to—protect and love her.

David returns to his seat and points to the flyer lying atop a stack on the desk. "Are you ready to get back to work?" he asks. "Because this looks like a promising case with a good payday."

He starts to fill me in and I pretend to listen though my thoughts are scattered. Can I do this? Can I continue, at least for a while, to live as both mortal and vampire?

Why not? My entire relationship to humans is based on lies.

This will be just one more.

Look for

THE WATCHER
An Anna Strong, Vampire Novel
by Jeanne C. Stein

Coming from Ace Books in
December 2007